Enough with the Secrets

2

Enough with the Secrets

Bobbie Jean

Home to Lake Louise
Book Two

http://bobbiejeansbooks.com

4

Author's Note

This book is a work of fiction. Names, characters, places, and incidents either are the products of the author's imagination or are used fictitiously. Any resemblance to actual events or persons, living or dead, is entirely coincidental.

Published by bobbiejeansbooks.com
Copyright @ 2012 by Roberta J. Kuhn

Original Cover Art by Jesse C. Kuhn   www.myspace.com/jesckuhn

Cover Formatting, Design, and Photography by Cory Zignego
www.littlelifemoments.com

Printed on Demand at lulu.com
Manufactured in the United States of America

ISBN   978-1-62407-854-5
eISBN 978-1-62407-853-8

This work is dedicated to my wonderfully supportive husband, children, grandchildren, extended family, and amazing friends. You hold me up!

The inspiration for this novel is a heart wrenching song I heard on the radio in 1969. I'll never forget the emotions that tore through me when I heard those lyrics. You can find the words to

Down from Dover
at
http://www.dollyon-line.com/archives/lyrics/dfdover.shtml

6

Chapter 1

CLAIRE

The flight from Phoenix to Minneapolis took an eternity. Claire couldn't get back to the Midwest fast enough; in fact, she'd be arriving a day early. No one was expecting her, and no one was home when she called from her cell the moment she landed. It didn't matter. She'd been single for her entire adult life and traveled alone, too, so she simply solicited the help of a tall stranger to rescue her carryon from the bin above her head and after dragging it down the ramp, hurried to the main entrance of the international airport and hailed a cab to take her the short forty miles over the border into Wisconsin.

It was a gorgeous September day. The noon sun warmed the interior of the taxi as the driver wove in and out of the heavy weekend traffic. And when the cab crossed the beautiful St. Croix River, Claire craned her neck to get a peek at the last of summer's bobbing sailboats. Her heart soared. She must have made the right choice when she decided to move back because she'd never been happier in her life. *Who said you can never go home?*

As the cabbie exited the highway and drove into the beautiful city of Lake Louise, Claire searched through her large, leather tote for the keys to her oldest daughter's house. Kate had made her a set one of the times she'd visited so she could come and go as she pleased. Now she'd been given a room of her own; albeit, a temporary solution to her housing dilemma. She knew she couldn't stay there forever, imposing on her daughter and her family, but she had no idea what she would do for money now that she'd left Arizona behind. Her meager savings wouldn't last long, and the job market had yet to recover from the most recent recession. Even updating her resume' could prove to be a waste of time.

Of course, the sale of her house in Phoenix could solve her money problems. Since her long suffering fiancé, Mel, had built it for her and her alone, he'd insisted she keep the profit. She had yet to decide if that was the ethical thing to do; after all, she was the one to end the affair to nowhere. He didn't owe her a thing.

Claire had to admit that even though their relationship never developed into the passionate love affair she was hoping for, she'd always be grateful to him for looking out for her and providing her with a gorgeous home in a safe, gated community. Still, she wouldn't miss it near as much as she'd miss Martha's House, the homeless shelter she'd built by tirelessly soliciting donations and writing grants for the better part of a decade. It had been her dream job, her heart's desire, but those days were over. She had another calling now.

After grabbing her luggage and generously tipping the cabbie, Claire dragged her carryon up the stairs and onto the porch of Kate's stately, two story brick home and rapped once before peeking through one of the rectangular windows that framed the door. Kate's house was dark, so she slipped the key into the deadbolt, turned it, pushed the heavy door open, and released a long grateful breath.

Once inside, Claire rid herself of her platform pumps and padded barefoot into the kitchen to see if she could find something to eat. Her growling stomach reminded her that she'd had nothing but a beverage on the flight to the Twin Cities, and she was starved. After swinging the refrigerator door open, she spotted the cardboard Pizza Palace box sitting cockeyed on a tightly packed shelf. Thanking God for leftovers, she wasted no time and threw a couple of pieces on a plate, nuking them before grabbing a Coke and heading to the back yard. She didn't get far; something else caught her eye. Claire knew that it was unusual for Kate to leave a mess in the kitchen. She was a neat freak, that daughter of hers. Had there been an emergency? Where in the world was everyone?

Claire stopped worrying long enough to wander over to the table and glance over the glitter covered mess. There was some sort of scrapbook, an assortment of colored markers, containers of colored glitter, and a glue bottle infused with more of the stuff. The thought that the mess belonged to her little, towheaded, eight-year-old granddaughter brought a smile to her face. She figured that it had to be a very important project if Abby was allowed to leave the kitchen table in such disarray.

Since the good sized scrapbook was open, Claire decided to snoop to see what her granddaughter was up to. After carefully lifting the scrapbook from its sacred spot on the table, she closed it to read the title…*FAMOUS PEOPLE IN MY FAMILY by Abigail Genevieve Fogarty*…and her throat tightened. She could keep her emotions in check most of the time, but when it came to her daughters and granddaughter, she seemed to have no control over the constriction of her heart muscle or the swelling in her throat. She decided to meditate more often, to calm down and find her center. It was very important to Claire that her children and grandchild view her as strong, independent, and self-assured. She hoped to become the role model she should have been from the very beginning.

As Claire opened the scrapbook, she imagined her daughter collecting memorabilia the day Abby began asking them about her birthmother. She remembered Kate telling her that when Abby understood what it meant to belong to a family, she was told that her mother was a relative and that they loved this woman so much that they agreed to raise her baby as their own because she couldn't. As far as she knew, they hadn't told her much more than that.

Forgetting about the pizza and Coke for a moment, Claire sat at the table to get a better look at the collection. The first couple of pages contained yellowed newspaper clippings, such as wedding announcements, followed by pages of antiquated photographs. She'd have to remember to ask her daughters about the man cozying up to their grandmother in a few of the pictures. She had no idea that her mother had a 'special' friend.

It wasn't long before she came across a copy of her birth announcement as well as those of her daughters. Included were their senior pictures and photocopies of their diplomas. Copies of all three of Kate's diplomas were there: one from Rock Creek High School as well as the B.S. from UW-Madison and the Master's from St. Mary's where she studied to be a nurse anesthetist. She noticed that Kate had thoughtfully added Maggie's certificates as well, including a copy of her PhD diploma from NYU. Claire's eyes burned with hot tears. *And they did all this without me!* Yet, the path to redemption was right in front of her, and Claire felt less like a loser when she spotted several articles about her homeless shelter along with pictures of the ribbon cutting at the dedication. *I hope they're as proud of me as I am of them!*

As Claire lifted the back cover of the scrapbook, she spotted one more clipping. She carefully turned it over and immediately stopped breathing. She hadn't seen the police report regarding assault on Maggie's life and forced herself to exhale as she read the article through tear clouded eyes. The charges against the perpetrator were listed…felony battery and attempted murder. Reality hit and Claire couldn't tear her eyes away from the printed page. *We almost lost her!*

As Claire struggled keep her rising anxiety in check, she wondered if she could have prevented the tragedy if she and Grant had been given the chance to raise Maggie themselves. She wondered if Maggie could have avoided getting mixed up with an abuser if her own mother and father had raised her. That's what she regretted the most; the fact that her daughters weren't raised by either her or their biological fathers, but by their maternal grandmother instead. Kate's father had given up his rights when he was sixteen and had never shown interest in connecting with his daughter; however, Claire hoped it wasn't too late for Maggie. And even though the venerable Grant Harrison had no time for her, even though he left her when she needed him the most, Claire believed that he was a changed man, a man Maggie could proudly call her father.

As much as Claire wanted Maggie to bond with Grant, she also understood that she'd have to stay out of their way, disappear when he came around. After all, the writing was on the wall when he'd abandoned her to give birth to their child on her own. He'd never cared about her, never truly loved her like he'd said, but none of that mattered any more; Maggie deserved a father. Suddenly, Claire couldn't wait a second longer; she wanted nothing less than a detailed report, a verbatim account of their very first meeting.

***

Filled with joyful anticipation, Claire backed her sports car out of her son-in-law's garage and drove the ten miles out of town to Maggie's rental. Since she couldn't reach her daughter by phone, she figured that she was simply walking her Great Dane on the paths through the woods behind her house and didn't have her cell on her. Or maybe she was with Kate. She had to remind herself that it was her own fault no one was around; after all, she was a day early.

As Claire left Highway 29 and pulled into the long gravel driveway that led to Maggie's refurbished farmhouse, she spotted her daughter's Lincoln parked in front. Next to it, however, was a vehicle she didn't recognize. She parked her Porsche behind Maggie's car, hopped out, and gave the unfamiliar car a once over. Claire knew her cars and grinned. The gorgeous, black Mercedes-Benz C-Class Luxury Sedan had new Wisconsin plates. She figured Mac, Maggie's landlord and colleague, had finally gotten sick of that old Jeep he drove and traded it in.

"Hey, Mom…I thought you were coming back tomorrow."

Claire turned from the cars to see Maggie coming out of the side door of the old red barn that separated Mac's house from his rental property. She simply waved and waited for her daughter to climb the hill toward her because she never wore the right shoes when she visited. She didn't own any sneakers or flip flops, and she did her morning routine barefoot. She knew she'd eventually have to buy something other than stilettos or platforms, but she had no idea what that would be or how she'd ever get used to them…even her slouchy winter boots had high heels.

"Where is everyone?" Claire asked as Maggie approached.

"There's a festival at one of the apple orchards today. You know…hayrides, corn mazes, all of that. Mac's aunt said the early apples, the ones she uses for pies, are ready to pick. They all went."

"Why didn't you go along?"

Her daughter didn't answer her question; instead, she turned and glanced toward the barn, and Claire, still wondering why Maggie stayed home, followed her gaze. Together, they watched as Maggie's huge black and white speckled dog, Horse, came out of the shadows, straining on her leash and yanking on some poor soul who had yet to come through the barn door. She expected to see Mac on the other end of the restraint, but when the man came out of the darkness into the sunlit yard and looked her way, he stopped abruptly, reining the dog to an immediate halt.

Maggie whipped her head around. "Mom…I thought you said you wouldn't be back until tomorrow," she stammered apologetically.

Even as blood rushed to her head and flushed her face, Claire was hard pressed to tear her eyes from his. She tried to run, but her feet were cemented to the ground. Then, as if in slow motion, she turned to her daughter. "Sorry to interrupt," she mumbled before attempting to leave.

"Mom, wait a minute," Maggie begged, reaching for her.

"Sorry," Claire repeated as she willed her legs to move, one right after the other; she couldn't get out of there fast enough. She'd figured he'd be long gone…the man who'd tossed her aside like so much garbage… but there he stood without a care in the world. She had no idea how she managed to start the car, but somehow she backed out, shoved the car into gear, and tore down the long, dusty road to the highway. She hadn't expected to see him, and she certainly wasn't prepared for the sickening punch in the gut she hadn't felt for decades. *Help me, Lord! This is going to be so much harder than I thought!*

Chapter 2

MAGGIE

Humiliated for her mother, Maggie could only stand and watch her speed away. She wanted to cry for Claire because she'd made no bones about the fact that it was all about the father/daughter relationship now, that it had nothing to do with her. In fact, she'd insisted that she be excluded from any of their get-togethers. Maggie remembered telling her that she'd be meeting Grant on Friday…she didn't know he'd be staying the weekend…and Claire agreed that it would be a good time for them to see each other because she'd be in Phoenix. So what was she doing back here already?

Maggie, her musings interrupted when she felt a cold nose pushing at the back of her arm, turned, wrapped an arm around her oversized dog and hugged her neck. She had no idea what to expect from the man holding her dog's leash, though, until she heard him clear his throat.

"Is she going to be okay?" Grant asked, barely getting it out.

Maggie choked up, but managed a nod.

"I didn't mean to upset her," he said. "I know I'm the last person she wants to see."

"What do you mean?"

"She probably hates me for leaving her. I mean, I was gone for two years, but I wrote her, explained everything, told her to wait for me, but I never heard from her."

Maggie reddened and raised her hands in the air, palms outward. "Hold it right there. She told me that you left when you found out she was pregnant, and she never heard from you again!"

Maggie watched her father's head jerk backward, his eyes pop wide open.

"What? I wrote her letter after letter for months. She's the one who never answered them, never returned my phone calls either. I had to give up the chase after a while, Maggie. If she didn't want me, I had to get on with my life." He rolled his eyes and simply shook his head.

Tears welled in her eyes, but she blinked them away. "Don't lie to me, Grant. Don't start this out with a lie. She told me you never contacted her until a year ago when you emailed her about making a donation to her project."

"Listen to me, Maggie. I've never lied about any of it. If only your grandmother were alive…I talked to her plenty. She always knew where I was…she knew I wanted to talk to Claire…she told me she'd make sure she got my messages."

"My mother never got one letter, one message, nothing. She thinks you led her on the whole time you were together, too, and that you never meant a word you said."

His shoulders slumped. "You've got it all wrong, Maggie." He stared a hole into the ground and kicked the dirt under his feet. "But there's no way to prove it now, is there?"

Maggie's heart lodged in her throat, but she managed to speak. "If I find out that you're not being truthful with me, I won't be able see you anymore."

"What?" he shrieked.

"Sorry, Grant, but I've never had a relationship with my mother before, and I'm not giving it up now. She's going to come first. Besides, I know she's not lying."

Grant gasped and grabbed her arm. "Neither am I!"

Chapter 3

CLAIRE

Claire had mistakenly assumed that her heart had hardened against him, but one momentary glimpse had cracked its exterior. It was the last thing she'd expected after all these years, especially since she'd had no problem communicating with him through impersonal email. She hadn't anticipated the pain either...the constriction of her heart muscle, the heavy weight upon her chest, or the realization that the damage to her heart had been permanent.

Thankfully, Claire knew exactly what to do to lesson unbearable heartache and cried in the shower until the water ran cold. At least she could cry now, she thought. After Maggie was born and she was hospitalized, her meds kept her from feeling anything; in fact, for years she felt nothing at all. But as her mental health gradually improved with years of therapy and hard work, she was allowed to cut back on or change her medications. Eventually, the ability to alleviate some of her emotional pain came naturally, and she was able to cry...and cry she did.

It didn't hurt that Claire was as healthy as she'd ever been in her life, both mentally and physically, and that she knew exactly what it took to brighten her mood. After searching through another stack of unpacked boxes on the bedroom floor, she found her favorite Victoria's Secret super soft, hot pink lounge robe, threw it on over her lacey underwear, and hopped onto the comfy bed. She blew her nose, crumpled the tissue in the palm of her hand, and pressed her towel covered head into her pillows. Meditation always helped at a time like this, so she concentrated on her breath and ignored the most recent shock to her system. After forcing her lungs to expand, she tried to focus on the warm, moist air that left her body through her nose. Tonight, however, she couldn't block her train of thought.

Grant looked great, and the salt and pepper hair did nothing but add to his good looks. She could tell that he'd taken good care of himself; she figured he worked out like everyone else these days. His shoulders were broader, his arms more muscular than she'd remembered. And even though she hadn't seen him in person for more years than she cared to count, she'd seen his image online. The first time had to have been about fifteen years earlier when he'd just been elected to a circuit court judge position. The Milwaukee Journal article told about his wife and son, and included a great photograph of the three of them taken during the campaign. Claire remembered crying after seeing the pictures because, at the time, she had no one, she was alone. Then some years later, after she found Mel, Grant had been elected to one of the state district attorney positions. He was being groomed to be the state's next Attorney General, but his party worried that his divorce might negatively impact the conservative constituents. At that time, she was considering marrying Mel, and Grant was alone. The irony of it all wasn't lost on her.

Claire's thoughts turned to Maggie, and she began to worry about how this looked to her, how running away couldn't have helped Grant's case. She was determined to be strong for her daughters, no matter what happened, and Grant was a good man, she knew that. Maybe if she shared something positive with Maggie, something to assure her that this wouldn't happen again.

After taking some time to reflect, Claire left the bed to grab an old cigar box she'd brought with her from Phoenix. It was one item she made sure to pack, to take with her whenever she needed to move on to the next job, the next town, or the next man. Another had to be her very first diary, the one filled with memories of Grant and her freshman year of college. She had yet to unpack it, but she knew exactly where it was and began to reminisce about the day her mother gave her the diary as a going away gift. It was the day before she was to leave home for Madison and the university. Martha told her that she'd thought of her when she spotted it in a second hand store. Claire behaved like a spoiled brat at the time; after all, it was ancient and tacky and she could barely make out the letters that read *Record of My College Days*. Obviously, it was a man's journal…how ridiculous for her mother to think she would like such a thing. But later, in the privacy of her own room, she laughed out loud. Inside the cover, on the first page, was a black and white sketch of a man in an athletic outfit, circa 1914, throwing a shot put. Because she was nothing if not creative, Claire grabbed her colored pencils and proceeded to draw over the likeness, turning the man into a girl with flowing yellow hair, wild eye makeup, and red lips. She even gave her creation an hourglass figure much like her own, clad her in a skimpy bikini, and took ownership of the diary. It became hers and hers alone, and before she left for Madison, she thanked her mother properly, giving her a great bear hug to boot.

With her precious diary out of sight, Claire could concentrate on the old cigar box as she cradled it lovingly on her lap. She allowed her small, delicate fingers to trace the painted pink rosebuds and purple violets on the cover before toying with the loose edging that ran along the edges of the lid. Just as she was about to lift the cover, she heard a gentle rap at her door.

"Mom, it's me. Can I come in?"

Talk about good timing, Claire thought. "Of course, darling."

The door opened ever so slowly, and her youngest daughter, the one that looked more and more like her everyday, cautiously poked her head into the room.

Claire laughed. "All the way in," she teased, patting a spot next to her on the bed before removing the towel from her head, giving it a shake, and threading her fingers through her damp, chin length locks.

Maggie warily entered the beautifully wallpapered bedroom and gently closed the door behind her. After hopping onto the bed, she wrapped an arm around her mother and gave her a quick squeeze. "I'm sorry, Mom. I had no idea you were coming home early," she whispered.

"I didn't know I was either, but then it hit me. The house was on the market, and the new director had taken over Martha's Place. I didn't have to pack up the house because the realtors want it to look lived in, so there was absolutely nothing else I had to do." She cleared her throat then and looked away. "I'm sorry if I ruined things for you."

"You didn't ruin things, Mom."

"I didn't know he'd still be here."

"He didn't tell me he was staying the weekend until last night."

"So, do you like him?" Claire asked, swallowing hard.

"I guess."

"So where is he now?"

"At the hotel downtown," Maggie said before noticing the cigar box. "What's this?"

Claire shook her head and sighed. "Seeing him there...I mean, it just brought back lots of memories."

"Can I see what's in it?"

"I was hoping to share it with you," she said, flipping the precious box open. "Ta da!"

Maggie giggled at her mother's antics and peered into the box full of notes, photos, and other memorabilia. Claire shuffled a few items around until she found what she was looking for and pulled out a perfectly square, black and white photograph. "Look, a Polaroid. I don't think they make these anymore. When you took a picture, it just popped out of the camera. You couldn't touch it until the entire picture magically appeared." She rubbed her fingers over the couple in the picture.

"Is that you and Grant?"

Claire nodded.

"When was this?"

"1973."

"Where were you?"

"Daytona Beach."

"Spring Break? You two are really cute. Grant was a hunk, huh?" Maggie said, poking her mother with her elbow.

Claire laughed. "You know it. He was in great shape. Skinner then, though. Good looking, wasn't he?"

"Still is," Maggie added, lifting her eyebrows. "You were pretty hot yourself. I see you tried to stuff yourself into a bikini top."

Claire stared at the picture and blushed. "Whoa, I guess I shouldn't have. Chalk it up youthful indiscretion."

"I can't believe Grandma let you wear a bikini much less go to Florida with your boyfriend. She'd never let either of us do that."

Claire chuckled. "She had no idea what I was up to most of the time as long as I came home on the weekends to take care of Katie."

"So how'd you pull it off?"

"I told you that Grant's family had money, right? Well, he had a substantial allowance, so he bought us plane tickets to Florida. We spent five days there, and I didn't miss a weekend at home."

"What about spring break? Didn't Grandma know when it was?"

"She sure did...she kept real good track of my schedule," Claire admitted. "But I was doing so well in school that when I told her I could use the week to study and that other kids were staying in the dorms, too, she believed me."

"She never found out?"

"Nope."

"But one weekend you were white as a ghost and the next, you had a tan, right?"

"You never lied to Grandma?"

"Little white ones...maybe."

Claire shook her head and sighed. "You were a good girl; I wasn't. I think I made up some story about how all the kids laid in the sun as soon as spring arrived. You know, how we all did our homework outside as soon as it was warm enough. It was true to some extent...I just wasn't one of them."

"Shame on you," Maggie said, joking and bumping shoulders with her mother before poking around in the cigar box. "What else you got in there?"

"It's just a bunch of junk."

Maggie shook her head. "Hey, if you kept it this long, it's not junk. Well, maybe these dried up flowers have seen their day," she said as the petals crumbled at her touch. "Oh, sorry, I didn't mean to wreck them."

Claire laughed. "It doesn't matter. It's foolish to keep them anyway."

"No, Mom, they're memories...memories that are obviously

very important to you. What's this pin from?" Maggie asked as she took it from the box and held it close to her face to get a better look. "Greek letters?"

"Yes…Phi Sigma Delta…Grant's fraternity."

"You were pinned?"

"Sort of …I mean, he gave it to me, but I didn't belong to a sorority, so there wasn't a ceremony or party or anything. He called it a promise, the first step to becoming engaged. And stupid me, I believed him."

"I don't think he was lying, Mom," Maggie ventured softly.

Claire ignored her daughter's naiveté. "Of course he was lying. First bump in the road and he was out of there."

Maggie got quiet then and leaned back against the headboard.

"He got to you, didn't he? He's charming. I'll give him credit for that."

"Something doesn't add up, Mom," Maggie offered cautiously.

"Then he hasn't changed a bit."

Maggie turned and moved closer to her mother. "Could we talk about what happened today when you came out to my place?"

"It's pretty simple. I dropped by and ruined everything."

"Stop it. None of this is your fault," Maggie scolded. "I just want to talk about what he said after you left."

Claire turned to her daughter and grabbed hold of her leg. "Darling, you don't have to. It's okay. I know where I stand with him."

Maggie looked her mother in the eye and shook her head. "That's just it, Mom. I think you've got it all wrong."

"What?" Claire asked, insulted by the insinuation. "I'm sorry, but you don't know a thing about it."

"Just listen, Mom. When you walked away, he was devastated. I'm not kidding you! Devastated!"

"So he's a good liar and a good actor," Claire concluded.

"I want to shake you right now."

"You sound just like my mother."

"I guess if you don't care about what I have to say, I'll just go," Maggie threatened as she started to slide off the bed.

The last thing Claire wanted was for her daughter to leave, so she reached over and grabbed her arm. "I'm sorry. Okay. I'll shut up and listen." She shifted on the bed so that she would be eye to eye with Maggie. That wasn't hard, they were the same height…just scraping five foot-two.

Maggie took one of her mother's hands in both of hers. "Mom, he was honestly upset because he didn't want to hurt you by being there. He said…and this is what I thought was strange…he said that he knew you never wanted to see him again."

"What?" Claire howled, eyes wide in disbelief.

"He said he knew you never wanted to see him because you never answered his letters or return his phone calls. He said he finally had to give up and get on with his life."

"That's B.S. Maggie. He knew I couldn't call him…his mother threatened me, told me never to contact any of them. He told me not to worry…he'd talk to them, he'd be back. I never heard from him again…no letters, no telephone calls, nothing."

"That's what I told him. But he said that Grandma always knew where he was, that she always knew how to get in touch with him if you came around."

Claire continued her denial, shaking her head vehemently. "You know I came home a couple times a year. Mama never told me anything about letters or calls."

Maggie nodded. "I think I know why."

"What are you talking about? She wouldn't keep that from me…I know she wouldn't. She knew how much he meant to me."

Maggie shushed her mother. Claire tried to pull away, but Maggie had a firm grip on her hand. "Listen, Mom. One time when I was about ten, I think, I was asking Grandma about my father. I had some project at school or something, and I just wanted to know about him so that I could write a believable story. I told her that if she didn't tell me, I was going to make up something really outlandish and embarrass the whole family."

Finally, Claire found a reason to smile. "You were a little stinker, weren't you?"

"Yup, like mother, like daughter. Anyway, Grandma got all grumpy and told me that he wasn't worth the ink I was writing with. She told me that he was a terrible man who hurt my mother so badly that she couldn't even raise her own two children. She said, God forgive her, but he was the only person she ever hated in her entire life."

Claire slowly shook her head, trying to control her breathing.

"He could be telling the truth, Mom. Grandma could have been keeping everything from you."

Claire sobbed. "No…she knew how much I needed him."

"But she knew how much he hurt you, too. Maybe she thought that she was protecting you or something. I'm not sure what happened between you two, but I think he was always trying to get in touch with you. I wish you could have seen him today. I think he might be telling the truth."

Claire swallowed her tears, took her daughter's hand, and looked her straight in the eyes. "Listen. When he emailed the first time, he asked about my projects, said he wanted to make a donation. After that, it was questions about you. Never once did he ask about my personal life, never once did he say he'd like to see me…that's how I know he really doesn't give a hoot about me. It's about you now, and I really do want you to get to know him…it's only fair. But please don't do this. Don't think you're going to get your parents back together or some such thing. He never loved me…he was just a college kid doing whatever he had to do to get his girlfriend into bed. That's all there was to it. It took me quite a while to figure that out, and the sooner you accept that the better."

***

Claire was fuming. What was she thinking when she told Grant that their daughter was in the hospital? For crying out loud, she'd been attacked and left for dead…she was just trying to be fair, just trying to give him a chance to meet her before it was too late. In hindsight, she should have left well enough alone because as far as she knew, he had no interest in meeting her before then. He said he was too humiliated to talk to her because he left us or some such thing. Bologna! And now Maggie believed every word that jerk was telling her. How dare he lie to her daughter, too? She was going to set him straight for once and for all. She didn't want him to break Maggie's heart like he did hers. She had to put a stop to this before her daughter wanted him in her life permanently, especially if he was going to continue with his lies. Yet, she had no idea how she would do it, how she would confront him, what she would say. After all, she'd seen him from a distance and scurried in the opposite direction as fast as her stilettos would take her. How in the world would she ever have the guts to talk to him in person?

Chapter 4

MAC

From the first moment Mac laid eyes on Maggie Borgerson…in a photograph, no less…she'd been invading his dreams. He couldn't believe his luck when she accepted a position at Lake Community and Technical College; he'd probably be seeing her 24/7…if she kept showing up in his dreams, that is. Then, just when he thought his life couldn't get any better, her brother-in-law convinced her to rent Mac's refurbished farmhouse, and she moved in right next door. Talk about system overload! Well, that was a month ago, and Mac had been riding a metaphorical roller coaster ever since.

Not that Mac thought he was a great catch for any woman. He wasn't perfect. Ask either of his first two wives if he were the ideal man, and you'd get an earful. He's nothing if not a quick study, though, and figured that he had to have learned from his mistakes. What mistakes were those exactly? Well, according to wife number one, he ought to have known better than to leave her immediately after their wedding and join the service. Of course, she'd get lonely and need someone. Too bad that someone was the person who'd bullied Mac throughout his entire childhood. He couldn't believe it…she was his high school sweetheart. Therein lies the rub, he guessed. Perhaps they were just too young.

The problem with Mac hinged on one thing…he wanted to be married. He wanted a family more than anything, and he figured he'd waited long enough. He finished his stint in the service, he went to college on the G.I. Bill, studied for his doctorate, and got a great teaching job. Then, he fell head over heals…in lust.

Mac had always heard that opposites attract, but it wasn't long before he learned that he and the exotic Carina had nothing in common at all…except for the fact that they both desperately wanted to be parents. They adopted their wonderful little girl, purchased his aunt's idyllic place in the country, and Mac was sure they'd live happily ever after. Instead, he ended up being accused of not trusting her, of never giving her the benefit of a doubt, and last but not least, of being a control freak. So, she left, and in the process, gave up rights to her little girl.

Okay, so three strikes and you're out! Mac certainly didn't want his relationship with Maggie to be strike three, but holy cow, she brought more baggage with her than anyone he'd ever met. He wasn't about to make another mistake either, and figured they had enough in common to make it. They each were raised with one sibling, in rural Wisconsin, and by a single parent or grandparent. He already knew that they had the same small town values. And, incredibly, they'd each been bullied by the same disgusting human being and built careers based on their familiarity with his personality type. As bad as that sounds, he hoped that what they'd learned from their shared experiences would cement their relationship. He understood her as well as anyone; besides that, all he wanted to do was make her as happy as she made him and for that to happen, he'd have to give up trying to control every little thing.

***

Mac and his daughter, Lily, had spent the afternoon at an apple orchard with their closest friends: Maggie' sister, Kate; her husband, George; and their adopted daughter, Abby. If Maggie could have joined them, the afternoon would have been perfect, but she'd apologetically bowed out because she was spending the day with her father.

After throwing a few apples into a paper bag, Mac left Lily and Aunt Galen in his kitchen slicing up some Paula Reds for pie. Maggie's Lincoln wasn't parked in the front of the house when they'd arrived home from the orchard, but it had been an hour since they pulled in, so he hoped she'd be home by now because he needed to see her; he couldn't shake the feeling that all was not well. How could it be?

Meeting her father for the first time had to hurt. As far as he knew, he hadn't even attempted to contact her once in thirty-seven years since her birth.

Chapter 5

MAGGIE

It was dusk, and Maggie thought she'd heard Mac's jeep roar past her house. She waited awhile before plopping onto the chair nearest the large picture window so she could watch for him. He came by every night after Lily had finished her homework and gone to bed. He wouldn't stay long…he just wanted to wish her a good night's sleep, he'd say. Usually, they spent more time together on the weekends, and she hoped it wouldn't be any different tonight because she figured that the only thing that would cheer her up was his goofy grin and silly antics. If he didn't drop by, she didn't know how she'd get Grant's visit out of her mind, not to mention her mother's reaction to it.

Maggie knew that Mac would do something to make her laugh; he always did. Sometimes she wondered if he thought it was his job to cheer her up. She'd even asked him once what he was trying to do because ever since she came home from the hospital, he'd become her personal class clown. He told her that he understood that she was dealing with some painful issues and simply wanted to lighten her load. Besides that, he reminded her that laughter was the best medicine. He loved those old proverbs and seemed to have one on the tip of his tongue no matter what. Could he be any more adorable? Still, she didn't want to be that person, the one everyone felt sorry for. For crying out loud, her family treated her as if she would collapse in a heap of tears if they looked at her cross-eyed. Sure, she was recovering from Rex's assault, but she wasn't the least bit fragile. Out of the blue, she realized that she was treating her mother the very same way, tiptoeing around, making sure that spending time with Grant didn't hurt her in any way. She guessed that it was too late now… she'd seen it with her own eyes…running into her father had put her mother into a tailspin, and Maggie figured that she'd soon be taking over as the caretaker, the mediator, and maybe as the only adult in their emotionally charged triangle.

Maggie stopped worrying about her mother when she heard the shuffling of feet on the steps to her front door. As she stood, Horse raced past her to greet their visitor. She must have recognized Mac because she didn't bark; instead, her huge frame wiggled out of control. With a gentle bump of her hip, Maggie moved her dog out of the way and reached for the door knob. She couldn't help giggling when she spotted Mac's clear blue eyes peeking through the curtains of the door window.

"Hi," she said, smiling warmly as she let him in. "How was the trip to the apple orchard?"

"Great," he said, "but we had to buy our favorites pre-picked. I'll give you a few for a kiss." Mac stood there, grinning from ear to ear, a small bag of apples dangling from his hand high above her head.

Maggie didn't have to be asked twice. She happily wrapped her arms around his waist, closed her eyes, and puckered up. He squeezed her tight, laid a wet one on her, and rocked her back and forth.

"Okay…you got what you wanted, now give," she ordered, laughing as Mac held the bag over her head, forcing her to reach for it. "No fair. You're a foot taller than me!"

"One more kiss and they're yours."

"That's what you said the last time. You can't be trusted," she teased, turning and walking away from him.

"Okay…here," he said. He handed her the bag when she turned around, grabbed her at the same time, and lifted her off the floor. When he began nibbling her neck, she dropped the bag of apples to hug him close.

"I missed you…the girls did, too," he whispered in her ear before releasing her.

"I bet you had fun anyway," she said, pushing him away as she bent over to scoop up the apples.

"It was a beautiful day, that's for sure. The orchard went all out this year…bales of hay for the kids to climb, hayrides, and even a petting zoo."

"So that's why Abby was so excited. I wondered what was so great about picking some old apples you can buy in a store."

Mac simply stared. "You mean you've never been to an apple orchard?"

She shook her head. "Nope, and we never did that as kids either."

"Huh? Well, it's big time around here. Cut up one of those apples…they're a brand new hybrid...the Zestar."

"What's the big deal?"

"You'll see," he said, following her to the kitchen counter. Maggie pulled out her cutting board and grabbed a knife. She washed the apple, dried it off with a paper towel, and sliced it up. He leaned on the counter, patiently waiting for her to take her first bite.

"Whoa," she said with her mouth full. The apple was crisp and exceptionally sweet.

"An apple a day will keep the doctor away!"

Maggie laughed. "I'd eat these everyday, that's for sure. They're delicious…no wonder you were so wound up."

"Well, half the fun is picking them, but we didn't get to do much of that…the trees were pretty picked over."

"So the girls didn't get to pick any?"

"Those two…really! The hay wagon kept circling as if there were apples to pick, so they hopped off every time it stopped. They were embarrassing…they'd grab whatever apples were left on the trees, take a few bites, then throw them on the ground. I felt pretty guilty about the half eaten apples littering the orchard, so I bought a couple of bushels on the way out."

"Abby shouldn't be acting like that," Maggie said with a shake of her head.

"Lily shouldn't either, you know. Anyway, I gave them some quarters so they'd forget about the hayride and buy some corn to feed the goats. Really, those two acted like preschoolers today."

"I'm glad I wasn't there. I might have overstepped my boundaries."

"I don't think so. Everyone had a really good time. I guess our daughters have to let their hair down once in a while, too."

Maggie flashed him a look. "Mac. Please don't call her that."

"Sorry... I didn't mean...talk about overstepping boundaries." Mac circled around the counter, grabbed Maggie and held her close, kissing the top of her head as he rocked her. "So tell me...how did it go with your dad?"

"I don't know if I can talk about it without bawling. You're going to get pretty sick of me if I'm crying about something every time we're together."

Mac chuckled. "No kidding...the old mascara smeared under your eyes and then there's that bulbous red nose."

"Stop it," she said, playfully punching him in the arm.

He didn't release her. "Okay, tell me anyway."

"Well, let's just say that it didn't go as well as I'd hoped."

"Didn't I warn you about that?"

Maggie nodded against his chest. "Still, I thought it would be different...I thought that meeting my father was...I don't know...something I needed to make my life complete. But, Mac, nothing he said made any sense."

"I figured he'd be a jerk."

"I don't know if he's a jerk or not, but for some reason, I want to get to know him anyway. You don't know what that's like...growing up without your parents."

"I do too, Maggie. My mom died when I was three, remember?"

"At least you had one parent who cared."

"Yes, my dad was great. But growing up without a mother is no picnic, believe me."

Ashamed of her self-centeredness, Maggie backed away and tried to look him in the eye. Lifting her hands to hold his face, she slid her thumbs across his cheekbones. "I'm sorry, Mac. I wasn't thinking. I wish you could have another chance with your mother, too," she said, trying unsuccessfully to hold back tears.

"Well, I can't, so I'll just have to live vicariously through you," he said, forcing a smile. "So what happened?"

"Okay…well, Mom showed up this afternoon and just lost it when she saw him. I needed him to explain what happened back then…he said he tried time and time again to get a hold of her."

"He did?"

Maggie nodded. "I told him that if he was lying, I didn't want see him again, so he left."

"I'm sorry it didn't work out."

"Mac…it's all so sad…tragic, really," she whispered into his shirt.

"What is?"

"What happened between Mom and Grant."

"Didn't you know that going into this?"

She looked up at him then and told him about the conversations she'd had, first with her father and then her mother. Mac grabbed a hand in his and led her to the antique brown leather sofa a few feet away. She curled into one of the soft corners to face him. He sat opposite her, but leaned into her with his arm over the back of the couch.

"Maybe you should all just step back, take a break, and wait until things calm down a little," Mac suggested.

Maggie became emotional. "Mac, I've already waited a lifetime."

Mac closed his eyes and released a sigh. Maggie had had enough and turned to stand when she felt his hand on her arm. "Wait…I'm sorry. I just don't want anything to interfere with you getting better, that's all. I don't want to fight."

"I know…me either," she said, giving in and sliding against the back of the couch and closer to him.

With his hand resting on the cast on her wrist, the last remaining evidence of the assault, he looked into her eyes and grinned. "Hey, when are you getting this thing off anyway?"

"I've still got three weeks to go…it's driving me crazy."

"You know, George and I are going to take the girls on a trail ride tomorrow afternoon. Do you want to come along? You should be able to ride, right?"

She caressed the hand on her cast, took a deep breath, and blew it out. "It's not my wrist, Mac; it's the head injury. Since it was the second one, they told me I should make sure I never get another injury like that again."

"What about your helmet?"

"You know I love riding, and I won't be able to resist it for long, but I've got so much on my plate right now. I don't want to take any chances. I mean, Mom needs me now, and I have to figure out how to tell Abby everything."

"Yes, and that's going to happen sooner than you think."

"What do you mean?"

"If your father starts coming around, Abby's going to be asking more questions."

Looking away, Maggie nodded. "I'll have to answer them, I know that. Kate and I made a pact never to lie to her, Mac, to explain things as they come up. Katie's told her that she'll meet her birthmother when she's ready. That wasn't a lie. I just don't know if I'll ever be ready."

Mac put an arm around her then. "But she is, Maggie. She keeps telling Lily that she'll be meeting her soon. Actually, she's been obsessing about it for some time now. I think she's mature enough to handle the truth. I know Lily could handle it if she were in Abby's place."

"I know, I know. I have to level with her, but how do I tell her about her father? What if she figures it out when we go to trial? She's pretty good at math, you know. She might read something in the paper or hear it on the news…then she'll know that he's the one. Jeez, he doesn't even know she exists, and I never want him to know."

"Why can't you just tell her that her father was cruel to you, and you didn't want him to hurt her, too? Then, if down the line she puts two and two together, you haven't lied. You don't have to go into the details of the abuse…I don't think that would be good for her anyway. Tell her that she has to wait until she's eighteen to meet him or something like that. Maybe that would be enough for now."

"I'll have to do it just right, Mac. I mean, I don't want her to think she'll turn out like him or something," she said, leaning into him for support.

Mac pulled her against him, wrapping his arms around her and patting her back. "The first step is the hardest. Everything will be fine. I think Abby might be angry at first, mad about you and Kate keeping this from her. But she has so many people who love her….she'll be okay. And you'll be fine, too. For some strange reason, they all love you, too… with or without mascara running down your face," he said as he moved a hand from her back to lift her chin so he could look into her eyes.

She smiled, chuckled, and focused on his lips. "How about you…is the mascara a turnoff?"

Without uttering a word, he answered her question with the kisses she seemed to love even though he longed for more.

***

In spite of the fact that she was comforted by Mac's visit, Maggie tossed and turned all night long. She couldn't get Grant's explanation for what happened between him and her mother out of her mind. He insisted that Grandma knew where he was, that she had letters, telephone numbers, and addresses to prove it, but she'd been gone for years, so there was no way to substantiate his claims.

As soon as the morning sun peeked through her bedroom window, Maggie jumped out of bed, started a pot of coffee, wrapped her cast in a plastic bag, and hopped into the shower. As the warm water washed over her, she began to wonder whether or not Grandma kept anything of value or if there was any evidence that she'd kept in touch with Grant. She and Kate had packed up Grandma's house and had given the clothing, dishes, and furniture to Goodwill before putting the house on the market. She didn't know why she hadn't thought of it before, but anything Grandma wanted them to have had to be packed in those plastic tubs…the ones with their names taped to the covers. The containers didn't mean anything to her at the time, but now she was beginning to wonder what kind of information was hidden inside. Didn't Kate bring them back here with her? She knew that she didn't have hers because she'd recently packed and shipped all of her belongings from Seattle to Wisconsin. Could there be anything in those tubs that could prove that Grant was telling the truth?

After drying her hair, dressing, and spending some time flipping through the Sunday paper, Maggie dialed her sister.

"Hello," Kate said hurriedly when she finally answered the phone.

"Hi, Sis."

"Just the person I want to talk to. What the heck happened yesterday?"

"It's a long story. Can I come over?"

"Please do. Mom isn't coming out of her room. I'm worried about her…she says she doesn't want to talk…says she just wants to be left alone."

"Where's everyone else?"

"George took Abby to Sunday School. I felt like I didn't dare leave the house with mom in such a mood. Anyway, after church they're heading out to Mac's for lunch and a trail ride."

"Oh, that's right. Hey, Kate? Did you bring some bins back with you after Grandma passed away?"

"Yup, two or three of them. I just went through Mom's a while ago to get a couple of pictures for Abby's scrapbook, but there's enough stuff in there to fill dozens of scrapbooks. I know right where they are. Why?"

"Did you see any letters or bundles of letters? Anything like that?"

"I wasn't looking for that kind of stuff. I just wanted some pictures for Abby."

"Okay, but I really think we should look through them. I'll explain when I get there."

"What's this all about?"

"I just want to do some snooping…help Mom out a little. Could you whip up some of your famous baked apple pancake? I'm coming over."

***

Sure enough, there were three bins in Kate's basement storeroom…huge tubs, at that. They were too big for the women to lift much less carry up the stairs, so Kate scrounged around for some cardboard boxes and plastic laundry baskets, and the women divided the loot into the various containers so they'd be manageable. While they were working, Maggie filled Kate in on her conversations with Grant and her mother, letting her know that she was hoping to find something, anything that would prove that Grant wasn't lying about trying to contact Claire. By the time they finished hauling all of it into Kate's kitchen, they were more than ready to eat.

"I'll get started on the pancakes. You go and get Mom down here," Kate ordered. "I just hope that whatever you're looking for doesn't make her feel worse."

"Most of this is probably just old school papers, report cards, diplomas…things like that. But wouldn't it be great if we found even one letter from Grant or something that would prove that he was in contact with Grandma?"

Kate turned from the kitchen counter where she was working. "I'm proud of you for caring, for doing this for Mom."

"Then you agree that we have to give it a try?"

"Yup," she said, waving crossed fingers at her sister, wishing her luck.

Maggie laughed. "I'll go and get her." She took a deep breath, left the kitchen, and climbed the stairs to the second floor of her sister's house. Her mother was staying in one of the four bedrooms on the second floor…the guest room on the left… and Maggie put her ear to the door when she reached it. She didn't hear a sound.

"Mom, can I come in," Maggie asked after lightly tapping on the door.

"I really don't want any company…okay, honey?"

"Kate's making her wonderful baked apple pancake. Come on…we've got something that'll make you feel better." There was no response.

"Want to help us sort through some of the old stuff Grandma saved for us? It could be good for a few laughs."

The door knob turned in Maggie's hand, and her mother peeked at her from the other side of the door. "I look like hell," she said.

Maggie laughed, pushed the door aside, and grabbed her mother in her arms. She leaned back then and took a good look at Claire. "Come on now…wash your face, throw on some sweats and join us."

"I don't own any sweats," she replied.

"Excuse me! Then how about some lingerie…I know you've got enough of that."

Claire relaxed and smiled for the first time. "I'll figure something out."

"Okay, now get a move on," Maggie said as she grabbed her mother by the shoulders, turned her around, and shoved her back into her room, only to have her spin around to face her.

"But aren't you seeing Grant again today…I mean, isn't that why he stayed for the weekend?" Claire asked sheepishly.

Maggie couldn't look her mother in the eye. "No, he left."

"When?" Claire asked, wide-eyed with surprise.

"Last night. I called the hotel to apologize for not letting him tell his side of the story, and they said he'd checked out."

"He checked out? He didn't stay the night?"

"No, so come on, Mom. Let's forget about all that and have some fun."

Chapter 6

CLAIRE

Claire's thoughts went into overdrive. Was it her fault he left? Maybe he was afraid he'd run into her again and that was the last thing he wanted. How did this happen? How did he end up hating her so? She'd never asked him for a thing, never hunted him down, and gave up wishing things were different a long time ago.

Thank goodness for her two sweet daughters. Claire knew she didn't deserve them, but here they were, asking her to spend a quiet Sunday with them. Besides that, if she knew what was good for her, she'd stop trying to analyze what went wrong in her past and concentrate on building a relationship with her girls instead. With renewed enthusiasm, she shuffled to the guest bathroom to wash up only to be shocked by what saw in the mirror; she looked as though she hadn't slept for a week. Her lips were chapped, her nose was red, and her normally beautiful, deep set, green eyes appeared to have sunk into her head. She groaned loudly, opened the medicine cabinet, and grabbed her prescription bottles. After twisting off the child-proof cap of the first one, Claire emptied a small white pill into the palm of her hand. She tossed it into her mouth and swallowed. She knew that she really needed it today even though she'd been on some kind of antidepressant for most of her adult life. She wished she didn't have to depend upon them, but she never, ever wanted to return to the state she was in before the doctors figured out how to help her. Next, she swallowed the only thing that kept her focused and on task for the better part of a day. She knew she couldn't live without the meds; she didn't dare try.

While Claire washed her face, brushed her teeth, and tried to do something with her unruly blonde curls, she thought about how far she'd come in the last few weeks. It wasn't that long ago that Maggie wouldn't speak to her. She was the daughter who, when she was younger, ignored her each and every time she visited. Now, a mere three weeks after they'd reconnected, she was inviting her to breakfast. Not only that, Claire could tell that both of her daughters truly cared about her well-being. She had to thank God for that one. She'd certainly done nothing to deserve either of them. The firstborn, Kate, the child she'd delivered when she was barely sixteen, looked nothing like her but exactly like her father...the tall, slender neighbor boy with dark, curly hair who'd seduced Claire in the hay mow and then denied everything, leaving Claire to bear the child and the humiliation alone. Her youngest daughter, the child she and Grant were going to raise together, took after her. Maggie had the same deep set green eyes, same cheekbones and dimples, and the same beautiful smile as Claire and her mother, Martha. Not only did they resemble one another, all three of them were blessed with the same body type...the enviable hourglass figure. Claire had struggled with her weight just like her mother; although, she got a handle on it after reaching middle age. She could see that Maggie still fought to keep off the pounds, running at the U or around the lake whenever she had a chance, but Claire thought she looked wonderful even with a little extra weight on her.

Claire rummaged around in her still unpacked boxes until she came up with some linen Capri-style pants and a relaxed fit, long sleeved summer big shirt. She felt better about herself now that her meds had kicked in, so she slipped her feet into her platform sandals and headed downstairs.

As Claire entered the kitchen, she saw her daughters sitting among boxes, baskets, and bins of all shapes and sizes. There were piles of folders, papers, and photographs everywhere.

"What in the world?" Claire asked, astounded.

"Oh, Mom, come here. Look at all this junk that Grandma saved. It's hilarious. There's every little drawing we did, every school project, pictures from the newspaper, cards we'd made..."

"Good grief...I had no idea she saved all of that."

"Neither did we. Your bin is over there. We took some of the stuff out and put it in that laundry basket so we could carry it upstairs. Want something to eat…some coffee first?"

"Sure, but why in the world did you drag all this stuff out?"

Kate gave Maggie a wide-eyed look, forcing her to confess. "It's all my fault, Mom. Don't get mad, okay, but I couldn't get Grant's story out of my head…how he said Grandma always knew where he was."

Claire released a sigh, closed her eyes, and slowly shook her head. "Maggie, don't. You're only going to be disappointed again."

"Maybe, maybe not. Let's just look through the stuff anyway, okay?"

"Think about it, Maggie," Claire said as she released a giggle. "If my mother had wanted to keep this big secret from me, she sure wouldn't put it in a box with my name on top!"

"Oh, jeez, what's wrong with me?" Maggie asked, shaking her head and chuckling as she rose to go to her mother. "I'm sorry. I don't know what I was thinking."

Claire hugged her daughter to her. "You just want everything to be perfect."

"I'm beginning to think you're right about that."

Kate turned from the stove where she'd pulled a cookie sheet of baked bacon and a pan of her apple pancakes out of the oven. "Well, that's it then. Let's eat!"

Maggie hurried to set the table while Claire poured herself a cup of coffee, leaned against the counter, and watched her daughters. *I definitely made the right decision. I know that this is exactly where I belong.*

***

The pancake dish was long gone, the dishes were picked up, and the kitchen table was wiped clean before the women refilled their coffee cups and got back to business. Claire finally relented and began looking through the stuff from her oversized bin. Her daughters' containers were full of childhood memorabilia, but Claire encountered something very different. Her tub and the basket were layered with old brown accordion files. There were stacks of them, and as she searched through the first few of them, she found legal papers such as marriage and baptismal certificates, shot records, diplomas, and old family photographs. She shuffled through the photos and passed on a few of people she recognized, explaining how they were related to them and so forth. Kate confessed that she'd looked at them and grabbed a few of the ones she knew for sure for Abby's 'famous people in my family' scrapbook. Claire smiled to herself, remembering how she'd found the glitter covered album. Still, there were plenty of photographs to go around; each woman's likeness could fill several scrapbooks. The women enjoyed comparing their school pictures and noticed that they could barely tell Claire's photographs from Maggie's. Kate asked if she could have some of the better pictures so she could make copies for all of them. Claire gladly handed her the files, and Kate carried them into her office.

While the women searched through the memorabilia in the various collections, they were surprised to learn that some of the items went as far back as the Civil War and her great-great grandfather's discharge papers. They were amazed by what they found there, but also flabbergasted by the fact that they had never seen any of it before. Together, they came to the conclusion that, Martha, their mother and grandmother, must have thought that the past wasn't important enough to share with them or, perhaps, she didn't think that they'd be interested anyway.

Claire continued digging, turning her attention to the laundry basket brimming with more of the old brown accordion folders. Kate and Maggie were content to enjoy their coffee and watch while their mother pulled out spreadsheets, accounting journals, and tax and bank statements.

"My mother, the accountant," Claire said, laughing.

"It's no laughing matter, Mom. She made a good living at it," Kate reminded her.

"I know. She made sure you girls never wanted for anything."

"No kidding. I mean, she bought that house in Rock Creek so she could work from home while we were growing up. Besides that, I think she was invaluable to lots of small businesses."

"But girls, I still don't understand how she could afford to buy that house? When I left home, the farm was mortgaged to the hilt. She couldn't have made any money when she sold it."

Kate shrugged her shoulders. "I don't know how she did it, but we lived in a good neighborhood. She always drove nice cars, too."

"Maybe she was a lady of the evening," Claire joked, making air quotes with her hands.

Maggie chuckled. "More like our Lady of the Cross."

"I think we spent more time in church than we did in school, and she always made us wear dresses or long skirts, you know? Good girls didn't wear jeans or mini skirts or any of that," Kate informed her mother. "If our high school friends hadn't shared their clothes with us, we would have been complete outcasts."

"Sorry…I didn't know…I thought she'd be easier on you girls than she was on me," Claire admitted quietly.

"She was strict, but somehow we knew we were loved," Kate said with a shrug of her shoulders.

Maggie cleared her throat and both Claire and Kate turned to look at her. "Mom, we hope you can explain why you left…when you're ready, I mean."

"What? You know why I left. It wasn't any kind of secret, that's for sure."

"No…Grandma wouldn't tell us anything…just something about you being sick…that's what she told everyone. We thought you were under a doctor's care somewhere, wasting away from some horrible disease, but you seemed fine when you came to visit. Then when you'd leave again, we were left more confused than before."

Claire expelled a defeatist sigh. "I'm sorry...I assumed you knew everything." She simply shook her head, asked to be excused, and hurried out of the room.

42

Chapter 7

MAGGIE

The younger women weren't surprised when their mother left so abruptly, and neither of them followed her. They were just getting to know her, and they'd learned early on that she preferred to be left alone when she was upset. Besides that, they were as stumped as she was and had no idea what to say to her anyway.

"Why do you suppose Grandma didn't tell us more about Mom?" Kate began.

Maggie was baffled. "I don't know, and I'm beginning to think that she didn't tell Mom everything either. And I don't think she's handling any of this well…Grant, her mother, what happened between the three of them."

"I don't get it…any of it."

"Do you think it would be okay if we looked at her stuff? I bet we'll find some answers in here," Maggie offered.

"Mom didn't seem to think there'd be anything of substance, so I guess it'd be okay," Kate agreed, albeit halfheartedly.

"Let's just look for anything that would connect her to Grant. A telephone number scratched somewhere, an address for him…anything that would indicate that they were in touch."

Kate got into the investigation then, telling Maggie that it might be kind of fun. Maggie began by reaching across the table and grabbing the file with all of the accounting paraphernalia that her mother had opened previously. When she began to sort through it, she noticed that her grandmother saved separate ledgers for each of her long time clients…the dry cleaners, the nursery, the local bakery, the movie theatre, a chiropractor, and the church, of course. There were entries for their receivables and payables, payroll and banking information. Maggie found nothing of interest there, handed those files over to Kate, and reached for the last one. As she untied the frayed, brown string and opened the tattered folder, she discovered that she was holding the file that contained their grandmother's personal financial records. *Bingo!* One by one, she pulled out a few household budget binders, outdated savings account passbooks, envelopes of bank statements, a manila folder entitled 'deeds', and a battered old address book.

After taking stock of the personal affects, Maggie began to have second thoughts. "Katie, you know what? Maybe we shouldn't. Mom should be the one to look at this personal stuff."

"Should we just take this up to her and let her sort through it in private? This is the end of it anyway…the bin is empty."

"I'll do it; although, I wish I could be a fly on the wall when she goes through it," Maggie confessed.

"No more wishing and enough with the secrets…let's look at it together," Claire said, surprising them as she unexpectedly re-entered the kitchen.

Maggie stood, threw an arm around her mother, and pulled her close. Kate slid out of her chair and joined them to initiate a group hug.

"Do you know how much I need you girls?" Claire asked, suppressing a sob.

"About as much as we need you," Kate said, affirming their growing affection for one another.

Chapter 8

CLAIRE

Because of the untold amount of admiration she held for her daughters, Claire decided right then and there that she would tell them everything no matter how long it took. She would be straightforward, honest, and strong. *Help me with this one, God...help me so I don't break down in front of them...help me so I don't turn into a blubbering idiot.* She was grateful that the rest of the family had gone on a long trail ride and wouldn't be back for awhile, just in case.

"How about we grab some coffee and settle in the living room where we'll be more comfortable," Claire suggested, moving steadily in that direction.

"I'll make a fresh pot," Kate told them. Meanwhile, Maggie stuffed her grandmother's personal records back into the old file folder, shoved it under one of her arms, and followed her mother.

Claire plopped onto the ample, linen sofa and adjusted one of the colorful throw pillows behind her to support the small of her back. Maggie sat down on the opposite end, curling her legs under her as she dropped the file between them. After setting a box of tissues on the large square teak coffee table and getting a laugh from the other two, Kate dropped onto the thick ivory carpet in front of her mother.

"The coffee's on...looks like we're going to need a lot of it," Kate joked.

"Is it too early for wine?" Claire pleaded.

"How about Irish coffee? That might do the trick."

Claire reached over and mussed her daughter's dark curls. "A girl after my own heart," she said before clearing her throat. "Okay then, let's get this show on the road. What do you want to know?"

Kate and Maggie glanced at each other. "You first," Maggie said.

"Okay. Just tell us why you went away…that's all I really want to know anyway," Kate admitted in an unusually subdued tone of voice.

Claire concentrated on her lap, nervously rubbing the palms of her hands over her thighs. "I don't want to blame my mother. She tried, I know she did, but no one…not her, not the doctors or teachers…really knew what was wrong with me."

"You mean when you were young?" Maggie asked.

"Yes," Claire answered, nodding. "I wasn't really a difficult kid, but my teachers told my mother that I was scatterbrained. Now I know that I suffered from Attention Deficit Disorder but nobody knew anything about that back then. I mean, I couldn't focus, couldn't pay attention at home or at school. I didn't make many friends…probably because they could tell I didn't learn the same way they did. But as I got older, Mama noticed that if I exercised, spent a lot of time outside, riding and taking care of the horses, that it helped my concentration. After you were born, Katie, I didn't want to go back to the high school in town…suffer the humiliation, you know? Anyway, Mama sent me to the Christian high school in Onalaska, and for some reason, I started to do well in school. I think it helped that the classes were very small, and I got a lot of one-on-one. I started to like school and got good grades for the first time in my life."

"We knew kids that went there, too, but wasn't it expensive?" Maggie asked.

"I'm sure it was, but Mama never said a word about how she paid for it. I think she liked that I was going to a church school. When I was little, she thought that the Lord would heal me. We spent a lot of time in church. I wasn't defiant or disruptive when I was young, but I couldn't focus…I thought I was dumb…Mama thought I was lazy and wasn't trying. You know, my self-esteem got pretty low, and by the time I was in high school, it was the attention from the boys that got me through those first couple of years. Actually, having Katie and switching schools in my junior year saved me from myself, that's for sure," Claire admitted, looking away and clearing her throat self-consciously.

"What about Grandpa? Where was he in all this?" Kate wondered out loud.

"Mama didn't tell you a thing, did she?" Claire said, shaking her head in disbelief. "Well, first of all, I don't think they had much of a marriage, but I don't think either of them had any choice in the matter either. Your grandfather was going to take over his parents' huge farm, and if he married the neighbor girl he might get theirs, too. And he needed a partner who was as hard working as he was…someone raised on a farm. His parent's were going to make sure of that. Then when his first born child was a girl, he had to have been disappointed. He needed sons to help run the farm, you know? Mama didn't have any more children…I don't think that helped their relationship. Do you remember that he had a series of strokes? Anyway, his personality changed for the worst. It had to have been hard for Mama, and a year or so before he died, I had you, Maggie, my second illegitimate kid. He said he'd never be able to hold his head up again. They were really ashamed of me, you know?"

Kate draped an arm over Claire's legs and hugged them. "Why did you leave us, Mom?"

Claire patted her daughter's arm and swallowed hard before continuing. "It's a long story, darling. You know about post-partum depression, right?"

"Yup," her well-educated daughters responded in unison.

"I was so despondent when Grant left me. He said his parents sent him away, but I don't know that for sure. Anyway, the depression just got worse and worse." Claire turned toward her youngest child. "By the time you were born, Maggie, I wasn't able to appreciate you at all. One doctor thought it might be post-partum depression. I don't know. All I do know is that I felt nothing for you. I didn't want to hold you, take care of you, nothing. I was in this constant fog that wouldn't lift, wouldn't leave me. Grandma did everything for you girls. I couldn't get out of bed. When I did, I'd just sit in the shower and cry. She couldn't leave me alone with you because she didn't know if I would hurt you or myself."

Claire felt Maggie rub her arm, but she couldn't look her in the eye and, instead, stared a hole into her lap. "This went on for way too long, turned into a clinical anxiety disorder. Since my mother couldn't get me to leave the farm...I had panic attacks if I did...one of my doctors suggested that I be hospitalized for awhile." She cleared her throat. "It was a psychiatric facility. Very scary, I know, but they saved my life. I got the therapy and the medication that I needed and eventually I moved from there to job training and a group home until I could live on my own."

"Couldn't you have come home then?" Kate asked.

Still focusing on her hands, Claire could only shake her head. "I was away for a couple of years, honey. I was so ashamed, you know, and all the therapy in the world couldn't take that away. By the time I got the nerve to come home, it was too late; Mama had custody. She wasn't going to give that up. Her husband was gone, and you two were all she had."

"But, Mom, we were yours, not hers," Maggie interjected.

"She knew that I wouldn't have been able to handle you, and she was right. I could barely take care of myself."

Kate was nodding her head. "So that's why she said you were sick."

"She wasn't fooling anyone, you know. The whole town knew about my mental health issues, and I'm sure my mother couldn't avoid the stigma, the stereotyping that went along with it. I bet she made up for it, though, because she had to have been respected for raising her grandchildren alone like that."

"So you didn't dare come home to stay, did you? Even if you wanted to," Maggie surmised out loud.

Claire shook her head. "No, Mama was the only mother you knew, and I knew that she would try her best, just like she did with me. Anyway, for many years, I could barely support myself much less raise two kids. Remember when I did come to see you a couple of times a year or so? I lived for those visits, you know? I would do any lousy job, work any hours as long as I could see a light at the end of the tunnel and a visit with my girls," Claire said as she looked from one daughter to the other. What she saw, however, broke her heart. Her daughters were both sobbing into their hands. Her reserve left her then, and she lost control.

In due time, Claire and her daughters were able to stop crying long enough to hug and tell each other that it didn't matter anymore. They had each other now and for the rest of their lives. In turn, they visited the lower level powder room or the guest bathroom upstairs in an effort to compose themselves just in case anyone came home early.

Claire was the first to return to the living room to continue to look through her mother's things, and the address book was the first item she attacked with vigor. Flipping through the yellowing pages of the tattered book, Claire searched for anything that would tie Grant to her mother. When she didn't find his name or accompanying address or telephone number, she checked for the initials G and H or GLH or any combination thereof. Determined to find something, anything, she didn't stop with the G and H sections of the little book, but scoured the pages under every letter of the alphabet. For the first time in her life, Claire became aware of the fact that her mother kept impeccable records even when it came to something as ordinary as an address book. Beginning with her own name and address, Claire noticed that whenever her own address changed, her mother crossed off the old address and added the new one with the date of the change printed in the margin next to it; her numerous address changes covered three entire pages.

Once she realized how precise her mother had been with the dates, Claire looked for any changes or additions for late 1973, when Maggie was born, and for other addresses or telephone numbers added during the following two or three years. Sadly, there was nothing that could corroborate Grant's story, reaffirming what she had always believed...he'd lied to her about everything, and he continued to do so to this very day. She didn't break down, though, because her motivation, her focus had changed. From now on, it would be all about her daughter, and she would continue the search for Maggie's sake, hoping to find something that would redeem Grant, something to verify his story. She understood that it was too late for her, forty years too late, and nothing had changed as far as she was concerned, but her daughter deserved to know the truth about her conception, her birth, everything.

Claire tossed the address book aside and moved onto the next folder. There she inadvertently stumbled upon a document that would change everything she thought she knew about her mother's livelihood. When she opened the old accordion folder that Maggie had tossed between them, she grabbed the first manila file, flipped it open, and picked up a real estate closing document and the buyer's agreement recording the sale of the farm. As she looked over the documents, she noted that the mortgage for the farm was held at a bank in La Crosse and was paid in full; in fact, the lien form was stamped 'paid' in bright red ink. There was also a purchase agreement for the house in Rock Creek. There was no mortgage, but she saw that the house in town was purchased the very same day and paid for in full by her mother. Claire had no idea about any of this and had always assumed her mother paid the mortgage off during the twenty some years she'd lived in town.

None of this made any sense to Claire until she began to look at the paperwork more closely. She searched for the name of the buyer at the bottom of the real estate closing statement and when she recognized it, she gasped involuntarily. Blood rushed to her head, and the room began to spin. Suddenly, the search through her mother's financial records took on new meaning, and she was going to get to the bottom of it if it was the last thing she did.

One by one, Claire yanked out her mother's bank statements. Her mother had them bound in groups by year. Claire started with the package that contained the statements from the year she sold the farm…the year Maggie turned two. She saw nothing out of the ordinary in the deposits for the checking or savings accounts. One of her bank statements, however, showed an unusual deposit for the month of January the year after the farm was sold. There in her mother's savings account was a deposit amounting to ten thousand dollars. Surprised by the size of the deposit, Claire searched through the statements for that year and spotted nothing suspicious. But, on the first day of the following year and just as Claire surmised, there was another deposit for the same amount, and her mother's savings account balance doubled.

"Did you find something?" Maggie asked when she re-entered the room.

Claire didn't answer her daughter. Instead, she handed her the lien release form and watched her reaction to the name at the bottom of the page. There it was, typed in the space labeled 'buyer' and signed *Grant Leland Harrison II.* Maggie gasped. "What? Is that Grant's legal name?"

"Indeed it is! Did you know anything about this? Did Mama ever say anything? Did she ever say anything about getting gifts from anyone or anything like that?"

Maggie could only shake her head, bewildered. "How could this be, Mom? How could Grant have afforded that…he would have been 23 or 24 in 1975."

After shrugging her shoulders, Claire told her daughter what she knew. "I swear that Grant said he wouldn't be getting anything from his trust fund until he turned 35. I don't get this at all. He couldn't have paid the lien on the farm, given her enough money so she could buy the house in town, and then give her extra money every year to boot!"

"Maybe his trust fund was divided up, and he got some of it earlier. Do you think it was his way of supporting me or something?"

"Could be, I guess. He'd have to do it behind his parents back, though. They threatened me, remember? I wasn't to put his name on the birth certificate or contact them ever again." Claire took a deep breath in an effort to compose herself before casting a serious look toward her youngest daughter. "Do you want to help me do some more digging?"

"Try and stop me!"

Eventually, Kate joined her mother and sister and together the three of them painstakingly sorted through Grandma's files. Just as Claire surmised, the monetary gifts continued until her mother's death when her daughters were in their late twenties, and according to her will, the profit from the house, the life insurance benefits, and the money in her bank accounts was split between Claire and her daughters. She remembered thinking that their inheritance was a lot more than she'd ever expected.

Claire could tell by the bank statements when her mother transferred money from her savings to her checking account, probably for the bigger expenses such as real estate taxes or automobiles. Kate told her about her mother's love for cars, that they were her status symbols. She figured if she drove expensive cars, the businessmen in town would take her seriously and come to the conclusion that she must have been a smart business woman at that. They told Claire that her mother got more and more clients as the years went by and along with that came better and better cars.

Kate said that she loved new cars as much as her grandmother and thought she might be able to remember when she bought them, so she made some notes about how old she was when she upgraded her vehicles, what kind of cars she bought, and whether they were new or used. Maggie went through the bank accounts and tried to match the withdrawals from her savings accounts to the purchases. She found some matches to the times Kate figured she'd bought a car, obviously putting those annual deposits to good use. Claire found real estate tax statements marked paid and was able to match these to withdrawal or transfer dates from her savings to her checking accounts. She figured her mother needed those yearly deposits to keep up her standard of living, yet there was nothing in her records to indicate their source.

When the women opened the bank statements for the year that Kate started college at Madison, there were no unusually large withdrawals from Grandma's account.

"This doesn't make sense. Grandma paid my tuition and room and board in full each semester," Kate said out loud.

"Mine, too," Maggie added.

"Did either of you see any other accounts in this mess?"

Both of the women shook their heads.

"There were no unusual transfers or withdrawals after we left home…just the real estate taxes, income tax payments…stuff like that," Kate confirmed, glancing at the mess on the living room floor to see if there was any folder or file they might not have opened.

"So you're telling me that you didn't have to take out any student loans, or get scholarships or grants to pay for your college education?"

Again, both of her daughters shook their heads, and all color drained from Claire's face.

"Mom, all I remember is Grandma telling me that she'd saved money to pay for our college and that we didn't have to worry about a thing. I never saw an invoice, a bill of any kind."

"But Maggie, as far as we can tell, it didn't come from any of her accounts. She couldn't have made some sort of deal with Grant, could she have?"

"What kind of deal? He never came to see me. There isn't anything here to suggest he wanted custody, so what was in it for him? His name isn't even on my birth certificate, for crying out loud."

"But, Maggie, didn't you tell me that he said Grandma always knew how to get in touch with him?"

Claire watched her daughter nod, a sheepish look on her face. She felt as though the rug had been pulled out from under her, and she collapsed into the corner of the couch, pulling her knees up to her face and wrapping her arms around them. Her daughters could do nothing or say anything to sooth her. They knew that the truth had to be too much for Claire to bear. Her mother could have been lying to her for most of her adult life. To make matters worse, Grant had been truthful to some extent, but there had to be a lot more to the story.

Out of the blue, Maggie said, "I'm calling him right now."

Claire lifted her head, shook it, and sniffed. "No, Maggie, don't. I'm the one who was lied to. I'm the one who is going to have to get to the bottom of this."

"What are you going to do?"

"Make a trip to Madison. I'll leave in the morning."

***

Later, alone in her room in her daughter's house, Claire lay wide awake on her side with a pillow covering her head. She wanted to bawl, she wanted to scream bloody murder, but, most of all, she wanted to fall into a deep sleep and awake to learn that the day had simply been a bad dream. Could the two of them have connived to deceive her? What had she ever done to deserve that? She always thought her mother was on her side…she knew her father never wanted her to begin with…but her mother? Her mother was her rock, her savior. Her mother knew she was different and did everything she could to help her overcome her difficulties. And when she became pregnant at such a young age, her mother was there to counsel her, to keep her from making a decision that she would forever regret. So, with her help, she kept the baby…her beautiful Katie.

Claire reached over to turn on the lamp on the nightstand so that she could see where she put her journal. It lay on the floor where she'd left it the night before, and she threw an arm over the edge of the bed to scoop it up. After arranging her pillows behind her and snuggling in, Claire searched for her pen, located it on her nightstand, opened her journal to where she'd left off the day before, and settled in to write her heart out.

Dearest Journal,

This has been a day to remember. In some ways, it might be the most disturbing day of my life. I just learned that my dear departed mother may have lied to me for years. Could it be that getting pregnant a second time sent my mother over the top? Okay, so maybe she could forgive one indiscretion, but two? Maybe that was too much to ask, but it wasn't like I did it on purpose. Grant and I truly loved each other…at least, that's what I thought back then…and we were careful, we didn't mean to get pregnant. Besides that, we were going to get married even if we had to run away to do it. And he loved Katie, too. We were going to be a family. What more could I ask for?

You remember that Grant's parents had other ideas, don't you dear journal? No way was the heir to their fortune going to marry a tramp with a kid. Grant was oblivious to all of it…living in la la land…thinking it would all work out somehow. But his mother had other plans. First of all, she insisted that I have an abortion. I refused, of course. You know I could never do that, especially since I knew what it was like to give another human being life. Then she said that if I went through with the pregnancy, I had better keep Grant's name off the birth certificate….if I didn't, there would be dire consequences. She scared me to death, and when I told Grant all about it, he told me not to worry. He would talk to her, she'd calm down, and he'd be back. I never saw him again. And he never contacted me until a year ago when his only daughter was more than 36 years old. Can you believe it?

The question remains…did he and my mother conspire against me? It doesn't make any sense to me. As far as I can tell, he never laid eyes on Maggie, never asked for custody, and never asked where I was either. But why did he buy Mama's farm? Was he giving her money, too?

Claire could no longer write. The questions she was asking were breaking her heart all over again.

***

It was the first time Claire had driven to Madison on I-94. When she lived in Rock Creek and drove to the capital city to attend the university, there were no interstate highways in Wisconsin, so she drove her mother's lackluster Ambassador Sedan down old Highway 14 for probably 150 miles, halfway across the state. Today, from Lake Louise, the drive would be 220 miles or so, and it would take an agonizing four hours if she followed the speed limit. Claire started out as early as she could manage…by 6 am. She hadn't slept well anyway, so she got up before the sun, showered and dressed, and then packed her carryon with what she might need the next day in case she couldn't see Grant when she got there.

Claire had become very good at self talk, and today, alone in her car with only her thoughts to keep her company, the inner dialogue began in earnest. She reminded herself that she was in charge of her own life, that no matter what she learned today, she alone would choose how to handle the calamity that was sure to come her way. But, more importantly, she needed to be in a positive frame of mind in order to conger up the confidence to walk into his office and ask for him. She could do it because she was grateful for the life she'd lived, with and without him, and whatever was in store for her today wouldn't change that.

Driving her high end sports car gave Claire comfort. As a woman of small stature, she could relax in her Porsche Carrera GT because every button and knob was within easy reach. Her throat automatically tightened, though, as memories of her dear, sweet Mel surfaced. She recalled the day that Mel gave her the car, telling her that he'd ordered it especially for her, that he wanted to make sure it was a perfect fit. It had served her well on the loops in and around Phoenix, and she had him to thank for that. She'd always remember him as one of the most decent human beings she'd ever met, and it shouldn't have surprised her when he told her that he understood her need to move to Wisconsin in order to reconcile with her daughters. He said he understood because he'd never be able to move away from his own children. With that simple statement of fact, Claire knew it was over. It was really too bad. Mel was as close as she ever got to being married and having a so-called normal life, and she missed him dearly.

Claire shook her head to stop her train of thought and began to focus on the road ahead. Before long, she was zipping in and out of traffic on I-94 without hesitation. In fact, Claire leaned back into her leather seat and began to relax as the highway unraveled before her. She'd be driving east and then south with the sun in her eyes much of the way, but it didn't matter today because the landscape to the left, right and directly ahead of her was gorgeous. She was sure that the lush vegetation in August and September in Wisconsin was unparalleled, and its beauty, along with her affirming talk, served to calm her inner turmoil.

Claire hadn't driven through the Knapp hills before, but the area reminded her of the foothills of the Great Smokey Mountains, one of her favorite vacation spots. When she passed through Wisconsin's driftless area, the deeply carved river valleys missed by the last glacier thousands of years earlier, her heart sang. She had chosen to live a life filled with joy, and she'd found it in Arizona. Today, she could safely say that Wisconsin offered her the chance to embrace that very same emotion, and she was grateful beyond words. That appreciation for everything in her life was exactly what she needed to keep her calm and steady today.

As she got closer to her destination, she began to pass through areas of Wisconsin that she'd never have visited if it weren't for Grant.

Her family hadn't traveled except to family reunions in Iowa and when she told him that, he said that he couldn't wait to show her all that her home state had to offer. About three hours into her drive she passed Wisconsin Dells and marveled at how the place had grown. In fact, she didn't recognize it at all, but remembered the day that she and Grant skipped school in the early fall so he could take her there. He wanted her to experience riding the army ducks, the best way to see the rock formations on the Wisconsin River. She wondered if there was still such a thing as 'ducks' because as far as she could tell the place had been overrun by monstrous water-park hotels. When she had driven another thirty minutes or so, she spotted the exit to Spring Green and recalled how Grant loved the place. He was a huge fan of Frank Lloyd Wright and insisted on taking her to Taliesin, the genius's home and architecture school. Grant dreamed of building a prairie style house someday; he told her they'd do it together. She wondered if he'd gone ahead and done it without her.

After one break along the freeway for a cup of coffee, Claire headed toward Madison and the Washington Avenue exit. Because she'd searched for the address ahead of time, Claire knew that Grant's office was in the new Dane County Courthouse, off of Fairchild on Hamilton, not more than a block from the Capital's inner circle. Luckily, Claire remembered her way around Madison and easily found the building she was looking for; in fact, she couldn't miss it if she tried because it towered over everything else for blocks around. Finding a parking spot so close to the Capital would be a problem, though, but Claire was determined to do just that. As she drove down Doty and turned the corner onto King, a car pulled out. She was just two or three blocks from the courthouse; she gave thanks and pulled into the now empty space.

It was a beautiful morning, so Claire didn't mind walking a ways to reach the massive ten-story, flatiron courthouse. Once inside, she found Grant's name and office number, 3000, listed on the directory near the marble columns in the brightly lighted lobby. The Senior District Attorney's office was located on the third floor, but before Claire hopped onto an elevator, she took a detour to the restroom. After relieving herself, she stood at the sink, washing her hands and asking herself what she hoped to accomplish. Would he tell her the truth or had he made a pact of silence with her mother? She shook her head at her reflection in the mirror. *Don't be silly. There has to be another explanation for all of this.* With renewed confidence, she ran a comb through her hair and leaned in to apply her lipstick. She was tired; she hadn't slept well the night before, but no one would be able to tell. Her eyes weren't bloodshot, and her concealer had done a good job hiding the circles under her eyes. She made a pact with herself, promising not to cry when she saw him, hoping to keep her makeup job in tact.

Five minutes later, Claire was standing at the door of Grant's office. Out of the blue, panic set in. Her pulse raced out of control; she felt the dreaded perspiration wetting her hairline. She didn't know if she could face him, and even more, she wasn't looking forward to the look of annoyance when she did. *Remember, this is for Maggie. It's her legacy I'm concerned about, not mine.* Her hand was shaking but she took a deep breath, turned the knob, and cautiously pushed the large, wooden door open; the office was empty. She thought that she would wait for a minute or two to see if someone was around when a voice came from the other room.

"I'll be right there."

Claire turned toward the sound of the voice and watched as a stately, well dressed, silver-haired woman come through a door and into the room.

"Good morning. What can I do for you today?" she asked in an unusually cheerful voice as she slid into the chair behind the desk.

Claire cleared her throat. "I'm looking for Grant Harrison. Is he in?"

"No, he's in court right now. Would you like to make an appointment to see him?" the woman asked, concentrating on her computer screen.

"No, I'm not a client. I just need a couple of minutes of his time."

"Okay. You're welcome to wait here, but I really don't know when he'll be free."

"Is there a coffee shop around here?"

The woman nodded. "Yes, about three blocks up on King...the Aurora Cafe. The early rush should be over, so you should be able to find a seat."

"On King? Great, that's where I'm parked. Would you mind telling him that Claire Holmes is waiting for him there?"

Claire turned to go, but the woman repeated her name, stood, and walked to the front of the desk, reaching toward Claire with her right hand. "You're Claire Holmes? I'm so glad to finally meet you. I'm Barbara Kimball, Grant's assistant. I know he'll want to see you. I'll be sure to send him over," she said with a smile.

"You know who I am?" Claire asked, taking the woman's hand in hers.

"Of course."

Claire was surprised that this stranger would recognize her name, and she felt the heat of a blush cover her cheeks.

"I'll be glad to send him over. Promise you'll stay put until he gets there, okay?"

"Sure...I'm not going anywhere."

Chapter 9

GRANT

Grant organized the folders in his briefcase and slammed it shut. The case he'd been prosecuting had encountered another delay. The defense wanted an evaluation of their client's mental health, insinuating that the man was not of sound mind. Grant wanted nothing more than to have this case over and done with. It had dragged on for weeks.

As soon as Grant left the courtroom, his mind was free to wander. He couldn't get Claire's face out of his mind, the way she stared at him when she ran into him at the farm. It was the face of a woman scorned, and it broke his heart to see her that way. And now there was no way for him to prove that he had never lied to her or that he didn't purposely abandon her because Martha Holmes had taken the truth to her grave.

After shaking his head as if to get Claire's image to leave him, Grant continued down the lengthy, pristine hallway to his wing of the building. When he reached his destination, he opened the door to his office only to find his capable assistant sitting behind her desk, a Cheshire grin crossing her aging, yet lovely face.

Grant knew her well, loved her more than his own mother, and laughed at her. "What's tickled your funny bone," he asked.

Barbara widened her eyes. "She's here. Claire's here!"

"Claire who?"

"Your Claire, who else?"

"What do you mean, my Claire? I'm the last person she'd want to see."

Barbara stood then and walked to the front of her desk so she could stand directly in front of her boss. "I don't think so. She's waiting for you at the Aurora."

Grant shook his head in disbelief. "Claire Holmes? Are you sure?"

"She was standing right here less than twenty minutes ago. She said she needed to talk to you about something and would wait for you at the coffee shop. So what are you going to do about that?"

After setting his briefcase on the reception desk, Grant pressed his fingertips into his eyes and rubbed. "I have no idea, Barb. I really don't know what this is about."

"You saw your daughter last weekend, right? Could it be about that?"

Grant dropped into a chair. "Yeah, and I saw Claire briefly, too. Needless to say, it didn't go well. That's why I can't figure out why she's here. I mean, if there was an emergency or something, someone would have called. She wouldn't have had to come all the way down here."

"Well, she did, and I'm going to ask you again. What are you going to do about it?"

"I have a full schedule today, don't I?"

Barbara walked behind her desk, glanced at her computer screen, and clicked her mouse a couple of times. "You don't have any appointments that can't be rescheduled. Why don't you take the rest of the day off so you can straighten things out with her, huh? I'll take care of the rest."

Grant rubbed a hand over his face and nodded his head, reluctantly agreeing with Barbara. "All I know is…this can't be good."

***

Barbara rescheduled all of Grant's appointments for the day so that he'd be free to talk to Claire. With trepidation in his step, he left the courthouse through the front door, crossed the street, and hurried the two blocks to King and his favorite coffee shop. Before opening the door to the Aurora, however, he backed up, sidestepped to the window, and peeked in. He didn't spot her right away and his heart stopped. *She's already left!* But then, a flash of blonde hair caught his eye. There she was, in the back of the café, alone at a table in the center isle.

Grant had no choice but to put on his best game face and walk through that door. Not only because he was meeting Claire, but also due to the fact that everyone he knew frequented the popular café. First of all, he'd be lucky to make it back to her table without someone inviting him to theirs or slapping him on the back, congratulating him on winning his last case and begging to hear the details. At nine in the morning, however, the place was only half full, and it would stay that way until about ten or ten-thirty when the crowd from the capital would swarm into the place for their coffee break. Secondly, if he did make it back to her table without incident, there'd surely be someone around who'd take note of the way in which he was spending his day, and the rumor mills would begin to churn.

He'd barely pulled the door shut behind him when a barista asked him if he wanted the usual. He nodded, but kept his eyes on the booth in the rear. Claire hadn't heard the barista or seen him; her eyes never wandered from whatever she seemed to be reading.

After fumbling in his pocket for some change, Grant grabbed the cup of dark roast, dropped a couple of bucks on the counter, and turned toward the back of the shop. He took a deep breath, attempted to steady his shaking hand, and prayed that he wouldn't be interrupted today of all days. When he stood a few feet away, she looked up and caught his eye. He couldn't help noticing that familiar blush and the way she chewed on her bottom lip. *My Claire!*

"Hi," he said as nonchalantly as possible as he set his coffee cup on the black table top, pulled out the chair directly across from her, and sat down. "You wanted to see me?"

Claire nodded, keeping her eyes focused on the tabletop. "I just need a few minutes of your time. I know you're a busy man, but I have some questions I need answered."

Grant guessed he shouldn't be surprised that she couldn't look him in the eye. "I cleared my calendar, Claire. There's no rush. What is it?"

She surprised him then by simply sliding a folded document toward him. "I just need to know what this is all about," she said.

"What's this?" Grant asked as he opened the certificate. "A real estate closing document? Do you need some legal advice? Is that what this is all about?"

"Just explain to me why you signed it," Claire said, suddenly in charge.

"What are you talking about?" Grant asked as he began to read the yellowing, extra long statement. Then his eyes slid over the signature at the bottom of the page. "Claire, that's my father's signature, not mine."

"But you're Grant Harrison II."

"No…that's my dad. I thought I told you all about that. I'm the third."

Claire looked dumbfounded. "Then why did everyone call you Junior?"

"Sad to say, that was always my nickname, and it followed me to college. So, where did you get this?"

Claire ran her trembling fingers over her brow and chewed on her bottom lip self-consciously. "I found it in my mother's things. Whoever signed this bought my parent's farm, giving my mother enough money to buy a house in Rock Creek."

"What?"

"At first, I thought it was your way of taking care of Maggie or something, but you never told me that you had access to that kind of money, so I couldn't figure it out. That's why I'm here," she stammered.

Grant glanced at the date at the bottom of the form. He was still trapped in Brazil with his missionary grandparents at the time of the signing. "Claire, if my dad did this, I had no idea about it. I had no idea he cared. I mean, they sent me away, didn't they?"

Claire nodded, and he watched her swallow hard. "Do you think he did this to support Maggie? I don't understand why I didn't know anything about this, why my mother didn't tell me."

Grant leaned back in his seat and simply shook his head.

After taking a ragged breath, she continued. "That's not all…my mother had gifts of $10,000 a year deposited in her savings account…every year until she died. We have all of her bank account information…she got it every year like clockwork. Besides that, the girls' college education was paid for. They thought my mother had the money saved for them, but there are no withdrawals or transfers for that kind of money from her accounts during the years they were in college. They said that they never saw an invoice, nothing."

"Oh," Grant said, looking down at his hands. "That was me."

"Huh?"

"I had money by that time, and I'd kept in contact with your mother…just in case you'd come home or she heard from you. Anyway, I thought it was the least I could do…pay for the girls' education," Grant said quietly.

Claire simply stared at him, looking stunned and about to burst into tears, so Grant continued without waiting for her to speak. "When Kate was beginning her senior year of high school, I called Martha and asked her if she had plans for college. She told me that Kate wanted to go to Madison, and that's when I offered to pay her tuition, room and board…Maggie's, too."

Claire squinted at him. "You did?"

After nodding, Grant's voice took on a somber quality. "She was skeptical at first. But during all the years they were growing up, I never once asked for custody or pressured her in any way, so I think she trusted me. "

"She never told me any of this," Claire admitted, shaking her head in disbelief.

"Listen, Claire, I really know nothing about what my father did back then. I have no idea why he did it…they were so vehement about keeping us apart."

"I always thought it was your mother's idea…she's the one who threatened me."

Grant nodded. "My mother was domineering, that's for sure. My dad never had a chance if he disagreed with her about anything. I always knew that. But you know what? Now that I think about it, Dad had his own money, his own businesses that had nothing to do with the family money…my mother's family money. I wonder if he just took things into his own hands. I know that's what I had to do."

"What do you mean?"

"Your mother wouldn't let me see Maggie no matter how often I asked, no matter how much I begged," Grant said, angrily clenching his jaw. "She said she had to get your permission and since you wouldn't give it, she said I couldn't see her."

Claire shook her head, tears brimming her eyes. She sniffed before speaking. "I swear, Grant. She never asked. She never talked to me about you at all."

Grant exhaled, frustrated. "So you never got any of the messages I left, the letters?"

"I never got a thing," Claire muttered quietly before asking for clarification. "So what did you mean…you took things into your own hands?"

"This is going to sound nuts, but every once in a while I'd drive to Rock Creek. I'd park across the street from your mother's place and watch Maggie play in the yard. When she got to be school age, I'd watch her on the playground. Creepy, huh?"

Claire smiled tentatively, briefly glancing upward. "Kind of."

"It got easier when she was in high school. I'd go to games and concerts and look for her. I don't think she ever noticed me. Your mother never did either."

"I'm sorry, Grant. I never knew," Claire said, still concentrating on her hands, folded in front of her.

"She was so beautiful. I thought she looked just like you." He watched Claire shrug her shoulders, ignoring his compliment. "Okay, then," he said, a bit sarcastically, "What do you want?"

"I'm at a loss for words," she sighed without lifting her eyes.

"Well, you came here for a reason. How about we take a drive? You never got to the family home in Maple Bluff. Dad still lives there. He needs some help getting around, but he has all his mental faculties. How about we pay him a visit?"

Claire finally lifted her head; her eyes popped. "Are you going to confront him about this?"

"Why not? Isn't that what you came here for?"

Claire nodded and then cleared her throat self consciously. "Your mother won't be there, will she?"

"No, she's been gone almost a year now. Anyway, they

separated a long time ago."

"I'm sorry."

"No you're not," Grant said, trying his best to keep it light. "So you coming?"

"Might as well."

***

Grant decided to drive ahead of Claire to make sure his father was up to having company; he'd call her cell if it wasn't a good time. As for Claire, she simply asked for the address to add to her GPS and said she'd meet him there. Twenty minutes later, Grant was on the front steps of the stately, hundred year old mansion. He couldn't wait to see his father's face when he walked in with Claire on his arm. That'll show him. On second thought, it might give him a heart attack or something. Still he wanted to see his father's reaction and secretly wished he could tell him that he and Claire were back together. *Talk about wishful thinking.* Grant knocked. Annette, the elderly man's housekeeper for the past twenty years, answered the door.

"Well! If it isn't Wisconsin's top-notch lawyer! What a nice surprise," she greeted with a wink.

"Good morning, Annette. Is Dad up for some company?" Grant asked, grinning.

"I'm sure he'd love it. He's in the study. Come right in."

"I'm waiting for an old friend to join me. Tell him I have a surprise for him. We'll be in shortly."

"Okay. Good thing I just took a pie out of the oven, huh?"

Grant smiled. What a sweet woman! The old grouch was lucky she was so dedicated to him. Grant decided that he must be nicer to her than he is to his own family; otherwise, there would be no reason for her to stay.

Grant waited on the steps, craning his neck and glancing now and then to the street leading to the brick circular driveway. Where is she? A half hour passed and his pulse began to race. If the truth be known, he was thrilled she'd come to find him no matter what the circumstances.

He'd learned from Maggie that Claire had left Mel and moved back to
Wisconsin for good, but after running into her at his daughter's place on
Saturday, he thought he didn't have a chance. By the look on her face,
he knew she wanted nothing to do with him, and he didn't blame her.
Something had changed since then. She hadn't actually looked him in
the eye, but she quizzed him without hesitation…she was a woman on a
mission, and he couldn't be happier. In fact, it didn't even matter what
they learned today because she was here, here in Madison talking to him
face to face. It was a dream come true as far as he was concerned.

Grant began to wonder if she'd chickened out when her Porsche
turned into the driveway. She pulled in behind his sedan and got out a
few seconds later. When he caught her eye, she blushed. He could see it
from yards away. His throat tightened, and his chest burned with shame.
I can't believe I didn't fight harder for her!

Grant all but ran down the steps to greet her. "So you found it," he
said, trying with all his might to keep his composure. She nodded
without looking at him.

His heart sank. "What do you say we get this over with?"

"Sounds good," she said as she climbed the steps ahead of him. He
reached in front of her when she approached the great white door and
pushed it open. She walked into the grand foyer, pausing underneath the
massive crystal chandelier while he closed and locked the door behind
them.

"Dad's in the study. It's this way," he said, walking ahead of her
down a long hallway adorned with professionally painted family
portraits encased in gold gilded frames. When he arrived at the door to
the study, he motioned for her to stop and poked his head inside.

"Dad? You up for some company? I've got a surprise for you."

Grant could see his father seated in his favorite leather armchair;
the overloaded, dark oak bookshelves looming high above him. His legs
were covered by an old plaid wool blanket, his book was turned upside
down on his lap, and he looked completely at peace with himself and his
surroundings. After removing his reading glasses from his nose, he
glanced up at his son.

"Long time, no see. Come on in, Junior."

Grant flinched at hearing the nickname, but turned toward Claire and indicated that she should walk in ahead of him. She did and he followed quickly, keeping his eyes on his father, gauging his reaction. Grant stared unabashedly as his father's jaw dropped and his eyes widened in surprise. His hands flew to his face. "Martha?" he cried.

Claire, in shock, turned to look to Grant for help. He grabbed her forearm.

"Dad...this is Claire...remember...Claire?" Grant asked quickly, astounded by his father's reaction to seeing her.

With great anxiety, his father blurted, "Oh, Oh...I thought you were Martha. Oh, my...I knew it couldn't be...I'm sorry."

Claire just stood there, stunned.

Grant, however, got right to the point. "Dad, that's why we're here. We want to know about your relationship with Claire's mother. What was that all about, Dad?"

To Grant's astonishment, his father began to sob. "I'm so sorry. I miss her so much."

"Who Dad? Who do you miss?"

"Martha...I can't believe she's gone."

Grant felt Claire grab onto his arm and lean into him. He pried her hand off his arm and slid it over her shoulders. After searching the room for a seat, he walked her to a rich brown, leather arm chair that faced his father and helped her slide into it. There was an identical chair nearby, and he left her long enough to shove it next to her and sit down. He glanced at Claire then. She was white as a ghost, her arms were wrapped tightly around her waist, and her lips were pursed as she concentrated on her breathing.

"Are you okay?"

She nodded.

"Want some water or something?"

She simply shook her head and stared stoically ahead. "I just want the truth."

Grant gritted his teeth and inhaled deeply before glaring at his father.

"Dad. What the ...? You and Claire's mom?"

"I'm so sorry, son. I just had to do something. Your mother…she couldn't stand the idea of you and Claire…you know, a girl with a kid. She had such high aspirations for you."

Grant nodded. "So?"

"At first, I agreed. I mean, you were headed down the wrong path. DUI's, flunking classes, totaling your car, and then getting a girl pregnant. We were beside ourselves. We just had to do something. She came up with the idea of sending you to Brazil to work with her parents. I had no idea what to do with you, so I agreed."

"I remember it well. But Claire's mother…what was that about, huh?"

"I couldn't ignore the fact that I had a grandchild out there somewhere. I hated that she might not be well taken care of. But even more, I hated that I might never get to know her."

Grant was livid. "Why didn't you tell me, Dad? Why leave me out of this?"

"Martha wanted it that way. I'm sorry, son, but after I convinced her that I wasn't after custody, that I just wanted to get to know my granddaughter, she made me sign legal documents to that affect and then and only then did she allow me to purchase the farm to relieve her of the debt. But she also made me promise never to tell you. She wanted nothing to do with you, said she hated you for taking advantage of her daughter…a girl who'd already made one mistake, a girl who was vulnerable. So in order to see Maggie, I went along with it."

"You mean that all the time I was sending messages for Claire, all that time you knew I wanted to see her and Maggie, you two were playing grandma and grandpa?" Grant had forgotten all about Claire sitting there, in shock, and grilled his father for his own sake.

The older man shook his head. "No, son…part of the deal was that I couldn't let her know that I was her grandfather. She said that, legally, I had no right to Maggie, but for some reason, she let me see her regularly. We got to be real good friends, as a matter of fact, Martha and me."

After checking on Claire, who was staring at his father, mouth agape, Grant asked how he got away with it, how his mother felt about it.

"After you'd grown and moved out, your mother and I drifted apart. I guess you were the only thing we had in common. Anyway, it started with separate bedrooms, and eventually, separate homes. I kept this house; she moved back to her family's estate after you left for Brazil. You must remember that."

Grant simply nodded and asked the obvious question. "Okay, so what you're telling me is…you had an affair with Claire's mother?"

His father was quiet at first, as if mulling the question over. That's when Grant saw tears overflow onto his father's cheeks and watched him dig in his pants pocket for a handkerchief. After, blowing his nose, he leaned forward and looked his son in the eye.

"Martha was a wonderful woman, son. I even told her once that I wanted to divorce your mother and marry her. I really loved her. She said she didn't want to be the reason for breaking up someone's marriage and wouldn't talk about it again. I had to resign myself to visiting her and the girls a few times a year. I even took them on vacation with me, but everything was always on the up and up." The elder man threw off his blanket and pushed himself forward and off the chair. "I'll leave you to take care of her." He slowly shuffled out of the room and gently closed the door behind him.

Grant slumped back into his chair and rubbed his face. What was so wrong with him that his own father would turn against him like that? Why did Claire's mother hate him so? She knew he was sorry he wasn't there for Claire when Maggie was born. She knew he was always trying to get in touch with her, and he was sure that Claire would have wanted to see him. They were soul mates; they'd made plans for the rest of their lives. Now he finds out that his father was in on it, even agreed to keep him away from Maggie and Claire. What kind of father does that?

Claire stirred and Grant turned to look at her. She had taken a tissue from her handbag and was blowing her nose. He watched her wipe away the mascara that had smeared under her eyes and then run her fingers through her hair. He had no idea how to handle this or take care of her like his dad said. And he certainly didn't know what to say to her after hearing his father's confession.

Suddenly, she stood and slowly walked in front of him. She looked exhausted.

"Wait Claire...where are you going?"

"I can't stand this. Why would he lie about my mother like that?"

After standing to block her exit, Grant grabbed her arm. "What do you mean...lie?"

"You're kidding me, aren't you? You certainly didn't believe that nonsense, did you?"

"It kind of makes sense."

Claire's chin quivered. "Grant...he's lying. Maggie never heard the Harrison name until you sent her the flowers in the hospital a few weeks ago. She called me right away and asked who you were. If he was in my mother's life while they were growing up, Maggie would have recognized the name. Now, please, just let me go."

She wrestled her arm from his grip and left him standing there, staring at her back as she left the room and probably his life, forever.

Shortly thereafter, Grant heard the front door slam. He could do nothing but fall into his chair and bury his head in his hands. He didn't know how long he sat that way, but presently, he felt a hand on his shoulder.

"I'm so sorry, son. At the time, it seemed like the right thing to do."

"Dad, Claire thinks you're lying about everything."

"Well, if keeping a secret is lying, then I lied. But all she has to do ask the girls about me, and they'll confirm what I told you."

"But, Dad, I was in Rock Creek, too, you know? I went to games and concerts, places where I might see the girls. I never once saw you there. Why was that, huh?"

"You were there?"

"I couldn't stay away either."

The elder man swallowed hard. "I had to follow Martha's wishes to a T, son. She was a very private woman and a good woman, too. After she moved into town, I'd meet her and the girls in La Crosse or Wisconsin Dells...someplace fun. She didn't want the hometown folks to see her with a man; she didn't want rumors to start. I don't think she wanted me to run into Claire when she came home either, so it was better if we spent weekends together out of town, went to small town festivals…things like that."

"Claire isn't taking any of this well," Grant bemoaned quietly.

"I think she'll be fine. She's healthier now, stronger, not to mention extremely successful. She's not the unstable girl she used to be, that's for sure. That girl wouldn't have been able to confront anyone."

"What are you talking about?"

"You know son…when she was sick."

Grant shook his head. "Sick…what do you mean sick? No one told me she was sick."

"Surely you knew why she wasn't around, right?"

"No…I wasn't told a thing, Dad. Martha just said she would give her my messages."

Grant's father rubbed his hands over his face. "I'm so sorry, son. I thought you knew, I thought you knew."

"Knew what?" Grant fairly screamed at his father.

"Son…she was ill, in bad shape mentally. Martha said she had to have her hospitalized, that she didn't have a choice or she would have hurt herself or the girls."

"What…hospitalized? I can't believe none of you told me. I could have been there for her, helped somehow. No wonder she can't talk to me…she's probably ashamed, she probably thinks I know all about it. For cry out loud, Dad, what were you thinking?"

"You were headed down the wrong path, don't forget. You two couldn't take care of yourselves, much less a baby!"

"That's not true…we were in love…we would have figured it out. You could have told me, Dad…someone should have told me."

"Son, I hope you can forgive me someday, but I was torn between telling you and losing Martha's trust. Claire needed help for a couple of years, and Martha didn't think that she'd ever be able to care of the girls, so she got custody. And you, son, you'd moved on, married Holly. Then when you had Greg, I thought it would take your mind off Claire and Maggie."

"Well, it didn't."

"Why don't you stay…have supper with me and we can talk some more."

"I just have one more question. What happened to my letters…all those letters I sent to Claire while I was in Brazil?"

The elder shrugged his shoulders. "I don't know anything about any letters."

"So Martha never mentioned them to you?"

"No. She told me that you called quite often in the beginning, but nothing about letters."

"I've got to get out of here," Grant said as he turned to leave the room.

Grant Harrison II cleared his throat and repeated, "It seemed like the right thing to do.

Chapter 10

CLAIRE

After leaving the Harrison mansion, Claire drove a block or two before pulling over. She was so angry that she pounded on the steering wheel and asked herself how Grant could stand to be in the same room with that awful man. Why would he make up such nonsense? Why did he hate them so? Claire knew that she wouldn't be able to drive all the way back to Lake Louise; she was physically ill. Yet, she was grateful for her foresight, her ability to plan ahead because she'd made a reservation at the Madison Concordia Hotel before she left home in case she couldn't see Grant that day. Even though she'd seen him and got more information than she needed, Claire decided to keep her reservation and steered her car in the direction of downtown Madison. All she really wanted was some peace and quiet, some time to think and sort this all out. Once she calmed down, she knew she'd be able to decipher what she'd heard. At least she hoped she could.

Claire drove until she came to the corner of Wisconsin Avenue and Dayton Street. There she made a right, pulled into the hotel parking lot, and checked the time. It was too early to check in, but she'd see if they had a room anyway.

Hotel management was happy to help and found her a room on the top floor…a Governor's Club guestroom over looking the capital just as she'd requested. After asking not to be disturbed, Claire grabbed her key, entered the elevator, and ascended to the top floor. When she opened the door to her suite, she spotted the huge window that ran along side the king sized bed and walked toward it, tossing her overnight bag on the bed as she passed. She didn't believe in wishing for time to pass, but at this particular moment, she couldn't wait for evening to descend on Madison so she'd be able to see the capital lit up in all its wonder. She needed something, anything to improve her mood. Suddenly exhausted, she dropped backwards, pulled the cover from the foot of the bed, and wrapped it tight around her shoulders. Momentarily, she fell into a deep sleep.

When Claire awoke, she couldn't remember where she was. She sat up and looked out the window. It was pitch dark, but the Capital shone like a Christmas tree in the distance. It was then that she remembered why she was there, remembered about the events of the day, and fell back into bed, covering her face with her hands as she wept.

Chapter 11

GRANT

Grant Harrison III should have been shocked upon hearing his father's confession, but he wasn't. Of course, he was as heartbroken as Claire, but what his father and Claire's mother had done didn't surprise him. After all, he'd always been considered a second class citizen, never doing well enough at anything to impress his own parents or their upper class cronies. Early on, he realized that he'd never measure up and gave up trying. Somehow he instinctively knew that his parents would always have control of his life anyway. Therefore, he never tried to win a science fair or run for president of his class. He wasn't interested in debate or learning to play chess or a musical instrument. He wasn't elected Homecoming King or Prom King, or even King of the Hill. He didn't get any credit for the Christmas wreaths he sold for charity, and he never made Eagle Scout. He loved sports, played them all, but never enjoyed competing. And even though basketball was his favorite sport, it didn't matter that he'd improved on his 60% free throw record because his parents never came to games to see him play anyway; they didn't even know that he'd spent his senior year on the bench. In hindsight, however, he did regret never making it to at least one state tournament; he thought he would have enjoyed the experience.

More than anything, Grant loved school. It didn't matter, though, because he didn't get good enough grades to satisfy his parents. After all, he needed to share the title of valedictorian with a classmate. He figured that once he left for college, he'd be free of their control; however, he quickly learned that his assumption couldn't be further from the truth when they sent him out of the country, effectively distancing him from the love of his life.

His parents might have thought that they were punishing him, but those couple of years with his medical missionary grandparents were the best of his life. He'd never let on to his parents, but he learned more from his time in exile than he cared to admit. The people he met in the favela of Sao Paulo, the people he served there taught him the real meaning of the word 'compassion'. His parents had no idea of the suffering he saw in a city where almost 20 percent of the people lived in poverty, where so many children suffered from malnutrition, so much so that they were unable to learn the basics because their brains were not developing. Not to mention the high infant mortality rates…that's what got to him the most. Too bad he didn't have the stomach to be a doctor like his grandfather, but he didn't. There were other ways to help in this world, nonetheless, and that knowledge would lead him back to school where he would figure out a way to work for the disadvantaged.

Now that he was a success in his own right, Grant wondered what his father thought of his election to the post of Senior District Attorney after spending an untold number of years as just one of many attorneys working for the state. He'd never said a word about it. Grant figured his father should be happy that he wasn't a dog catcher or that he wasn't just volunteering at an animal shelter somewhere; after all, that was the most they expected of him and had no problem telling him so. If he didn't want to go into the family banking business, what in the world would he do? How would he ever make a decent living? Maybe his dad was waiting for him to become governor. But then that wouldn't be good enough either. How about President of the Universe? Perhaps that would do it. Somehow, he doubted it.

Grant was having a hard time sitting still. He felt as though he'd been punched in the gut, punched so hard the pain would not go away. So, he paced. He paced back and forth in his kitchen while he ate a ham sandwich. He paced in front of his fireplace while he read the Wisconsin

State Journal. He stood in the shower until the water ran cold and then paced to and fro as he dried himself. He asked himself if he were at fault somehow, if he were unintentionally responsible for the state of Claire's mental health. He wondered how she was taking the news, wondered if he'd ever have a chance to see her again, and worried she'd have a setback. That one would be his fault; after all, he was the one who insisted they visit his father. When his cell chimed, bringing him out of his musings, he recognized the music he'd chosen for Maggie's number and ran to his office to grab it.

"Hello?" he said anxiously.

"Grant?"

"Yes, Maggie."

"I'm sorry about the weekend. It's just that I'm very protective of Mom right now."

"No need to apologize. I understand."

"So you're willing to give it another try?"

"You don't even have to ask. I can't wait to see you again."

"I'm glad…I feel the same way."

"Good…that takes a load off."

Maggie laughed. "I have one more question. Did you see my mother today?"

"Yes, earlier, but she should be home by now."

"No, she's not coming home. She's in Madison at the Concordia. I called there, but she isn't taking calls, and she's not answering her cell."

"How did you know she was there?"

"She told us that's where she'd be if she couldn't see you right away, but I guess she decided to stay anyway. Um, did she get her questions answered?"

"Yes."

"So you bought the farm?"

"No, it was my dad."

"Your dad?"

"Yes, my father." Grant cleared his throat self-consciously. "Maggie…do you remember a friend of your grandmothers…a guy who took you on vacations and spent time with you and Kate?"

"Sure. What's that got to do with anything?"

"What was his name?"

"Harry…Uncle Harry…some relative of Grandma's. Why?"

Grant heart tightened. "What was his whole name?"

"I have no idea. What does that matter anyway?"

"Maggie…Uncle Harry is your grandfather…my dad. He just told Claire and me the whole story about how he and Martha took care of you girls and how they kept it from us."

"What are you talking about?"

"You heard me. They decided together to keep us away from you."

"He admitted that?"

"Yes, and he said he knew nothing of my letters…the ones I sent to Claire from Brazil. There wasn't anything in all that stuff Claire said you went through, was there?"

"No, there weren't letters of any kind. And your name wasn't even in Grandma's address book. Oh…Grant…Mom…what about Mom? She's not answering her cell."

"You said the Concordia…they told you she'd checked in?"

"Yes, but said she didn't want to be disturbed."

"Should I go over there…see if I can talk to her?"

"Please, Grant. It's not like her to ignore her cell."

"Okay, okay. Don't worry. I'll call you as soon as I know something."

Grant snapped the cell shut and covered his face with his hands. "God help us!"

***

Less than twenty minutes later, Grant stood at the reception desk of the Concordia, having little luck convincing them that Claire might be in trouble. He'd dialed Maggie and handed the telephone to the attendant. They talked and the attendant finally said there was one thing he could do. It wasn't long before a manager appeared and got on the line with Maggie. After hanging up on her, he turned to Grant.

"Mr. Harrison. I'm so sorry, but it is our hotel's policy not to let calls through if a patron requests it. But I could hear the fear in her daughter's voice, so this is what I'll do. I'll go to her room and knock on her door to see if she'll answer. You know, it's possible she just went out for dinner or something."

Grant nodded.

"If you don't mind waiting here, I'll see if I can get her to answer the door, okay?"

"What if she doesn't?"

"We won't worry about that now. Please. Just take a seat in the lobby. I'll be back."

Grant couldn't sit still now if his life depended on it, so he paced down the first floor hallway and back again. While he walked, he kept an eye on the elevators. Even if his back was to them, he would turn if he heard them open and watch as strangers entered the lobby. It seemed like an eternity before the manager reappeared, spotted him in the hallway, and ambled toward him.

"Mr. Harrison. She's okay. It took her awhile, but she came to the door. I told her that her daughter had called you because she wasn't answering her cell and that you were downstairs to make sure she was okay. She said I should thank you and tell you not to worry. She said she'd forgotten her cell in the car when she came in…said she was upset when she arrived. I asked her to please call her daughter, and she said she would."

"Good, okay then," Grant stuttered. "Thanks for doing that."

"Anytime, Mr. Harrison."

Grant didn't want to leave. He'd hoped to be able to see Claire, but it didn't look like that was a possibility. The manager wouldn't give him her room number; he was sure about that. He figured he would call Maggie later to see how Claire was. That was about all he could do now anyway.

While Grant was driving through town to his home on the lake, his cell rang, and he quickly hit his cell phone button on the steering wheel.

"Hello?"

"It's Maggie."

"Hi. How's your mom?"

"Okay, I guess. She says she has lots to mull over, lots to think about."

"Yeah, we both do. I think she was in shock when she left my dad's place."

"Me, too. I told her about Uncle Harry."

"How did she take it? She was sure my dad lied about that."

"That's what she said."

"She did?"

"Yes, but she needs some time now to sort things out, okay?"

"Okay, but Maggie, what do you think about all of this, my dad, your Uncle Harry?"

"I'm having a hard time believing any of it. I just loved him. He was so good to us. And Grandma…well, she just lit up when he was around. She was a different person then, so happy and relaxed."

"Maggie. Do you want to see him?"

"Someday, maybe. I just have to wait until I talk to Mom in depth about it. Okay?"

"I understand."

"Grant. How do you feel about my mother, if I may ask?"

"You know the answer to that one…but she hates me, doesn't she?"

"No. She just never got over the fact that you never came for her like you promised."

"I hope she understands now…after today."

"Just give her some time."

"And you can put a good word in anytime."

Maggie laughed. "I'll make sure I do. Talk to you soon."

"Good night, honey."

***

The bedroom was dark, almost pitch black. Grant had read that any kind of light can keep a person from sleeping well, that a human being needs darkness to send the brain a signal, telling it that it's time for the body to rest. On this particular evening, however, it didn't help one iota;

Grant was not going to fall asleep no matter what.

He dozed fitfully for awhile before getting up, finding his way to the kitchen, and pouring himself a glass of milk. He wondered if he was supposed to warm the milk before he drank it or if that was that just an old wives tale. He couldn't remember and drank it cold. After stretching while he walked down the hall, Grant hit the sheets one more time. He wiggled his toes, flexed the muscles in his legs, and tried deep breathing while rolling his shoulders. He beat his pillow into a more comfortable shape, turned onto one side and then the other, but no matter what he did, he could not keep the events of the day from interfering with his sleep.

Grant was wide awake because he was second guessing, wishing he could go back and start all over. If that were possible, he would've reacted differently to his father's confession. He would have been angrier; he would have ranted and raved. After all, what his father did was despicable, and it would serve him right if he never spoke to the old man again. But he was the only father he had so he would have to live with it. As for Claire, she didn't have to live with any of it, did she? No, Claire could move on and choose never to see either of them again, and he wouldn't blame her. Her heart had to be broken and his father was to blame, at least partially. Her mother wasn't innocent either, but Martha was gone, wasn't she? He didn't know if that was easier on Claire or if she wished her mother were alive so she could confront her about what she now knew of their conspiracy. And where were the letters? It's as if they never left Brazil. Would he ever know the answer to that question? Would Claire ever speak to him again? After seeing her today, he knew one thing for sure. She was the one, had always been the only one for him. Besieged by feelings of regret, it suddenly became difficult to hold back the tears.

***

The early morning sun lit up the sky and brightened the den where Grant was asleep in his well-worn leather recliner. He opened his eyes, held a hand over them, and squinted at the window. Automatically reaching for his stiff neck, he massaged it and groaned in pain. It took him a moment or two to get his bearings and when he did, the memories of the day before flooded his foggy brain. *How did I end up in this chair and what in the world am I supposed to do now?* The answer to the second part of his question came quickly. *Check on Claire.*

It didn't take long for Grant to whip through his morning routine. The only thing he skipped was his usual thirty minutes on the treadmill. He'd have to get it in later because tomorrow he'd be lifting weights instead, and there'd be no time for both.

Before he knew it, he was sitting in the parking lot of the Madison Concordia Hotel. When he drove in, he searched for Claire's Porsche and spotted it where she'd parked the day before. He breathed a sigh of relief and figured that since it was only 7:30, he could wait to make sure she was all right and well on her way home. He decided to park a couple of rows away, facing her car so he could see her when she came out of the hotel. Then he turned his attention to the knob on his radio and scanned the stations until he found one broadcasting the national news. After releasing the seatbelt, he settled into the bucket seat, grabbed his travel mug, and enjoyed the first sip of morning coffee.

The parking lot was bustling with travelers packing up and heading out to who knows where. A couple approached the car parked next to Grant and eyed him suspiciously as he sat there facing in the opposite direction of the other vehicles in his row. He waved; they frowned and hastily entered their car, buckled up and backed out, one or the other of them keeping him in their sights the entire time. He hadn't thought of it before, but he supposed he did look a bit suspicious. This didn't count as stalking, did it? No…he was just making sure the woman he never forgot was okay and his daydreaming took him back to the fall of 1972, the day he first laid eyes on Claire, the girl from Rock Creek. Grant closed his eyes, leaned his head against the seat, and smiled. He'd been in the throes of a hangover on the first day of the first semester of his junior year. He remembered running from the frat house because he'd overslept and then frantically searching for a good looking girl to sit next to. Claire had been in a hurry, too, and rushed passed him on the steps of the huge lecture hall. When she did, he'd lost his balance, and the students coming in behind him had to help him up. Grant shook his head at the memory. He might have been under the influence, but he never lost sight of her curly blonde ponytail, swishing seductively back and forth as she raced ahead of him. He'd stumbled along, followed her down the second row from the front, and plopped down right next to her. He'd never forget the look on her face when he opened his mouth to talk to her. She yelled 'you reek', jumped from her seat, and got as far away from him as she possibly could. He thought he'd never have a chance with her then, and now, almost forty years later, he sat there thinking the very same thing.

It was about eight-twenty when Grant noticed Claire in the parking lot. How could he not notice her? How could anyone miss the classy way she dressed or how the stilettos she wore changed the way her hips moved when she walked? Then there was the thick, wavy, blonde hair. He ran his hand through his own thinning mane. She was one lucky woman, he thought. He figured something he did caught her eye because all of a sudden she was staring in his direction. *Do I get out of the car? Do I talk to her? If I don't, she will think I'm a stalker!* Grant fumbled for the handle of his door, lifted it, and quickly stood, watching her all the while. For a second, she didn't move; she simply stared. *Okay...she thinks I'm a maniac!* Then, chewing her lip like she always did, Claire very slowly mouthed 'I'm sorry'. She turned immediately to face her car, opened a door and threw her bags onto the passenger seat before getting in. She backed out and left the lot before he knew how to react. *What did she mean 'I'm sorry'?* When he tried to swallow the huge lump that had suddenly formed in his throat, he felt the ache of his clenching jaws, licked his lips, and shook it off. As he reluctantly dropped into the seat of his car, Grant remembered what Maggie told him the night before...Claire now knew that he had suffered, too. Was she sorry that their parents had both conspired against them? Or, was she saying she was sorry, but didn't want to speak to him or have anything to do with him ever again? He wouldn't be able to stand that...not now that he knew what was still in his heart. What he needed was another plan...a plan to win over the woman he'd fallen in love with thirty-eight years ago when he was twenty-one years old and continued to love, mostly sight unseen, for his entire adult life. But would a plan be enough? He doubted it…it would be a fight to win her over…he'd just have to hang in there until he did.

Chapter 12

CLAIRE

What was he doing waiting for her in the parking lot? Did he think she wanted to talk to him? There was no way she could talk to him face to face with everything that just happened. And what was that look he gave her? She couldn't tell, but she had a feeling it was the same look she'd gotten from her daughters lately. Just then, it became abundantly clear; everyone felt sorry for her…her daughters, first of all, and now Grant. For some reason they thought that she was emotionally fragile, that she couldn't handle rejection or hurt, and that she couldn't take care of herself. Little did they know, but over the last few decades of her life, she'd faced unimaginable challenges, overcome them all, and ended up being more self-reliant and stronger than anyone she knew.

Claire was just getting to know her daughters and they, in turn, were learning her ways. She figured that they attributed her need to be alone as a sign of sadness or depression. But in times of stress, Claire simply needed to regain her focus, her center, her energy, and she needed to do that in the privacy of her own home or, for the time being, her own room. She guessed that she needed to explain that to them when she got home because ever since Grant entered the picture, they'd become overly sensitive, overly cautious around her. And now he was behaving the same way…coming to the hotel to look for her, having the manager check to see if she were okay, then waiting in the parking lot to make sure she was capable of driving out of there. In fact, it was written all over his face…he thinks she's a fragile little thing, that she must have broken down after hearing his father's confession, never to be the same again. He probably even thought she'd attempt to end her life. Please. Sure, she could become emotional at the drop of a hat, but that didn't mean she was weak or helpless. She simply lived life to the fullest and when you live that way, you're likely to endure heartbreaking disappointments. But in Claire's case, life's disturbances only served to make her stronger. Maybe she couldn't talk to him right now, maybe the wounds were just too fresh, but none of them need worry about her; she was as tough as nails.

As Claire wove through the streets of downtown Madison, a wave of nostalgia took over, and she slowed her car to take in the familiar panorama. A smile crossed her face as bikers turned in front of her or passed her dawdling car; others walked on the crowded sidewalks with their buddies, heavy backpacks weighing them down. As usual, college students swarmed the street and sidewalks of University Avenue, and Claire chuckled at the memories. She'd decided, however, that recent events left a bad taste in her mouth and now Madison had become the last place she'd ever want to visit again, so she decided to pay her respects and say goodbye to her favorite haunts. She'd been lucky enough to spend an entire academic year on that campus, and it had given her self-esteem a boost. She knew after that first year that she could do it, that she was capable of completing a college degree. Of course, she didn't begin studying again until a decade later, but when she did find the wherewithal to return to school, she knew what to expect, how to study, and how to make the most of her education.

Traveling on University Avenue until she came to North Mills Street, Claire turned south and then left on West Johnson. She continued at an unhurried pace until she passed by her old dorm, Susan B. Davis Hall, and pulled to the side of the road. She noticed the no parking sign, but chose to ignore it; she just needed a moment to gaze upon the dorm that had been her first home away from home. Out of the blue, she remembered being peeved with her mother for insisting that she have a room to herself. Martha had done her homework and knew that the dorm was one of the smallest on campus and that the housemother was the type to keep tabs on her girls. She understood that her daughter had trouble staying on task, and the housemother agreed to keep Claire accountable, even to the point of finding her a tutor when she lost her way for a while. Her mother had her back, and she couldn't have survived that first year of college without her planning and foresight.

Yet, Claire remembered wishing that she could have a roommate like everyone else, but she wasn't like everyone else, was she? It wouldn't have worked in her favor. She wouldn't have passed one class if she'd stayed up late chatting, or playing cards, or ducking out to fraternity parties. No. Back then, Claire had to focus. To do that she had to be left alone, she had to have peace and quiet. In fact, she never grew out of it, she'd never changed in that respect.

After pulling out and continuing on West Johnson Street, she noticed Victor Communication Hall on her left and her heart skipped a beat. There it stood; the building that housed the huge lecture hall where she took her first college course. She remembered how intimidated she felt the first day. She almost lost her nerve when she entered the hall; the place was buzzing with activity…over a hundred freshmen filing into the room at the same time. But that wasn't all. It was also the place Grant first noticed her, the place where he followed her to wherever she sat, never failing to sit right next to her every Monday, Wednesday, and Friday morning for an entire semester. In the beginning, she wasn't impressed. After all, he'd already taken the journalism course once and flunked. He'd admitted to that on the second day of class. She remembered thinking that the kid must learn the hard way because he showed up with a hangover the second time he took the course, too. Initially, she didn't want anything to do with him, but his persistence eventually wore her down. Of course, those big brown eyes, the square jaw, the full lips, and that shock of black shaggy hair didn't hurt.

Claire recalled wanting to make out with him the first time she saw him, hung over or not. She also remembered holding herself back, trying so hard to resist him day after day. She knew how easily she could get into trouble; she was already responsible for one child, and she had to prove to her parents that she wasn't a loser. In fact, she felt that she needed to prove it to the entire population of Rock Creek and if that was her goal, then there was no room for a guy in her life. The problem was…boys had always been the number one distraction during her teen years. She loved the way they flirted and fawned over her; she loved all the attention. Of course, she knew they liked her because she'd make out with them. She wasn't stupid like her mother said, she knew what they wanted. Still, it had gotten her in trouble, and she had a kid to prove it.

Claire truly loved her little Katie and after having her, decided that she'd be the best mother ever. To do that, she'd have to give up boys and concentrate on doing well in school. She remembered thinking...easier said than done...because she had a hard time concentrating on school work with that high energy level of hers. Sometimes she just wanted to scream, sometimes she wanted to run. Other times she wanted the boys to notice her, to tell her she was pretty, to ask her out. But she needed a good education and a high paying job, so she made the most of her last two years of high school, passed the ACT with flying colors, and applied to the University of Wisconsin-Madison.

As Claire headed out of the college town for the last time, her thoughts returned to her mother, the woman she thought she knew, the woman who praised her and pushed her to excellence so she could accomplish that almost impossible goal for a girl who couldn't concentrate on a thing. With her mother's help, Claire learned the skills she needed to study, to retain information, to concentrate on what was important. And what was important to her mother was for her daughter to support herself and her child and to do it without a man. Claire remembered thinking that it didn't sound like any fun, living a life without guys. But what else could she do? Her mother had sacrificed everything for her...she volunteered to take care of Katie during the week and even figured out how to pay for room and board. To this day, Claire didn't know how her mother accomplished that. Did she just up and sell some of their prized dairy cows or take out one more loan on a farm already mortgaged to the hilt? Claire thought that she'd be forever grateful to her mother for giving her the chance to turn her life around, but now she wasn't so sure and wondered why her mother turned on her the way she did, why she conspired against her, but most of all, why she had never mentioned that Grant wanted to see her. She guessed that she'd never know the answer to that question.

Chapter 13

ABBY

It was already after seven on a school night, and Miss Abby Genevieve Fogarty, age 8 1/2, still hadn't finished her keyboarding homework. In order to do that, she had to get permission to use her mother's computer. Since her mother was already using it, Abby had to admit to her that she had not finished her homework and beg to let her use her precious PC. She figured her mother wouldn't be upset about it, though, because she knew that she'd been busy every day after school. She and Lily had registered for the cheerleading workshop that started this week and went through the next. It lasted two hours, and Abby couldn't believe how much one simple extracurricular activity cut into her free time. But she was not about to give it up, especially since she got to spend time with the real Lake Louise High School cheerleaders. 'Cheerleaders' was a good name for them, Abby thought. She had never met such a happy bunch of people; every one of them was always in a good mood. And they loved teaching the third grade girls. She figured they must…they'd repeated the workshop year after year. The cheerleading camp was one of the reasons Abby and Lily couldn't wait until third grade not to mention the fact that they would get to cheer during the junior varsity football game in less than two weeks.

Abby rapped on the office door, and her mom answered, telling her to come on in.

"Is it okay if I use the computer now, Mom? I have to prove I did my keyboarding assignment."

Abby got a warning look and waited for the grilling to begin.

"Do you have any other homework?"

"Nope."

"You sure?"

"Yup."

"Keyboarding again?"

"We don't have time for it at school."

"Okay…just a sec…I have to log off."

Abby stood patiently while her mother exited the internet. As she waited, she began to snoop in the ancient accordion folders on one end of her mother's large, antique desk.

"What's all this stuff?" she asked, curious.

Kate reached over and abruptly closed the cover to the top file folder. "Just some stuff Grandma, Maggie, and I found in our bins in the basement," she rattled off quickly. "We might want to pull out some of it for your famous people scrapbook. How does that sound? Maybe we'll get to it on the weekend. Now get to that keyboarding and promise not to go online."

"Promise," Abby said with a roll of her eyes.

Kate grabbed her and hugged her hard before kissing the curly blonde locks that covered her head. "I think you need a shower, kiddo."

"Mom!! I need to get this done!"

"Okay…I'm out of here." With that said, Kate grabbed the pile of folders full of whatever, ambled over to the bookcase, stood on her toes, and set them on the highest shelf she could reach. Then she stepped into the kitchen and gently closed the door behind her.

"I thought she'd never leave," the sassy girl whispered to herself. Then, after retrieving her keyboarding disk from a pocket in her backpack, she inserted it into the D drive, and waited patiently for the program to load. Since it seemed to take forever, Abby's mind wandered to the old brown folders her mother had taken from the desk. *Why had she put them up so high? Was she afraid I'd look at them instead of doing my homework? Or is there something there about my adoption, about my birthmother? I've been asking a lot of questions lately…are the answers in those files?* It didn't seem likely that her mother would hide things from her…she'd never done that before as far as she knew.

Curiosity got the best of the petite third grader, and she left the desk to grab the rolling library ladder and slide it across the floor to where her mother had placed the folders on the top shelf. She'd have to climb awfully high, higher than she ever had before. She couldn't explain it, but whatever was in those files seemed a lot more important than keyboarding, so she took the first step and then a second. Once she was standing on the forth step, she realized that retrieving them would be trickier than she thought, so Abby grabbed just one file, the top one, and held it against her chest with one hand while holding onto the ladder with the other. Slowly, she backed down the ladder until she was standing firmly on the carpeted floor.

Instead of returning to the desk, Abby plopped down on the worn leather couch at the other end of the room. With the folder balanced precariously on her lap, she read her adoptive grandmother's name on the flap, lifted it, and pulled out the contents, setting them next to her on the couch. She quickly shuffled through the report cards, drawings, and other boring stuff to look for photographs of her adoptive mom, Kate, and any other women in the family. She'd been told that her biological mother was a relative. Would there be a picture of her in the files? Would she immediately recognize her? Or was the relative on her dad's side of the family? She'd been told that she'd have to wait to find out. Her biological mother got to choose when and where they'd meet, and she just had to live with that. *Maybe I don't want to wait!*

Abby had learned about the process of elimination at school. If she went through the folders and no one looked anything like her, she'd assume that her birthmother was from the other side of the family. That would narrow it down some, but it wouldn't help. There were very few pictures of people on her dad's side around, and the ones she'd seen were of really old people. It wouldn't do any good to ask her dad about it; he never talked about such things. It came to her then that she knew very little about her adoptive relatives because all she ever heard anyone talk about was how Grandma Claire and Maggie had to make up. She remembered that her mom talked to Grandma a lot, but Maggie didn't until she moved to Lake Louise. Now they seemed to be together all the time! She wasn't sure what that was all about, why Claire and Maggie didn't see each other, but she knew that it had something to do with the fact that her mom and Maggie were raised by their grandmother, not their mother, Claire. She'd never heard an explanation for that arrangement…it was almost as though her mom didn't know her biological mother either until a couple of years ago when they all went to pick up Claire at the airport. Abby figured her mom understood exactly what she was going through.

Spurred on by natural curiosity, the little girl continued to sort through the photos. What she found, however, were her own pictures, not those of her adoptive mother…at least, she thought they were hers. She grabbed one of the school pictures and studied it. It seemed kind of old to her; the edges were brown, and the picture was in black and white. She knew that all of her school pictures were in color, but the girl in the photo looked just like her except for the fact she was wearing a plaid blouse…she'd never owned one of those as far as she knew… and her hair was never cut like that! Abby swallowed hard and turned the photo over. It read *Claire Genevieve Holmes, 1961.*

Abby's mind began to race. *So if this is Claire and she looks like me, my biological mother is from that side of the family!* The process of elimination had worked. Her biological mother was a relative and now she knew that the woman had to be a relative of Grandma Claire's. Suddenly, she became more determined than ever to find out who this woman was, and the creepy old folders might just hold the secret she was beginning to wrap her brain around. Her homework, the keyboarding assignment, would have to wait.

Hiding the old school photograph in her backpack seemed like the logical thing to do while she continued her search. It wasn't long before she found more pictures of Grandma Claire and possibly her parents. There were pictures of Claire on horses, Claire alone in front of Christmas trees, Claire lying in snow banks making angels, and Abby saw her own likeness in all of them.

After setting the first old file aside and without cleaning up her mess, Abby made another treacherous trip up and down the ladder. This time she held the file labeled…*Katherine Claire Holmes.* Upon dumping the contents onto the couch, she spotted photographs of her adoptive mother who, of course, looked nothing like her. That didn't make sense to her now. Why didn't she look more like Grandma Claire? It didn't matter at the moment, because Abby had waited a long time to see pictures of Kate as a child, and she looked through the folder anyway. She saw all of her adoptive mother's school pictures, a couple of Kate on a horse, and a few with her grandmother, not Claire, at someplace like Wisconsin Dells. She smiled knowingly when she spotted her mother in her cheerleading outfit and when she found the familiar senior picture, the only picture she'd ever seen of her mother as a kid.

After she'd been digging around for a while, she found the type of picture she'd been hoping to find; one with all of them together. It was an old photograph, shiny, black and white. It had been taken in the summertime. The person she recognized as her grandmother was sitting in the grass behind a big metal tub. Her hair was in a pony tail; she looked like a teenager. Peeking over the rim of the tub were two little girls, one with dark curly hair and the other, light, light blonde. Abby could do nothing but stare. It shouldn't have raised any red flags because she knew that Claire was mother to both Kate and Maggie, but it did, for Abby could not take her eyes off of the little blonde toddler. *I know that can't be me!* She had no choice. She had to hold onto that one, too, and shoved it into her backpack before leaving the mess that had accumulated on the couch to make a third run up the ladder to grab the last wrinkled old folder.

Once again in the safe confines of the comfortable old couch, Abby's heart began to beat wildly in her chest as her trembling hands lifted the flap to the third and last folder in the pile. The name on the flap read *Margaret Jean Holmes*. This was Abby's first clue that there was a lot she didn't know about her mother's sister, Maggie. Why is her name Borgerson now? Why didn't she come to visit much? And why weren't there more pictures of her around? She'd seen her senior picture right next to her mom's and dad's in the hallway and noticed Maggie in her parent's wedding picture on the dining room wall, but that was it.

Very slowly and with much trepidation, the nervous child lifted the cover. There, inside the old brown folder, was a professional photograph of her mother's sister, Maggie. Abby grabbed it with her forefinger and thumb, carefully touching only the white, outside rim of the picture. She lifted it, bringing it closer to her face, and squinted hard as she studied to make sure it really was a photograph of her adoptive mother's sister. The tears came unabated, and the little girl began to sob. And while hugging the photo to her heaving chest, her mind began to race. *Could it be? Is she the relative they keep talking about? Could Maggie be my birthmother? But why would she leave me? She has money...she could have taken care of me. Why didn't she want me? Why haven't they told me? Is Maggie here to take me back? Is that why Mom wanted her to move here? Is that why Maggie looks like she's going to cry every time she sees me?*

After quickly wiping her eyes and nose on her sleeve, Abby took the third and last photograph for her new collection and added it to the others in the inside pocket of her backpack. All she could think about was comparing them to her own school pictures as soon as she got to her room. But first, she had to grab the keyboarding disk from the computer drive, shove it into the backpack, and sneak past her mother so she wouldn't catch her crying. Fortunately, there were two entrances to the home office. Peeking through to door into the kitchen, she saw her mother and father at the kitchen table, sitting next to each other drinking wine, reading newspapers or doing puzzles, and chatting away. After shutting the door as quietly as possible, she went for the one that opened into the hallway near the stairway and stepped out of the room. Since she figured she had to let her mother know that she was done with her keyboarding and the office was free, she yelled that she was going to take a shower and go to bed. Her mother shouted back. "Whoa...who are you and what have you done with my daughter?"

Abby shook her head. Would her mother ever get sick of that tired old joke?

Since she wasn't a liar, Abby took her shower, making sure that she shampooed her hair twice because her mother would be sure to give it a sniff. After dressing in her two-piece, sock monkey short sleeved pajamas, she pulled the pictures from her backpack before shoving it against the door. That way, if her mother decided come in and give her a hug, she would have to push the backpack out of the way, giving Abby time to hide her precious photos.

Abby's own photograph albums were on her bookshelf. Her mother had been scrapbooking ever since she could remember, and there was an album for every special event in Abby's life, including one for every year of school. Sitting on the edge of her bed after grabbing her baby album and her first and second grade scrapbooks, the very excited girl lined up the photographs she'd taken from the office along the edge of her pillow so they'd stand up. The first one in the row was the picture of the little girls in the washtub. Abby put the one of Claire right next to it because it looked as if it was taken in early elementary. Finally, she added the picture of Maggie. It had third grade scribbled on the back; an early attempt at cursive writing, Abby presumed.

After blinking away tears as she studied the photographs, Abby opened her baby book and searched for a picture of herself at one or two years of age. It wasn't long before she found a print of herself, sitting naked on a blanket. In fact, she recognized it as soon as she spotted it. It was as if she and the baby, Maggie, were the same person. After carefully peeling the photograph away from the photo tape, tearing some of the colorful paper as she did, Abby stood the pictures side by side and couldn't help but notice that the two blonde babies had the same chubby cheeks, the same little smile, and the same, almost bald, round head. Abby remembered hearing that all babies looked alike, but Abby didn't care because she was on a mission, the most important mission of her life. For that reason alone, she laid a kiss on both of the baby pictures before putting the scrapbook aside and grabbing a second one from her unruly pile.

All Abby needed now was just a little more proof, and she began to study the newly discovered school pictures of Grandma Claire and her aunt, Maggie. She figured they were about a year apart in age in those pictures and that's exactly the reason why she chose them for her investigation. She figured she'd have proof positive that she was related to them if any of her school pictures looked like either of them. After opening her first grade scrapbook, she grabbed her school picture for the year. Her picture wasn't close up like the two she was comparing it to. In her picture, she was standing and her whole body was in the picture, from the top of her head to the top of her knees. Needless to say, she was more than a little disappointed and basically threw the scrapbook and offending photograph onto her bedroom floor.

Fortunately, there was one more scrapbook, and Abby remembered that last year, in second grade, the pictures were close-ups. A grin spread across her face as she opened the album and found exactly what she was looking for. After turning to grab the two photographs leaning against her pink pillow case, she set the pictures of Claire and Maggie on either side of her own second grade close-up. The resemblance she saw on the faces of the three little girls in the photos was uncanny, and Abby knew the truth, gasped out loud, and covered her mouth with her hands. *Maggie is my birthmother, the relative who wasn't ready to tell her? Not ready...she's been around since the beginning of the school year. She's been around forever! Now what, now what, now what?*

Suddenly, Abby was afraid, afraid her mother would be upset, afraid that Maggie never loved her, afraid of causing unnecessary trouble. Maggie already had a lot of trouble...she was beat up and almost died. It came to her then; she would ask her best friend what to do. Lily would be able to confirm her suspicions. Then, she would help her figure out what to do next. No, it wouldn't be fair to Lily...she'd never be able to find her birthmother. But she loved her birthmother, Abby knew, because she prayed for her every day, prayed that she had a good life, and prayed that somehow she knew that Lily had a good life, too. And Lily would want to help, she would want to know what her best friend had found. With new resolve, Abby took her three precious photographs plus her second grade likeness and returned them to the pocket of the backpack, moving it away from the door before racing to her bed to crawl under her covers. Should she have been praying for her birthmother, for Maggie? She came to the conclusion that she'd always prayed for her, that she and her mother had asked God to bless Maggie and everyone they loved every night since she could remember. She'd leave the light on because her mother would come in to give her a goodnight kiss and ask God to bless everyone.

Chapter 14

KATE

Kate left her husband, George, to clean up the kitchen while she finished what she'd started before Abby needed the computer. She knew that she should go upstairs first to give her baby a good night kiss and tuck her in, but she just had a little to do and then she could retire for the evening herself. As Kate sat down on her high back office chair to finish an email she'd begun earlier, something to the left of the monitor caught her eye, and she turned to stare at the couch in the shadows at the other end of the room. Standing immediately, she flew to the couch to examine what she already knew to be true. The old accordion files she had put away were strewn all over the couch, the photographs and other papers were scattered every which way…it was a mess. She knew she hadn't left them that way because she remembered purposely putting them where her daughter couldn't reach them. She also knew that she and her sister needed to have a heart to heart before showing the contents of those old files to Abby. Suddenly, her breaths came in short spurts and her chest tightened. *Abby has looked through the file folders! But did she notice anything? Maybe not because she didn't try to hide the fact that she messed with the stuff her mother had purposely put up. But the kid always left messes wherever she went…that was a normal everyday occurrence!*

This time it was different, though. Seeing the photographs in the old folders had simply confirmed what Kate had always known and had become the reason to hide them. Her daughter strongly resembled her mother and her sister, and if Abby ever laid eyes on those old photos, she'd be bound to notice it, too. She thought she was doing the right thing when she encouraged Maggie to move back to Wisconsin to be part of Abby's life, but she was already having second thoughts. Was she ready for this? Was she in any way, shape or form ready for the consequences? After swallowing back some tears while straightening the mess on the couch, Kate decided she'd better leave it to check on her daughter...just in case.

"Hey, baby," Kate whispered as she slipped into her daughter's bedroom, stepping around the usual mess on her daughter's floor. "You sleeping?"

There was no answer, so Kate leaned over to kiss the top of her daughter's head. "You smell so good. Night sweetie." After lifting the light covers over her daughter's exposed shoulders and tucking them in around her neck, Kate turned off the light and tiptoed out of the room, pulling the door shut behind her.

It was a short walk down the hall to the master bedroom, and tonight, Kate was more than grateful. She simply dropped on top of her bedspread and curled up on her side. She had a lot to sort out before she approached her sister with her suspicions. *I think Abby knows!*

"What are you doing? You alright?" George asked when he came in right behind her.

Out of the blue, Kate began to sob, and her husband joined her on the bed, curling up and squeezing her shoulders from behind. "Sweetie, hon, what is it?"

"Abby knows, I think Abby knows."

"Knows what?"

"I think she suspects that Maggie is her mother."

"Oh, good...then we can get this over with."

Kate turned toward her husband. "What are you talking about?"

"Sweetie...remember...that's one of the reasons we wanted Maggie here. Abby is more than ready to have a relationship with her birthmother."

"What if she wants to live with her instead of us? She's our daughter, George...not Maggie's...we raised her...we're her parents."

George gently turned his wife to fully face him, pushed an errant hair from her forehead, and looked into her eyes. "Maggie, of all people, knows that. I was worried for awhile, too. But Maggie's been here a month and still hasn't asked Abby to stay overnight with her or do anything special with her. She's behaving just the way we thought she would. You're just afraid, sweetie. Sure, things might be tough for a while. Abby might be angry and maybe we'll have to get some professional help…she'll have lots of questions, but the kid is ready…she never shuts up about it, and we said we would never lie to her. So if she asks if Maggie is her mother, you'll have to tell her the truth. It's going to happen soon, so you and your sister have to figure out how you're going to handle this."

"I know, I know."

"Besides, honey, Maggie stayed away for almost nine years, not only because of Rex, but because she wanted you to be Abby's mother, she wanted you to have the full experience. We always said we wanted Maggie and Abby to have some kind of relationship…you always felt a little guilty about that, that she didn't feel she'd be safe coming back here. We felt bad she wasn't around more, that she was missing so much. Now it's time."

"God, George…I have to talk to Maggie right now…we have to tell Abby before she figures it out herself." Kate sat up quickly, grabbed the phone next to her bed, and dialed her sister.

***

Cheerleading Camp had ended and the girls were ready to perform during half-time at the junior varsity game…a mere week away. Their golden tee shirts emblazoned with the Lake Louise Leopard had been paid for and laundered, and Kate managed to find the requisite navy blue shorts needed to complete their outfits even though it was the end of summer and the store shelves were stocked with clothes for the coming fall and winter months. The girls would be allowed to wear their own tennis shoes with navy knee highs, and the high school cheerleaders would provide them with pompons.

Kate had Mac's permission to bring Lily home with her, so she picked up the girls after practice, and to her chagrin, they practiced their cheers all the way home.

"Push 'em back, push 'em back…way back!" The cheering continued after they entered the house, while they poured chocolate milk into plastic glasses, and when they ran into the back yard, their beverages spilling and splashing onto the kitchen floor.

After wiping up their mess, Kate listened to the girls repeat 'first and ten, do it again, come on leopards, let's win' over and over until they got the giggles. She was chuckling to herself when she sat down with Claire to watch them from the kitchen table.

"How'd your day go?"

"Good…I found your stew recipe…it's in the slow-cooker."

"Mom, you don't have to make supper every night."

"I have to pay my way somehow."

"No you don't. You're our guest. We're just happy you're here."

"It's the least I can do until I can afford a place of my own."

Suddenly, a very loud and obnoxious scream came from the backyard, and the women turned toward the window to make sure everything was okay. They concluded that the girls were fine, just more rambunctious than usual.

Sheepishly, Claire spoke. "You were a cheerleader, weren't you?"

"Yup. Were you?"

Claire shook her head and looked away. "Nope…I was pregnant by fifteen, remember?"

"If you hadn't had me, would you have been on the squad?"

"Probably not. We lived an awful long way from town. I don't think they would have let me anyway. The cheerleaders were the partiers."

"I wonder why Grandma let me do it then…well, we had moved to town by then and she trusted me. I guess because I was the good girl…never did anything wrong."

Claire smiled widely and grabbed her daughter's hand. "Thank goodness she got a chance to know what that was like, huh, raising a good girl?"

As long as she had her mother's hand in hers, Kate knowingly broached the most sensitive of subjects. "Mom...what are you going to do about Grant?"

"I have no idea."

"Have you talked to him?"

"Who? Grant? Why would I want to talk to him?"

"Don't you think it would help...if you two talked, I mean?"

"You know, sweetie, I don't know if I want to go down that road...hashing it out all over again. I really don't know what good it will do."

"Maggie thinks he's still in love with you."

"Katie! She doesn't even know that she's in love. Please!"

"Okay, okay...calm down...I just want to tell you something."

"Oh, man...what now?"

"Well, Maggie and I are going to talk to Abby this weekend. We're going to tell her everything."

"You are?" Claire's hands flew to her face covering her mouth, eyes wide.

"Now hear me out. If we tell her everything, we're going to have to tell her about Grant...that Grant is Maggie's father, her grandfather. Do you follow me?"

"Jeez, is that necessary right now? I mean, I knew it would have to happen some day, but now?"

Kate nodded purposefully. "Yes. We want her to know about her whole extended family. We have it all planned. We drew out a little family tree and everything."

"So then you'll tell Grant that she knows, and he'll want to come here to see her, and you wonder how I'll take it." Claire rolled her eyes and looked away.

Kate grabbed her mother's arm and tenderly shook it. "Of course. We don't want to hurt you. We have some idea of how tough this is on you, you know. Sorry, Mom, but we're worried about Abby...how that's all going to go. That's all."

"I'm sorry. I get it. You don't have to worry about me."

"Are you sure? Because if things go as planned, we'd like to invite him to the football game so he can watch her cheer and then come over for pizza afterwards."

Claire dropped her head into her hands and groaned. "That's next week, isn't it?"

Kate nodded and Claire whimpered obnoxiously.

"Mom, do you think you could talk to him a bit beforehand so you'll feel comfortable when we're all together?"

"I don't know if that'll ever be possible," Claire replied quietly.

Kate wrapped her arm around her mother's shoulder and whispered in her ear. "Just think about it, okay?"

Claire swallowed hard and blinked back tears. "Do I have any choice?"

Pressing her head to her mother's, Kate felt her eyes burn. "Sorry, Mom, but Maggie and I both want him in our lives. I mean, when I was little I thought he was going to be my dad, too. Remember?"

While nodding vigorously and wiping her eyes with her fingertips, Claire pushed her chair from the table and stood. "I know. I'm so sorry it didn't work out."

"Me, too."

"Just give me sometime to think, okay?"

Kate could only nod as she watched her mother scurry from the room.

104

Chapter 15

CLAIRE

Claire leaned against the sham covered pillows on her bed and simply stared out the window, watching the early evening dusk settle on Lake Louise. After closing her eyes, taking a deep breath, and exhaling uneasily, she thoughtfully considered Kate's request. She guessed that it didn't matter how she communicated with him as long as they began some sort of dialogue; although, she wasn't sure how she'd do it until one memory resurfaced to lead the way.

It had been an ordinary day at the shelter beginning with a breakfast meeting with her advisory board. She remembered being grateful when everyone left because she had a lot of work to do. In fact, she'd asked her assistant to take all her calls; she needed uninterrupted time to add some heady facts to her tired old speech before her presentation the next evening. Little did she know, but checking her email that day would spiral into a series of events that would turn her life upside down. First of all, there was the shock to her system when she saw his name; she gasped out loud. Then, after reading the email through to the end, she collapsed in a heap on her desk and sobbed. When she calmed down enough to use her mouse, she printed a copy of the email, folded it, put it in her purse, and gave herself permission to leave for the rest of the day.

Grant wrote that his father had seen her at a banker's convention in Phoenix, that her speech inspired him to donate thousands of dollars to her cause, and that he wanted to do the same. He wanted to write a check, wanted to know who to make it out to, and wanted to know exactly where to send it. There was nothing personal about it at all; it was strictly business.

It took Claire a few days to recover. Nothing was the same after that; in fact, she lost interest in everything for a while. It became hard to get up the gumption to go to work, hard to find the energy to give her fund raising presentations, and even harder to look Mel in the eye when she tried to explain her mood. A few days later, she sent a reply, simply answering his questions. Then she waited and wondered if she'd ever hear from him again; she did. First a check arrived in the mail, followed by an email a day later. This time he asked about her business, how and when she started it, and whether or not she did any fundraising in Wisconsin. Initially, it didn't matter that he didn't want to discuss their personal lives; it was enough to be communicating on some level, any level. She looked forward to each and every message he sent, telling her about his work, his plans for the future. It thrilled her to be able to write about her projects, her struggles and successes. After a while, she understood why she was happy to be corresponding with him. She simply wanted him to be proud of her and her accomplishments. She wanted to be held in high-esteem. If he didn't love her, if he never loved her, at least she knew what he thought of her professionally, and as it turned out, he held nothing back in his praise of her accomplishments.

Eventually, questions about Maggie began appearing in the messages. They were the only personal questions he ever asked. Claire answered them, keeping the focus on Maggie's education and successful career. He asked for pictures; she had a few, made copies of them, and sent them to him. Her cooperation must have spurred his interest because then he wanted stories about her childhood as well as her hobbies and her interests. She told him as much as she knew, embellishing on the bits and pieces she'd gathered when she visited her daughters or from the letters her mother sent on a regular basis. Of course, Claire left out the fact that she was missing for most of their daughter's childhood.

Everything changed, however, when Maggie was attacked on

Labor Day while Claire was visiting Kate. In fact, the incident scared
Claire to death. It suddenly became of paramount importance that Grant
be informed, giving him the chance to meet his daughter before it was
too late. He'd mentioned briefly in an earlier email that he never
contacted Maggie because he was too humiliated to do so. Claire told
him about her anyway, and he sent flowers to the hospital. Maggie
survived and began her own correspondence with her father.

Grant's last email had come to Claire's business address two
weeks earlier; he couldn't know her new email address…she hadn't
shared it with him, but she knew that she missed the connection they'd
had and decided that perhaps she could do it again. She'd be the one to
initiate the email this time and, hopefully, they could begin to sort things
out that way because she wouldn't be able to hold it together if they
needed to talk face to face. Claire concluded that she'd do it for Abby's
sake because she fully understood why Grant had to be included as a
member of Abby's extended family, and she also knew that she needed
to suck it up for the sake of her granddaughter, her daughters, everyone.

After grabbing her laptop and setting it on top of the quilt covering
her thighs, Claire turned the computer on, went online, and logged into
her email account. There were a few messages she needed to reply to,
but hit 'compose' and typed in Grant's email address instead. *Now
what?* When he'd emailed her last year, they'd talked business for
months until he suddenly broached the subject of their past. What had he
said again? Wasn't it something like 'he never stopped looking for her'
or some such nonsense? He'd mentioned it once, and when she didn't
reply to the comment, he never brought it up again. At the time, she was
sure he was lying, but ignored her feelings so she could communicate
with him…something she was thrilled about at the time. *And I never
forgot about you either.* Ignoring the way her pulse raced when she
thought about him, Claire swallowed the lump in her throat and began
typing.

RE: Can we talk?
Grant,
*   I know you're going to be involved in Maggie's life… that's what*

I've prayed for all these years…and now I've been told that Abby will be hearing about you soon. I know we'll probably run into each other now and then, and for the sakes of our daughter and granddaughter, I believe we need to make an attempt to get along, but I can't imagine rehashing everything when we see each other again.

Would you be adverse to the idea of emailing for awhile? Perhaps we'd get our questions answered that way. Then, down the line, if we're ever in the same room, we'll know where we stand with each other. What do you think?
Claire
PS Thanks for checking on me at the hotel. It meant a lot.

Before hitting 'send', Claire read and reread the email. She thought it would be so easy, emailing him, but she'd put herself out there by doing so, by thinking that he'd even want to hear from her. She reminded herself that he'd waited for her in the parking lot in Madison earlier in the week. He probably wanted to talk to her then, but she knew she couldn't face him and four days had gone by since she'd seen him; she had yet to change her mind. Would she have to forgive his father so they could move on? Oh, God help her, she knew that this would happen…even sending off a simple email had stirred everything up again, causing her an untold amount of grief. She shook it off as well as she could and after giving her shoulders a roll, she hit 'send', logged off, and slammed the computer shut.

Chapter 16

ABBY

Eager to share what she had found, Abby hustled Lily upstairs and into her bedroom immediately after supper. They had lots to talk about, according to Abby, and the adults couldn't know anything about it. Her mother didn't eye them suspiciously when they asked to be excused and Grandma, who seemed preoccupied all through supper, had gone to her room, too. So far, so good...they were alone.

Just to make sure they wouldn't be interrupted, Abby shoved both of their overstuffed backpacks against her bedroom door. If anyone wanted in, she and Lily would have time to hide their contraband before moving their school bags and allowing a visitor into their private sanctum. That old trick had never failed.

After shoving the clutter on her multi-colored area rug aside, Abby patted a spot on the floor indicating that Lily should take a seat. Lily understood and sat crisscross applesauce on the floor facing her best friend. Across from her, Abby stretched out on her stomach, braced herself on her elbows, and began setting her precious photos face down on the floor.

"We're going to play one of your made-up games?" Lily asked. "I thought you were going to tell me a secret or something."

Abby nodded. "I am, sort of. It's part of the game. Okay, these are the rules. Each of us will draw a picture from the pile, turn it over, look at it, and guess who it is."

"But haven't you seen them all...don't you know who they are?"

"I covered up the names on the back so I wouldn't remember and replaced them with numbers. And I made up an answer sheet to tell us who they are. Okay?"

"Oh, okay then," Lily conceded with a roll of her eyes. "Who goes first?"

Abby tossed her a die. "Whoever gets the highest number on the first roll."

Lily rolled and got a five. Abby followed with a two.

"I guess you're first," Abby said.

Lily chose a picture at random, picked it up, and looked at it. "It's some baby...I have no idea who it is," Lily said, frowning. "This game is stupid!"

"Just wait...it gets better. Now turn it over and put it back on the floor. My turn." After rubbing her hands together gleefully, Abby chose a picture and flipped it over. "Hmm...let me see. Oh, this one's easy."

"Let me see," ordered Lily.

Abby turned the photograph to face her friend.

"That's you."

"Yup."

With a sly grin on her mug, Abby set the photograph aside, face up, picked up her pencil and drew a slash mark under her name on the yellow legal tablet next to her. *This is going just as I suspected!*

"Why did you have such a weird haircut?" Lily asked, still staring at the picture.

Shrugging her shoulders nonchalantly, Abby motioned for Lily to take a turn.

Lily did what she was told and turned another picture face up. "Ah, ha...last year's school picture...it's you again."

"Right on. Put it next to the other one of me, okay? I'll give you a chicken scratch for that one."

Abby drew and came up with the picture of two youngsters in a metal tub.

"Is that me again?" Abby asked, feigning ignorance.

"Let me see," Lily said, grabbing the picture out of her friend's hand. "I don't know...who's that other kid?"

"Who knows...where's that other baby picture...is this the same one?" Abby asked as she picked up the first baby picture and held the two of them together. "What do you think, same baby?"

Lily held the two photographs just inches from her nose, her eyes bouncing from one to the other. "Yup, looks like the same kid to me."

"That's what I think, too," Abby said quietly.

Momentarily forgetting about the game's rules, the curious girls simply stared at the last photograph on the floor between them, face down. It was Lily's turn, and she lifted it from the floor. "OMG…it's you again? But where are you? Why does it look so old?"

Losing her composure, Abby rolled over onto her back, covered her eyes, and began to sob, her cries coming in spurts. Lily sat still as a stone, stunned by her friend's behavior.

"Abby…what's wrong?" Lily asked, compassion filling her voice.

Reaching toward a pile of papers and markers near her, Abby grabbed the answer sheet to the game and shoved it at her friend. Lily snatched the pink construction paper and looked at the rundown. After scooping up the photographs littering the floor, she turned them upside down and put them in order by number. Slowly, she turned them over one by one, checking the corresponding names on the answer sheet. She didn't say a word.

Abby's sobs subsided somewhat, and she rubbed a sleeve under her nose before speaking. "What do you think this means, Lil?"

"You're all related?"

"Yup, I think so. What else?"

"I don't know."

"Don't you see? Grandma Claire and Maggie looked just like me when they were little. Grandma is Maggie's mother, and they look just alike. Really, do you think Maggie could be my biological mother?"

Lily's hands flew to cover her wide open mouth. "No way!"

Abby nodded. "Way!"

"So she came back here to get you or something?"

Abby shrugged. "Maybe."

"My dad would know. He'd know all about it. Want me to call him? I could call him and find out right now."

Shaking her head vehemently, Abby lost her nerve. "No. What if it is some relative like they've been telling me, not Maggie at all? Some cousin or something…cousins can look alike, right?"

The darling Asian girl rolled her eyes. "How should I know?"

"Oh, sorry. I just don't know what to do."

Out of the blue, Lily got a strange look in her eye and Abby caught it.

"What?"

"What would be so bad about her being your birthmother, huh? I really like her, don't you? And what if my dad wants to marry her? Then that would make us sisters, wouldn't it? You could move in with us; you could share my room…we could do everything together!"

***

Later that evening when all was still in the house except for the hourly chime coming from the grandfather clock in the living room, Abby lay in her twin bed, listening to the intermittent snoring coming from her friend on the trundle bed next to her. Her mind wouldn't stop racing. What if Maggie was her birthmother? What if she wanted to raise her now? What if it's not Maggie? She came to the conclusion that she wouldn't want it to be a stranger; it would be better if it were Maggie. *But I want my mommy!* The tears started up again, and the worried child pressed her face into her pillow.

Chapter 17

GRANT

There is nothing quite like an average Friday night in Madison, Wisconsin. Grant's son had invited him to dinner, but on this unusually warm September evening, the great places to eat on State Street would be packed with happy, hollering, bar hopping students; therefore, Grant talked his son into meeting him at a pub on the capital's outer circle, walking distance from the courthouse so he could leave his car in his reserved parking space. Later, as he strolled down Doty Street toward The Capital Pub and Brewing Company, he noticed that he wasn't the only one headed in that direction. So much for hoping the college kids would stay on State Street. He should have known better; the pub was well known for its award winning ale and huge billiards room...what kid could resist that.

Grant, seated at a table in the dining room, savored a fine, pale pilsner while he waited for Greg. It had been a while since they'd talked face to face instead of texting, which was the kid's preferred means of communication these days. Besides that, he was looking forward to talking about something other than his relationship, or rather his non-existent relationship with Claire. He'd already taken as much advice as he could stand because his assistant, Barbara, made sure she put in her two cents worth every day, and there was no stopping her. Before the foam was off his beer, Grant spotted the tall, gangly young man coming in the door, his redheaded, freckle-faced girlfriend, Jolene, glued to his arm. He got a kick out of his kid and his fashion sense and could see that the punk craze was alive and well. His son's oversized baggy pants just resting on his hips, looking as though they'd drop to the floor at any moment. The kid loved the look and the anti-establishment music that spawned it since middle school, and he never grew tired of it. Grant always thought it was a strange choice for his son, the science geek; it didn't matter, though, because the kid always had his head on straight.

After waving to get their attention and standing to greet them both with bear hugs, the young people pulled out chairs and sat directly across from Grant. He envied them…youngsters in love…and wished for a time machine so that he could start all over. He'd give just about anything to change the way he handled things when he was their age.

"Don't you two have anything better to do on a Friday night?" Grant joked as he settled into his chair.

Greg's eyes widened and he winked at his girlfriend before he spoke. "Well…I just thought it would be nice to share some good news with you in person."

"Really," Grant said, watching the two of them closely, wondering whether or not they had a personal announcement to make. They'd been dating two years or so now, hadn't they?

"Hold on to your hat, Dad…I finally got a job interview!"

"Wow, congratulations! When and where?" Grant asked, happily giving his son his undivided attention. This was big. The kid had been on a relentless job search since getting his Master's in June, but with little success.

"With the Environmental Protection Agency…I'd be working out of Minneapolis."

"Right up your alley, buddy," Grant said proudly.

"Isn't it great?" Jolene interjected with glee, squeezing the life out of Greg's arm.

"Yeah, they need engineers experienced in environmental fluid mechanics. Exactly what my internship was all about. It's about the protection of the St. Croix and Mississippi Rivers, you know, the land runoff and infiltration of the rivers."

"Actually, I don't know a thing about it, but I'm thrilled that you do. Somebody had better take care of the environment. When you doing this?"

"Bright and early Monday. I've already got the address loaded in my GPS."

"So your resume' got you in the door. Have you practiced for the interview?"

Greg shook his head and rolled his eyes. "Yes, Dad."

"Just checking," Grant said, eyebrows raised. "What about a haircut?"

Jolene piped up then. "Tomorrow...I'm taking him myself."

"You should wear a suit or at least a shirt and tie."

Greg released a sigh, obviously annoyed by the fatherly advice. "You got me a suit for graduation. Remember?"

"Oh, that's right. I forgot." Grant decided not to mention the facial piercings since the only one visible today was the one in his nose. On the other hand, Jolene had yet to cave to convention, silver jewelry covering her ears, nose, eyebrows and lips. Piercing the lip had to hurt like the devil, he thought.

Greg smiled at his father as if he knew what he was thinking and shook his unruly locks in feigned disbelief.

The waiter stopped by then, taking drink orders and dropping off the menus. While he waited, the three of them talked about getting an appetizer to share. Grant remembered how much he liked the cheese and artichoke dip and fresh boule loaf that came with it. He ordered it, and their drinks showed up shortly thereafter.

"Jeez, I'm proud of you, son! Wow...the EPA!"

"Yeah, a government job...I knew you'd like that," Greg said, laughing.

Grant raised his glass in a toast to his son. "Here's to you, Greg."

They clanked their glasses, drank heartily, and laughed out loud.

"I bet you thought this day would never come, huh Dad?"

"Oh, I knew it would come...but with the economy the way it is, the government cuts. I feel bad for the kids just starting out, that's for sure. What about you, Jolene? Any leads?"

"Nothing yet, but if Greg gets this one, I'll probably concentrate harder on the Twin Cities. Maybe there'll be enough teachers retiring that I'll get lucky."

"You never know."

Grant heard his son clear his throat and glanced his way.

"Dad, I want to ask you something," he said sheepishly.

"I know. Sure, you can borrow my car," Grant joked.

"Hey, great...but that's not it. Um, I just wanted to know that since I'm driving right by Lake Louise on my way to the Twin Cities, could I, I mean, would it be alright if I gave Maggie a call and met up with her?"

Taken aback by the question, Grant simply stared at his son. He'd shared the saga of Claire and Maggie with him, little by little over the past year or so, but this was unexpected. He never got the feeling that his son cared.

"Dad? Is it okay? Do you think she'd like to meet me?" Greg continued.

Grant's heart swelled with pride. Greg was an only child. He had no idea how he would take the news of a half sister; he couldn't be more pleased. "Well, yes...I think that'd be great."

Greg's eyes widened. "No kidding, Dad?"

"Sure...want me to call her and give her a heads up?"

"Yeah. Jolene is going along for the ride. I want them to meet, too."

"Wow...sounds like a party." Sadly, a party he wasn't invited to. "I'll give her a call later and remind me to give you her cell number before you leave."

Greg nodded. "Will do. So when are you seeing her again?"

"Not sure."

"What about Claire? Have you talked to her since Tuesday?"

Just the subject he'd hoped to avoid. "Nope."

"Why the hell not?"

Jolene backed away and jabbed him in the arm. "Greg...it's none of your business," she scolded.

"It sure is my business," Greg insisted firmly. "I finally have a sibling and Claire's her mother...that makes us family."

Nodding, Grant agreed, but had nothing to say.

"Why aren't you talking to her? I mean, you were so glad she was back in Wisconsin. No, let me rephrase that, you were thrilled when you heard she was back!"

Grant laughed at his son. "Maybe you should get a job as an interrogator."

"Dad, come on, I know you care about her; you told me that you never forgot her. And Mom's in a good place now; you deserve to be happy again, too. You know I'm behind you one hundred percent, don't you?"

"Yes, thanks, son, but it's complicated," Grant said, staring a hole into his beer.

"So you're just going to sit there…do nothing? What about that BS you're always preaching…that 'go for what you want' spiel, that 'stop at nothing till you get it' bologna?"

"Jeez, Greg, stop it. Don't talk to your dad like that," Jolene scolded, squirming uncomfortably in her chair.

Grant held a hand in the air, palm forward. "Jolene, it's okay. He's right. I should practice what I preach. I hadn't thought about it that way, I guess. I kept thinking if I could just come up with a plan, a plan where I'd be in her good graces again, but Maggie says she's having a hard time. Did Greg tell you what his grandfather did? I mean, she needs time to sort it all out, so I guess I'm going to have to play it by ear."

Jolene nodded. "Greg told me everything, and I know it's none of my business, but can I offer a woman's point of view?"

"You've got the floor," Grant said, leaning back in his seat, amused by his son's bright, down-to-earth girlfriend.

"Okay, you don't have to take me seriously and this might sound like psycho-babble, but if I were her, I sure would want to know how you felt about me…even if we weren't on speaking terms. I mean, Greg told me that she thought you lied about everything, so she might not believe you, but since she knows what your dad did, it might be a good time to tell her. Might be risky, but…"

"Yeah, and it scares me to death," Grant admitted.

"Sure…you'd be putting yourself out there," Jolene added. "But, you don't want her to go back to Phoenix, do you?"

"I never thought about that."

"Or, another guy could come along," Greg interjected.

"That never entered my mind either."

"Sorry, Dad, we don't mean any disrespect by bringing this up. We were just thinking that Grandpa might have opened a door for you by telling the two of you everything. You know what happened now, and you know that neither of you are at fault. You have a clean slate, a fresh start."

"Man, you really thought this through."

"We've been talking about it a lot," Jolene said. "We couldn't help it; we felt so sorry for you and wondered what we would do if something like that happened to us."

"Don't worry, you're safe. I couldn't lie to my kid like that."

"So you're not mad?" Greg ventured cautiously.

"Are you kidding? Any parent would be proud to have a couple of kids like you!"

"So what are you going to do?"

"I appreciate the input, guys, but I think it's time to change the subject."

***

Home alone in his den, reclining in his well worn, but comfortable, leather chair, Grant closed his eyes and tried to think. The kids were probably right. Claire had no idea how he felt and maybe that did add to the heartache. Couldn't she tell how he felt just by looking at him? Wasn't it written all over his face? What in the world would he say and how would he say it? When? Where? He'd spend the weekend coming up with a way to tell her, he thought. He would say it in such a way that she'd find him irresistible; he'd overwhelm her with his charm, and she wouldn't be able to stay away from him. He laughed out loud at the thought of it. For crying out loud, he was sixty years old, practically an old man. Irresistible? Highly unlikely. Besides that, how could he charm her if she couldn't even talk to him, couldn't even look him in the eye? He'd have to sleep on it and think about it again in the morning when his brain was fully functioning instead of floating on fine pilsner.

***

As soon as Grant awoke, his brain went into overdrive. He figured the only thing that would take his mind off of Claire was his Saturday morning routine. After separating the newly printed sections of the State Journal and Journal Sentinel, he organized them in an orderly manner on his lap, the sports' sections on top as usual. Nothing relaxed him more, and he couldn't wait until retirement age so he'd be able to begin every single day of his life the same way. He inhaled the dark roast blend that filled his coffee mug to the brim and relaxed against the back of his favorite chair while taking in the splendor of his backyard and the maple leaves that would soon wear a golden hew. Was there anything more beautiful than the change of seasons in Wisconsin? He doubted it; he'd traveled the world, gazed upon foliage of all kinds, and nothing thrilled him like autumn in Wisconsin. He smiled to himself, feeling fortunate for the life he'd lived. When he returned his focus to the printed word, however, the sting of his father's betrayal prevented him from fully concentrating on the news. Frustrated, he finally gave up on the newsprint and decided to check his email instead.

Leaving his newspapers in an unruly pile on the floor of his den, Grant shuffled into his office, plopped into his rolling office chair, and accessed the internet. After skimming a few newsworthy articles online, he logged onto his email account. Barbara had promised to forward his schedule for the following week, and he wondered what he'd have to prepare for, what amount work he'd have to do at home before Monday morning. The email and attachment were there, but he didn't want to read them now and spoil his carefree Saturday morning. Instead, he allowed his eyes to roam over the list of his most recent emails and after deleting the junk mail and spam, Grant's cursor landed on a new address with a familiar name. In the subject line of the email, he read: *Can we talk?*

Stomach bile made its way into his throat; his cheeks and ears burned. Isn't this how women start conversations when then want to break up with someone? *Can we talk...is she going to tell me that she never wants to see my ugly mug again?* How could it be over before they'd had a chance to start again? Grant inhaled and rubbed his face nervously before hitting the mouse. It wasn't until he'd perused the entire note that he stopped holding his breath. *She really did want to talk!* She said that they'd be running into each other now and then, so she wasn't cutting him out of her life totally, and she didn't say she hated his guts! Thank you, God! So far, so good, except for the fact that he had to reply, and he was sure she wasn't ready for what he'd really like to say. If only he could lay a kiss on the computer screen and then magically, she'd know how he felt.

This was going to take awhile, so he left his office and found his way to the kitchen where he dumped his cold coffee down the drain before pouring himself another cup. After rummaging through the cupboards looking for something to eat, Grant poured himself a bowl of bran flakes and raisons, laced it with skim milk, and carried both the bowl and his coffee cup through the French doors and into his sunny living room. After setting the coffee cup on an end table, he remained standing, eating the cereal and taking in his backyard and the sparkling lake beyond. Honking geese flew over head, and he searched the skies for their familiar formation. Afterwards, he couldn't help noticing that his bird feeders were low; he'd have to take care of that this weekend, too. Gray clouds appeared on the horizon, and he cringed involuntarily at the thought of a cold, miserable winter and the possibility of yet another record snowfall.

Okay, so procrastination was his middle name, and he'd have to fight it hard today. Out of the blue, an idea popped into his head. If he answered the email right away, perhaps she would, too. He got carried away with his fantasy, like he always did when he thought about Claire, and imagined that after emailing incessantly, she would tire of it and simply give him a call. Well, except for the fact that he'd been corresponding with her for a year now, and the only time she called was to tell him that Maggie had been hospitalized. This time it would be different, though. He figured she'd call as soon as he told her how he really felt. The fantasy propelled him forward; he grabbed his coffee, sprinted into his office, and sat on the edge of his chair…recharged and full of vim and vigor.

Hitting 'reply' was the easy part. Now he had to come up with something intelligent to say. Jolene suggested he tell her how much he cared, and it gave him pause. Was she right about that? She was a level headed young woman…could she know what she's talking about? Well, Claire had given him an opening, hadn't she? She'd started this and now he hoped he could be as sincere without offending her or coming on too strong. In addition, now that his father had leveled with him about why Claire left the girls, he needed her to confirm the story. He wondered if she'd be able to tell him or if she'd prefer to keep it under wraps. If only he could get a do-over…that's all he really wanted anyway.

Claire,

I was just sitting here drinking my morning coffee when I saw your email. I think it's a wonderful idea, and I believe you're right; it would be better than talking in person. It hurts way too much, doesn't it? I just want you to know how sorry I am about what they did to keep us apart. I am not sorry, however, that we found out because learning the truth has unlocked the mysteries that have haunted us both, and I, for one, will no longer question why you never got back to me, never answered my letters. In any event, I believe my father inadvertently wiped the slate clean, giving us a chance to reexamine our past without recrimination, and I hope that you agree.

If I may, I'd like to start the dialogue with a question that has haunted me since I first returned from Brazil to find you gone, and it's really the only question I need answering. Why did you leave Maggie and Kate to be raised by your mother? I can't imagine that this was in any way easy for you because I saw what a good mother you were to Katie. I have no doubt that you had a very good reason for doing so. I'll wait until you're ready to tell me…no pressure. I just hope and pray it wasn't because I didn't come to see you right away. Two years had passed before I was allowed to return to the states, and by then, you were gone.

I really appreciate the email, and it is a good way to talk about the past without our emotions getting in the way. But to be honest, though, I

don't really want this to replace seeing you in person because I've spent most of the last forty years wondering where you were and now that I've found you, I can't imagine living another four decades without you in my life.
Grant

There, he did it; he told her how he felt. The ball was in her court now, but it didn't stop him from second guessing. He questioned whether or not he was too forward, whether he'd gone too far, and he couldn't let it go. Eventually, he opened Barbara's attachment and groaned out loud at the amount of reading he'd have to do before Monday. He hadn't been able to concentrate on the morning paper, and the briefs would be no different.

Chapter 18

MAGGIE

When Kate suspected Abby was on a mission to learn the truth about her birthmother, she told her that it was time for a heart to heart talk. Today was the day, the day that secrets would no longer be secrets, the day that everything they thought was right could go wrong. Their precious Abby may be heartbroken by the truth; Maggie couldn't stand that, but it was a possibility she had to face…no wonder a good night's sleep escaped her. In fact, Maggie spent the dark hours of the night trying to imagine how this day would go. Did Abby know the truth as Kate suspected? Or was Kate imagining things? No one wanted to hurt the kid…that was one thing she knew for sure. The facts would have to be introduced in a loving way, and she would be forever grateful to her sister for handling that part. She owed Kate so much already. What would she have done if she hadn't agreed to adopt her baby? What if Rex had found them instead? She knew from personal experience what he was capable of. He would have killed her and her baby to boot.

After today, Abby would know that everything they did was for her sake, for the sake of a child she wanted more than anything. Abby's reaction to her birthmother's decisions might prove to be a different story, however. They had to be prepared for that; they had to be prepared to answer questions and even expect an angry response to their revelation. But after the initial reaction, after they worked on repairing their relationship, Maggie prayed that Abby would gain a sense of belonging instead of facing a life of unanswered questions.

Maggie didn't know a thing about her own mother. Even though she grew up under her grandmother's watchful eye, even though she was well cared for and felt loved, she never understood why Claire left her at such a young age, and it had haunted her. Why didn't she want her? How could she just show up once in a while, only to leave almost immediately? She'd waited thirty-seven years before learning the truth, and that was the last thing she wanted for Abby. She wouldn't wish that on anyone…waiting a lifetime like she did. What they would do today was the right thing to do. Today, Maggie would admit to her child that she had no choice, and the very mother who'd abandoned her almost four decades earlier would be there, too, lending her support and with complete understanding of what needed to be done.

Chapter 18

KATE

Kate had decided early on that they'd have lunch together…Maggie, Kate, Claire, and Abby…just the four of them. Lily had gymnastics at ten, so Mac would pick her up from her sleepover by 9:30 or so. That would mean a good two hours of shooting the breeze until lunchtime and Maggie's arrival. Kate thought that she and Abby could play a game of Sequence or something until it was time to make lunch. She'd be sure to have Abby's favorite foods…peanut and jelly sandwiches cut in cookie cutter shapes, the crusts tossed aside. The kid loved carrot sticks and apple slices, so she wouldn't forget those. Chocolate cupcakes with creamy centers topped off the kid's menu.

Her mother and sister would expect a more adult fare, however, so Kate prepared a nice cold salad with pasta, chicken, grapes, and walnuts, laced with raspberry vinaigrette. Coffee was a staple, and Maggie would want half and half to go with it. If they were lucky, Abby would share her cupcakes with the older women; then they would sit down and talk. Maggie had pleaded with Kate to lead the conversation, and Kate agreed. This was much harder for her sister than she'd ever imagined it would be. She'd always thought that Maggie would be eager to tell Abby, that she couldn't wait for the day. Now that the day had arrived, nothing could be further from the truth. There was a time when Kate worried that her sister might renege on her promise to stay out of it, to let them raise Abby. It never happened, and Kate's heart swelled with love for the woman who sacrificed her own child so her barren sister could raise that child as her own.

Kate knew her husband well and fully understood when George begged to be excused for the afternoon. He told Kate that he wanted to leave this very important task to the women because the simple thought of it turned him into a blubbering idiot, and he didn't want to fall apart in front of the kid. Eventually, Kate agreed. Her husband was such a softie when it came to Abby, and she knew he couldn't stand to see her hurt in any way. He said he could get a lot of work done at school if that was all right with her, telling Kate to call him when it was over. His eyes already brimming with tears, it was all he could manage to say on his way out the door.

At about 11:30 or so, Kate heard a knock on the front door and ran to greet Maggie. After turning to make sure that Abby had not followed her, Kate gave her sister a huge bear hug and asked her if she was okay. Maggie nodded.

"You look really pretty," Kate said, trying to boost her sister's confidence.

"Thanks. I thought some makeup might brighten my mood," Maggie answered, mustering a smile.

After hugging her reassuringly, Kate cooed, "It'll be fine. Come on. Let's have some lunch."

Abby was sitting with Claire, tossing dice into a tin pie pan and playing her own version of Bunco. Kate watched as her sister came up behind Abby like usual, kissing her on top of the head and hugging her from behind. Abby didn't turn to look at her, but mumbled some sort of greeting. Maggie glanced at Kate who shrugged her shoulders in response. *It was going to be a long day!*

The four of them ate around the kitchen table. Kate kept her eyes on Maggie and Abby, watching for any sign of Abby's suspicions. What she saw confirmed her every fear. Her daughter would not look Maggie in the eye, even if she spoke to her directly or tried to engage her in anyway. Kate could barely swallow; the great mass in her throat made that simple involuntary act impossible. Then there was her mother, Claire. Obviously distracted, she wasn't eating much either and spent a good deal of time staring out of the sliding glass doors leading to the back yard. Kate had a feeling that her mother's preoccupation had nothing to do with the problem at hand; she had a lot on her psychological plate right now, and not one of them could help her with any of it.

Maggie was the first one to bus her dishes; Claire followed. Abby watched them closely as if she knew what was about to happen. The kid looked scared to death, Kate thought. *Time to intervene!* As Kate walked to where her daughter sat, Abby moved and looked right past her, never taking her eyes off of Maggie.

Tapping her lightly on the shoulder, Kate spoke. "Abs...we have something to talk to you about."

The child, wise beyond her years, nodded. "I know."

"Should we sit in the living room? You know, snuggle together on the couches?"

Abby nodded, left her dishes where they were and headed out of the room ahead of everyone. Kate entered the room to find Abby curled up on one end of the full-sized sofa, staring at her hands and cracking her knuckles. Kate plopped down on the other end, close enough to touch her if need be. Claire followed and sat on the loveseat, throwing off her platform sandals and tucking her feet under her. Maggie came in then, pushed her mother over, slid in next to her, and grabbed a hand in hers as she nestled in.

Kate waited until they were all settled and cleared her throat. "Honey, we've decided to tell you all about your birthmother. Is that okay with you?"

Abby nodded without looking up.

"Okay, hon," Kate said, patting her daughter on the knee. "First of all, I want to tell you how much she loved you. I mean, she loved you more than life itself. And the last thing she really wanted to do was let someone else raise you."

In an almost inaudible whisper, the girl spoke without looking at Kate. "Why'd she do it then?"

"Women have lots of reasons why they feel they cannot raise their own children. Your mother had plenty, but it still broke her heart to leave you."

"Then why'd she do it?"

Glancing toward the women on the loveseat, Kate stared at her sister, hoping for permission to continue. She got what she needed…a nod as well as a tentative smile. "First of all, you were born long after your mother left your father. He never wanted children, so your mother didn't tell him about you. Your mother no longer loved him either. He didn't treat her very well when they were together, and she knew that he wouldn't know how to treat a child either. So she left."

The child looked across the room at Maggie before asking a very courageous question. "Why didn't you take me with you?"

Kate's heart was breaking for her sister. Just as they'd suspected, Abby had guessed the truth. Kate watched as Maggie took a deep breath, blew it out through quivering lips, and stood to walk toward the couch. She knelt on the floor in front of Abby and tried her best to explain.

"I couldn't take you with me in case he followed me. I'm sure he was very angry that I left him, and I had to protect you somehow. I kept thinking that if he found me and learned about you…he might hurt us both. I couldn't stand it if anything happened to you."

"So you left me because you loved me?"

As Kate watched tears begin to make trails over Maggie's cheekbones, she grabbed a tissue and handed it to her sister. She took it, wiped away the tears under her eyes, and blew her nose as she nodded.

"That's what Lily says…her birthmother loved her and let her go so she could have a better life."

"Sometimes that's what we have to do even though it's tearing us apart inside."

Abby broke down then and Maggie reached for her, but the little girl jerked away, jumped from the couch, and ran from the room. In a split second she returned, pointed a finger at Maggie, and yelled. "Why did you wait so long to tell me? I've wondered about this my whole life!" And she was gone.

The women sat, stunned. Maggie slid upward and onto the couch, crying and blowing her nose intermittently. Kate stayed in the corner next to her, putting on a brave face, and patting her sister's knee.

Claire, alone on the other side of the room, spoke first. "What now, girls?"

"I suppose I should see if she'll talk to me," Kate said.

"What if I went up there," Claire suggested unexpectedly. "What if I told her what happened to me...well, a child's fairy tale version of what happened. Maybe that would put things in perspective for her. Maybe it would help her understand the family dynamics, help her see where she fits in. What do you think?"

"Really? You'd do that, Mom?" Maggie asked, a grateful tone to her voice.

"Yes...I would. Where's that family tree you drew? I'll take that with me."

Chapter 19

CLAIRE

On her way to Abby's room, Claire stopped in the guest bathroom and shook the tension from her hands before purposefully blowing her nose. Her throat and mouth were parched and, grateful for the paper cups that Kate kept there, she yanked one from the plastic tube before filling it to the brim. After draining two cups of water and staring intently into the mirror above the sink, Claire reminded herself that she'd come full circle, that she was capable of offering hope and healing, and that she could support her daughters in their time of need. Hopefully, she'd be able to prove to them that she was worthy after all.

A few short minutes later, she was standing in front of little Abby's bedroom door, smoothing her clothes, making herself presentable. She rapped and called to her granddaughter. "Honey, it's Grandma. I have something to show you. Want to see?"

"No!"

"Please, sweetie, you'll really like it. I promise it'll make you feel better."

No sound came from the other side of the door.

"Honey, please?"

Claire heard a shuffling, then a scraping, as if something was being moved away from the door. "Okay."

Slowly turning the knob, Claire pushed the door inward. "Hi, sweetie," she whispered when she saw her granddaughter curled up on the bed, a big, pink, furry sham covering her head. Slowly crossing the room, she slid onto the pink and white bedspread at the foot of the bed.

Lying on her side with one arm bent, she rested her chin in her hand. Taking hold of one of Abby's ankles, she straightened a leg before tickling the bottom of a sock covered foot.

"Stop it, Grandma," Abby ordered, her voice muffled beneath the pillow.

"Thanks for letting me in, sweetie pie."

"You can come in, but not them! What do you want?"

"I want to show you a little drawing."

"Of what?"

Claire swallowed hard. "Of our family."

It came, barely audible, but a scream nonetheless. "I hate this family!"

Tears brimmed Claire's eyes. "I believe you do. I would, too."

The room became quiet then and time passed at a snail's pace until the little girl lifted the pillow from her head and tossed it onto the floor.

"You'd hate them, too?" she asked rubbing her face with her hands and facing the wall without as much as a glance at her grandmother.

"Yes, I would…because of the secrets, Abby. Secrets can hurt you. They hurt me, I know that for sure," Claire claimed, drawing the girl's interest.

"What secrets, Grandma," Abby asked as she sat up, scooting closer to Claire.

"Well, for one, my own mother didn't tell me that Maggie's father was looking for me, that he wanted to see me and Maggie, and that he wanted to take care of us. That was a secret she kept from me."

Little hands flew to wipe away new tears. "That's terrible, Grandma."

"Because I didn't know he wanted us, I got sicker and sicker. I had to be in a hospital, and my mother got to take care of Kate and Maggie."

"But Mom loved her grandma. She told me she was the best ever."

Claire nodded. "She was real good to them. She thought she was doing the right thing by not telling me about Maggie's father. She thought he was bad for me and Maggie, so she kept the secret. She thought she was protecting us from him. Do you understand?"

"Was he a bad guy, Grandma?"

"No. He was a good guy, but my mother didn't know that."

"Was my father a bad guy?"

"Sometimes. He could be real nice. That's why Maggie loved him. He was so good to her in the beginning, but later he became angry, even cruel."

"Why was he so angry?"

"Nobody knows for sure, but I think that when he was a little kid…maybe his parents didn't treat him right so he grew up mad at the world and took his anger out on other people. Sometimes it happens that way."

"So Maggie gave me to Mom and Dad so he couldn't take it out on me?"

"That's right."

Out of the blue, Abby changed the subject. "Grandma, what did you want to show me?"

Claire looked for the piece of printer paper she'd brought in with her. It had fallen off the end of the bed and onto the floor. Abby spotted it and climbed over her grandmother to get it. Claire laughed when the child kneed her and again when she apologized.

"It's okay, honey. It didn't hurt much," Claire joked. "Now, let's see what we've got."

Abby leaned into her grandmother as she smoothed out the wrinkled piece of paper. "I know what this is, Grandma. It's a family tree. We read a book about it in school… *Lucy's Family Tree*…so we could make our own family trees. I checked it out, and Mom and I read it a bunch of times."

"So you've already made a family tree?"

"No, we didn't have to…we could do anything we wanted. I started my 'famous people in my family' scrapbook instead."

"Good. Well, this is your family tree. Do you want me to tell you all about it?"

Abby nodded and Claire began explaining the branches on the chart and who everyone was until Abby got a strange look on her face. "You have two branches coming off your name."

"Yup. One for your mom and one for Maggie…they're my

daughters. See what happens when your name is added to theirs?"

"Why are there lines to both of them?"

"Well, that was the only way Maggie could think to do it. Kate is your adoptive mom and Maggie is your birthmother, and since they're sisters, they're both related to you. Understand?"

"Yes, but I don't know why Maggie has a different last name. Mom says she never got married so why isn't Maggie's last name the same as Mom's was?"

"I think Maggie wanted to start a whole new life when she left here. Changing her name was one way to do that."

"And that's when I got Mom and Dad's last name."

"Yes, when they adopted you."

"So you really are my grandma, aren't you?" she sniffed.

"Uh huh."

After latching onto Claire's arm, Abby laid her head on her grandmother's shoulder. "I'm not mad at you, Grandma. Just them."

"Someday you won't be mad at them either."

"Why not?"

"Because we're related, we're family...we have the same relatives going back hundreds of years. Let me tell you, sweetie, you've been an important member of this family since the day you were born. We all love you very much, and we'll always take good care of you."

"But Lily isn't related to her family, and they still take care of her."

"Yes, they do. Their family just came together a different way. You know that there are lots of different kinds of families, right?"

"I learned that way back in Kindergarten, Grandma."

"Okay, smarty pants. Lily's family is one kind; we're another kind. Both kinds are good because people in both families love each other. Families come with lots of relatives, too. Lily has relatives in another country, but now that she's part of Mac's family, his relatives are hers, too."

Abby gave a nod in agreement. "But she has way more relatives than I do."

"You have plenty of relatives."

"No, I don't. Mom, Dad, and now Maggie and you. Isn't that it?"

"Nope. Look at the family tree. Look at the name next to mine."

"Grant somebody? I don't know that person, do I?"

"Not yet, but you will soon. He's your grandfather. You know, the man my mother thought was a bay guy?"

"No way!"

"You'll probably get to meet him the next time he comes to visit Maggie."

"Nope...not going to. I'm not talking to her; she could have told me a long time ago. They just kept me guessing, Grandma. I don't think that was very nice of them. That was mean."

"Okay, sweetie, I understand what you're saying, but if you wouldn't have run out of the room, they would have explained everything."

"Nope...they're mean, mean, mean."

"Okay, mean. But can I just tell you one more thing about your grandfather?"

Abby gave a roll of her eyes.

"There are a couple of other relatives."

"Huh...really?"

"Yup. Your grandfather, Grant, has a son. See?" Claire said as she pointed to a name on the family tree. "So what do you think he would be to you?"

"I don't know."

"He'd be your uncle and Maggie's brother. Well, don't worry about that part...you know what an uncle is, right?"

"I think so. Lily has an uncle and cousins. Like that? Do I have cousins, too?"

Claire laughed and mussed with Abby's hair. "No, Greg just graduated from college...he's pretty young. He doesn't have any children yet."

"When do I get to meet him? Is he cute?"

"I don't know...probably. His father is very cute."

"Grant is cute?"

"Yup."

"But isn't he really old?"

"Well, so am I, I guess."

"But Grandma, you're pretty."

Claire grabbed her granddaughter and hugged her hard, both of them falling backwards onto the bed. "Oh, thanks sweetie. So are you."

"I'm going to look like you when I'm old, aren't I?"

"I guess so."

"I know so…I have your school pictures, Grandma. I figured it out a while ago."

"We guessed as much."

"Grandma, why did Maggie wait so long?"

"She was scared."

"Scared of what?"

"This…scared you would hate her and scared you wouldn't understand why she left you."

"Oh…I didn't know she was scared. I don't want her to be scared, Grandma." New tears appeared in the child's eyes. "You know I don't really hate her, don't you?"

"Yes, but you need to tell her that."

More tears. "But she was mean; Mom was mean to keep secrets, too."

"Okay, sweetie, but the only way it will get better is if you give them a chance to explain."

Abby wrestled her way out of her grandmother's arms. "They think I'm just a little kid, Grandma. They aren't going to do that, because I want to know the whole story! I won't talk to them ever again unless they tell me every single thing!"

After reaching for her granddaughter, holding her close, and kissing the top of her golden curls, Claire tried to calm her down. "Sweetie, please…you know that there are things that adults have to keep between them, but I'll be glad to tell them what you said, okay?"

"I'm not kidding, Grandma. They have to promise…no more secrets!"

"Okay, okay. I'll tell them for you. Anything else?"

"I'm going to stay in my room, and I'm not coming out until you tell me they promise."

"Then you'll be ready to listen to them?" Claire felt the child nod as she held her close. "Anything else?"

Pushing off, lifting her chin, and looking her grandmother in the eye, Abby added one final request. "Grandma? Do you think my grandpa would like to come to my cheerleading show next week?"

Kate had mentioned the very same thing; still, Claire was at a loss for words.

"Well, Grandma? Do you think he'd come?"

Claire cleared her throat and stuttered. "I don't know for sure," she answered truthfully.

"Will you ask him? Please!"

"He's a busy man…he might not…"

"But all the kids are having their grandmas and grandpas come. He wants to see me, doesn't he?"

"I'm sure he does."

***

By the time Claire returned to the lower level of Kate's house, Maggie was gone and Kate and George were in the kitchen, talking quietly. She sat with them for a while, relaying the conversation she'd had with their daughter. Kate nodded appreciatively, her head resting on her husband's shoulder while Claire told them of Abby's ultimatum. She said she'd be glad to run interference until Abby settled down.

Suddenly, Kate's head popped up, her eyes wide. "Mom, I think I know what you can tell Abby. When Maggie and I talked about how we would handle this, she suggested that we let Abby ask the questions…the questions she most needs answering. Our answers might satisfy her for a while, and we might be able to avoid some of the more adult topics until she's mature enough to handle them."

"Might work. Want me to help?"

Kate finally smiled. "I believe you're the appointed one!"

"You want to tell Maggie where we're at?"

"Yup…she's been waiting on pins and needles. I'll call her after I see if Abs will talk to us."

Claire raised her brow. "Okay, just let me know if you need me to get you in the door. I'll be in my room."

Unexpectedly, Kate stood, walked to her mother, and wrapped her arms around her. "I'm glad you're here," she said.

"Me, too, darling. I'll do anything you need," Claire said, patting her daughter on the back before turning to grab a bottle of water and head upstairs, giving her daughter and her husband the privacy they deserved.

Once she'd firmly closed the door to the guestroom, Claire breathed a sigh of relief. She believed they had a good start with answering Abby's questions, and she'd be forever grateful for the chance to be involved, not only to support her daughters but as a necessary step in her search for redemption. As she opened the plastic water bottle and raised her chin to take a long drink, she became aware of the painful tension in her neck and shoulders and remembered that she'd been interrupted by her daughter earlier and hadn't had time for her daily stretches. She decided that she had time to perform the routine that lessened her stress and melted away the tension that had held her hostage for so many years.

After throwing off her shoes, her linen top and Capri's, Claire grabbed her yoga mat from under her bed, unrolled it, and placed it on the floor. Starting with the twirls and stopping when she began to feel dizzy, Claire continued with all the stretches in her routine. Usually, she could do each one twenty-one times, but today she accomplished half that many. That was good enough, she thought, because it calmed her mind enough to concentrate, to think about her future. She recalled that when she'd decided to build her homeless shelter, performing the movements before each business day gave her the ability to concentrate on her goals and allowed her to focus on her plans one step at a time, using her brain to accomplish the goals she held in her heart. This time, however, her goals were personal and her decisions would be controlled by her heart, her brain taking a back seat. Since she never got the chance to shower earlier, Claire stood under the hot water longer than usual. Of course, whenever she did this, the tears would start to flow. This time, however, the tears were for the lost years, the years she and Grant should have had together. For the first time in forty years, her tears were for him as well. *I knew it!* She screamed out loud because deep down inside her very soul she knew he wouldn't have purposely left her. She'd always known it, but could never reconcile it with the fact that he never came to find her. That's why she never hated him even though she was humiliated, abandoned, and left to deal with their unborn child on her own. She remembered thinking he had to be dead, he had to have had some horrible accident; otherwise, he would have come for her. She also remembered blaming him for everything that had gone wrong in her life since he left. But, in the end, she knew that she had only herself to blame for her mistakes.

Wrapped only in towels, one around her head and the other hugging her torso, Claire grabbed the laptop from her nightstand and hopped onto the bed. With the computer on her lap, she lifted the cover, typed in her password, located her email icon, and opened her account. To her surprise, Grant had already responded to her email; her hand shook as she hit the key to open the letter. Her nerves got the better of her, and it took several attempts to read the letter through to the end. Longwinded…that was Grant alright…she couldn't believe how he could go on and on, his personality jumping right off the page.

Claire couldn't help questioning the whereabouts of the many letters he said he wrote, but she did agree that his father's confession had given them a fresh start. She worried, however, about answering his heartbreaking question; he wanted to know why she left the girls. *The mother I thought I knew would have told him, the mother I trusted with my own children would not have betrayed me by keeping him in the dark.* Claire's chest burned with humiliation; she had no other choice but to answer his question. She reminded herself that this is the reason they were emailing…to get it all out in the open so that someday they'd be able to be in a room together, to get along for the sake of their children. But her life wasn't a fairy tale and telling him the truth might not lead to a happy ending. She figured that after he learned why she left the girls, he might decide to take a different path and choose to see the girls when she wasn't around. He'd told her once that he thought she was strong and independent and that's what attracted him to her, and she knew she was those things…in her professional life anyway. But nothing could be further from the truth when it came to her personal life. She was ashamed and overwhelmed by feelings of guilt because she couldn't take care of her own children and mortified by the fact that succumbing to mental illness was something she needed to fight against everyday of her life.

Claire decided that it would be best to do as he asked and tell him everything because she never wanted to talk about it again. She would tell the whole story, leaving him to decide whether or not he wanted to continue communicating with her. She figured she'd be lucky if his first email to her wouldn't be his last.

After rubbing her hands over her face as if erasing the tearstains, Claire shook her hands, pressed her hands together, and stretched her fingers before placing them on the keyboard.

Dear Grant,

So you're going to live another 40 years? Good luck with that. And as I said before, I imagine that I'll be part of your life because we'll probably run into each other at family events now and then.

You want to know why I left the girls. It's because I'm not who you thought I was. Do you remember what you said when you learned I already had one child? You said you knew that I didn't need a man because I would have reeled you in the day we met. You said that just because I was a single mother, you figured I needed rescuing, but you learned early on in our relationship that I needed nothing of the sort. As it turned out, though, I did need rescuing after all.

Remember how I couldn't focus, how I needed tutors, and how I had all those strategies to help me concentrate on my school work? I know now that I suffered from ADD and depression as well, but back then there wasn't a label for what ailed me. Then after Maggie was born, something changed, and I could no longer be trusted to care for her or Katie, for that matter. I was exhausted when I came home from the hospital, but I never got my strength back. I couldn't get out of bed, and I was consumed by a prevailing sense of panic and a sadness that never went away. I can remember wanting to die. My mother had to do everything for the girls and for me, as well. I didn't bathe or dress myself, and Mama forced me to eat. She forced me to hold Maggie, too, but I felt nothing for her. Poor little Katie would climb on me and beg me to read to her, but I was so dizzy I couldn't focus on the words. One day I told Mama to take the baby away because I couldn't remember what I was supposed to do with her. That's when Mama took me to the emergency room, and I ended up in a locked unit for two weeks.

Long story short, I went from the hospital to a sanitarium for a few months, followed by a year in a long term mental health facility. There was a lot of experimentation to see which drugs would work to keep me stable. It was tough because they needed to treat the ADD as well as the post-partum depression. When I started to get better, I moved to a group home and job training until I could live on my own and support myself. By then, Mama had custody of the girls, and I was a stranger to them. Still, I saved every penny I could to come home to see my babies a couple of times a year, but I didn't feel welcome and never lived at home again.

So there you have it. Truthfully, I think the depression would have come on whether you were there or not. My brain chemistry would have been the same no matter what, and I've tried everything known to man to eliminate my dependence on medication but to no avail.

You know, I blamed you for everything even though I was the one who wanted to take our relationship to the next level. The pregnancy was my fault, so when you didn't come for me, I assumed that you hated me for causing the predicament and that's why you stayed away. You say you tried to get in touch with me, but I was the one who went to the mailbox everyday until I was hospitalized, hoping I'd find a letter. My mother couldn't have kept them from me.

Here's my question: why were you out of the country for two whole years?
Claire
PS We told Abby the truth today. She's angry right now. Maggie went home, upset, because Abby wouldn't listen to her explanation. I spent

some time with Abby, showed her the family tree…you and Greg are on it now.

Chapter 20

KATE

Kate gave her sister a call and asked her if she'd like to come back to town. She told her how Abby would talk to them only if they'd tell her everything, that she wanted no more secrets between them. Maggie agreed to come for supper, and they would try to talk again. That being settled, Kate made her way to the second floor of her house and knocked on her daughter's bedroom door.

"Abs…it's Mom."

There was no answer but Kate thought that she heard sobbing.

"Honey, can I come in?"

There was no answer, just sobs. Kate pushed the door inward and for once there was nothing blocking it. Abby was curled up on her bed, completely covered by her pink striped quilt. Kate choked up, but managed to hold back tears as she sat on the edge of her daughter's bed. After wrapping her arms around the lump under the covers, Kate laid her head against her daughter's.

"I'm so sorry, honey. I know we should have told you earlier, but Maggie had to be ready, too. Do you understand?"

Abby said something; it was muffled by the covers.

"What sweetie? What did you say?"

The lump under the covers began to stir and wiggle its way out. Kate backed up and watched her daughter break free of the cocoon. The curly blonde locks appeared, followed by the familiar green eyes, the same emerald orbs she'd inherited from Kate's mother and sister.

"What is it sweetie? You can talk to me," Kate sniffed.

There was another sob. "I don't want to.."

"You don't want to 'what'?"

It all came tumbling out then...something none of the adults had thought of, something they'd never even considered. "I don't want to live with Maggie. I want to stay here, Mom. I don't want to move."

Kate grabbed her little girl and held her tight, rocking her back and forth, kissing her head repeatedly. "Oh, sweetie, no! You're our daughter, you'll always be ours. Maggie agreed to it years ago. She knew what would be best for you. She loves you more than anything, but she knows you belong to us."

"But isn't that why she came here, doesn't she want me back?"

Kate took a deep breath and let it out. "I invited her here, hon. I always wanted her to be part of your life. I never wanted her to leave in the first place. I didn't think it was fair that she wouldn't be able to see you grow up."

"Then why did she go, Mom?"

"I can't speak for her. All I know is that I wanted her to stay. You're going to have to ask her. She's coming back in a little while to talk to you. And no more secrets, right?"

"So I can stay here, right, Mom?"

"Forever and ever."

"Then can we order some pizza?"

"Sure...I'll let Maggie know we're having pizza so she won't eat ahead of time."

Suddenly, Abby latched onto her mother. "I don't want to see her right now, Mom."

"Okay."

"I just want one mom like everybody else."

"Okay, sweetie. But lots of people have two moms. Lily does, too."

"But this is different...Maggie's going to be right here all the time."

"You don't want her around?"

"Not right now, Mom, not right now," Abby sobbed.

Kate held her daughter close and rocked her back and forth. Her heart was breaking for her baby. "We'll do whatever you want. You just let me know when."

After a while, Abby calmed down some and asked her mom if she wanted to play a game until it was time for supper. Kate told her to go downstairs, and she'd be there soon. She needed to talk to Grandma first. Abby took off like a shot leaving Kate time to talk to her mother, so she wandered down the hall to her room and knocked on the door.

"Mom, can I come in?"

"Sure…the door's open"

Kate opened the door to see her mother stretched out on the bed, reading some old diary.

"What's that?"

"My first journal. Mama gave it to me before I went to college."

"Can I see it?"

Claire giggled, shook her head, and grasped the book against her chest. "Oh, no! I don't want you to know what I was up to most of the time."

Kate laughed as she crawled onto the bed. "Okay…I get it."

"What's up, honey…do you need help with something?"

"As a matter of fact, I do. I just talked to Abby, you know, about having Maggie come back for supper so we can talk again." Kate choked up. "But she doesn't want to see her yet. I don't know what to do, Mom. I thought this would work out a little differently…that Abby would be thrilled. Needless to say, she's not."

"Want me to give her a call? She'll understand. She waited all these years, didn't she? She knew this wouldn't be easy."

Katie nodded and started to leave.

"Just stay put," Claire said, gabbing Kate's hand in hers. Kate watched her mother grab her cell from the bedside table and hit Maggie's number, listening as she spoke.

"Hi darling," Claire said, her eyes on Kate the whole time. "What are you doing?"

Kate listened intently, unconsciously holding her breath.

"Listen, hon, there's been a change of plans. Abby isn't up to seeing you right now, okay?"

Kate's hands flew to her mouth, muffling a sob.

"Well, she thinks it was mean for you and Kate not to tell her the truth a long time ago. She's just processing, that's all."

Claire nodded. "Okay…say hi to Mac. We'll talk to you tomorrow."

"What'd she say?" Kate asked, anxiously.

"Mac was there. She said he wanted to go to dinner anyway."

"Was she crying?"

"Yup."

Tearing up, Kate collapsed in her mother's arms. "Abs thought Maggie wanted her to live with her…that's why she came home. I explained how I asked Maggie to come here so she could get to know her, but that she would always live with us."

"Good. Listen, you don't have to worry about either of them. Abby loves Maggie. She told me that she didn't want Maggie to be scared to tell her."

"She did?"

Claire nodded. "Now, go and order that pizza."

Chapter 21

GRANT

After checking the TV listings to see who'd be the guest on *Saturday Night Live*, Grant decided he'd seen enough rappers and turned the television off after the ten o'clock news. Out of habit, he stood next to his desk like he did every night and checked his PC to see if there were any new messages, clicked the appropriate icon, and let his eyes roam over the long list, most of it junk. When he noticed Claire's name, he turned on the desktop lamp, dropped onto his chair, and leaned into the monitor. His heart attempted to beat its way out of his chest, and he gasped out loud as he read her reply to his one and only question...*why did you leave the girls with your mother?*

She wrote that she couldn't bond with Maggie or be a mother to Kate and that she'd endured postpartum depression, mental hospitals, and group homes. He'd had no idea about any of it until his father had hinted at it, and it hit him hard. Where in the world was the love of a parent for a child, where was the caring, the compassion, and what the hell was wrong with his father or her mother, for that matter? She was suffering like that and those two didn't care? Besides that, she needed his support...not just financially, but emotionally. They should have told him because he could have helped...he could have saved her from years of misery. No matter what she said, no matter whether she took the blame for the pregnancy or not, the truth was...he was responsible, responsible for it all. He could have refused to sleep with her. But...he was a man in love...madly in love and he wanted her, too. Of course, it was his fault...all of it.

Grant, beside himself with guilt, leaned back in his flexible desk chair, covered his eyes, and sobbed. His heart was breaking for her, for what she'd endured alone. He cried because he hated his father...the one parent he could trust. He bemoaned the lost years and the marriage that failed because he'd never truly loved anyone but Claire. He hadn't been there for her and assumed she hated him for leaving her; she had every right to, but she didn't. In fact, it was the other way around. She said that she thought he hated her for the trouble they'd gotten themselves into, and even though she didn't say it, he hoped that she understood that it couldn't be further from the truth. He decided that he'd better not forget to tell her that he never hated her, couldn't hate her if he tried. He believed, however, that she still felt responsible for their mutual dilemma, not only because she said so, but also because she had yet to look him in the eye. A week ago, when she ran into him at Maggie's, she looked flustered and hightailed it out of there rather than speak to him, and when he met her at the coffee shop, she never looked at him directly, but stared a hole into the table instead. Then, when they visited his father, she blushed and looked away just as their eyes met. Now she says that she wants to email instead of talking to him in person. It all made sense and it had nothing to do with their relationship, but rather rested with Claire's sensitivity to her mental health struggles and the disgrace that came from her inability to raise her own children. He knew enough about psychological problems to understand the inevitable havoc it could inflict on one's self-esteem. More than one of his friends had suffered with its repercussions, and he'd personally witnessed the life-long stigma it carried; therefore, he knew for a fact that it was the indignity of it all that was holding her back, and he was the only one who could convince her that the burden of shame was his to bear.

Instead of heading to bed and because he'd never be able to fall asleep on this particular night, Grant searched for something to calm his nerves. He liked beer and wine as well as the next guy, but tonight he needed something stronger and decided to pour some of the expensive brandy his father had given him over a glassful of ice. While he searched for a glass, he thought about his father's confession and what Claire had said in her email. It was no longer a simple matter settled by parents who didn't think their children belonged together. Oh, no, it was so much more serious than that, and Grant would have to confront his father again. He just had to make sure he didn't have a brandy bottle in his hands when he did because he'd kill him for sure.

Iced drink in hand, Grant headed back to his office, his chair, and his computer. He opened Claire's email, read it, dissected it, and read it all over again. He wished he could talk to her in person...this seemed much to urgent to leave to email...but he had to follow her wishes if he wanted to get anywhere with her. And he thought about what Greg had said about going after what you want, and he wanted her more than ever now that he'd seen her, now that they'd spoken. As far as he was concerned, it was as if they'd never been apart. Obviously, she wasn't in the same place. He had to be patient, had to wait for her to catch up to him, and he didn't dare dwell on the alternative.

According to the digital numbers in the corner of his monitor, it was past midnight. Grant held the drink to his forehead while he pondered his response to Claire's declaration of guilt. He had to remember where she was coming from and forget about his own wishes and desires when all he wanted to do was call her and hear her voice. He reminded himself once again that it was after midnight; still, he couldn't quit thinking about her so he'd never be able to fall asleep. He figured he might as well tell her how he felt.

Dearest Claire,

Thank you for telling me about the depression. To be truthful, my dad told me a little about it after you left that day. I didn't give him a chance to share much...I was too angry that I hadn't been told...especially considering the circumstances, and I am so sorry that you had to go through that alone. You know that I would have been there for you if I had known, don't you? In fact, I would have been there no matter what.

I get the feeling that you're ashamed that you suffered from depression and that you couldn't take care of the girls. You know that it's not your fault. It's your brain chemistry, like you said. Besides, one in four people has some sort of mental health problem. You're a professional…you know that. And your mother did one thing right…she got you some help. But she could have told me when I first contacted her. Together we could have cared for the girls until you were better. Wouldn't that have been great?

As far as the pregnancy goes…it takes two to tango. We waited months to sleep together…you were strong and resisted temptation, knowing where you could end up if you didn't. If anyone is to blame, it's me.

Okay, you want to know why I was gone for so long. Remember how livid my parents were? First of all, there was the drinking, flunking classes, and all of that. Then the pregnancy. They were out of their minds, but I thought I could smooth things over, come up with a plan so we could be together. I'd have given up everything, including my inheritance, for you. I'm afraid that they figured that out, and it scared them to death. You know that we visited my grandparents in Brazil every year. Usually, it was during the winter months when it was unbearably cold here in Wisconsin. That summer you were pregnant, they suddenly needed to take a trip there…said my grandfather needed them and off we went. I was sure I'd be back in a couple of weeks, but I'd underestimated what my parents were capable of. You want to know why I was gone for two years? My parents left me there to work with my grandparents and took my passport with them. They said it was for my own good, so the only recourse I had was to write to you. I wrote you so many letters from there. I had to sneak off to mail them, of course, but I figured it out. I even got a post office box so you could get back to me without them knowing it.

Claire, it broke my heart when you didn't write back, and it was broken again when I returned to the states and you were gone. I'm sure you can say the same, waiting for me, not ever getting my messages. So what are we going to do about it now? I, for one, would like to stop wasting precious time blaming each other as well as our parents and just accept what happened and get on with our lives. Is that possible? Grant

He hoped he was clear enough this time. After all, she didn't seem to understand his previous comment about not wanting to live the next forty years without her. In fact, she just blew it off. Would she understand that he wanted to start over…the two of them, together? Or was he jumping the boat? He'd never be able to sleep now unless he took something, but he hated it, hated that groggy feeling the next day. Suddenly, he thought of Claire and berated himself…she had no choice…she had to take her meds or else. Overcome with sadness at the thought of it, Grant left his office, climbed the stairs to the master bedroom, and flopped face down onto his bed. He grabbed his pillow, pummeled the life out of it, and gave God a piece of his mind while he was at it.

Chapter 22

MAGGIE

After sleeping in, Maggie dragged herself out of bed and let her dog out. When she realized she'd slept until noon, she looked around the room to make sure that Horse hadn't had an accident. She saw nothing to suggest she didn't get outside in time, so she padded to the kitchen, thought about making a pot of coffee, but decided on tea instead…the quick way…in the microwave. Just as she filled her cup with water and added the tea bag, her cell rang. She slid the cup into the microwave, hit number two, and ran to her bedroom. Maggie hoped against hope that Abby wanted to see her and that the telephone call was from her sister, but the cell number she saw did not belong to Kate, but to her father. Maggie swallowed her disappointment, held the cell to her ear, and said hello.

"Maggie? Hi…how are you?"

"I'm fine. How are you doing?"

"Pretty good. Say, I don't want to keep you, but I have something I want to run by you."

"Okay."

"Well, uh, my son, Greg…well, he's going to Minneapolis for an interview tomorrow, and he wanted to know if he could stop by and meet you on the way back."

"Greg wants to meet me?"

"Yes, he and his girlfriend…they both do."

"Is it okay with you?"

"Certainly…I think it would be great. I mean, I never thought this day would come."

"Well, okay. How much does he know about me? What about Abby and all that?"

"Well, I filled him in about the attack, without mentioning your history with Rex…I figured I'd leave that up to you. Anyway, I told him about Abby and about your great career. I hope you don't mind, but I've been talking to him about you ever since I reconnected with your mom last year. I had no idea what he thought about all of this…he never let on he cared…but he told me that since he finally has a sibling, he wants to get to know her."

"That's one way to look at it."

"So it's okay if I give him your number?"

"Sure. So he'll be coming through sometime tomorrow? I could meet him for early dinner or something. I'll be working until four or so."

"I'll tell him. Hey, Claire told me that you were going to talk to Abby. How did that go?"

"Mom's talking to you?"

"Not exactly. She emails though."

"Well, it's a start, huh?"

"I'll take what I can get. So is everything with Abby okay?"

"She's upset. She doesn't want to see me right now."

"Shoot."

"It's okay. It's a shock to her. I guess Abby knows about you, though. Mom told her about you and Greg."

"Yes, she told me. The family tree."

"You might be getting an invitation soon."

"Really?"

"Cheerleading…Abby and Lily are cheerleading during a football game."

"When's that?"

"This coming Thursday. It should be hilarious. I hope she's speaking to me by then…I don't want to miss it."

"I don't want to either. Will you call me later with the details?"

"Sure will."

"So, I hope you like Greg…and Jolene, too…you'll notice they're joined at the hip."

"Oh, cute! Tell him I can't wait to meet him."

"That's great…just great."

"Okay…I'll call about Thursday when I know something."

"Good. Take care."

After ending the conversation with her father, Maggie wondered how long it would take before they'd be able to say "I love you" when they said goodbye. Abby entered her thoughts just then, and she wondered the very same thing. Now that the truth had surfaced, she couldn't wait to say it to her little girl as her biological mother, not her aunt, and she prayed that Abby would give her the chance to do so.

Maggie finished brewing her cup of tea, removed the tea bag, and plopped on the couch only to have her dog bark to be let in. It was already way past noon, and her dog needed her long awaited walk, but she felt the weight of the world on her shoulders and couldn't imagine leaving the house, so she let her in. It wasn't fair to the dog, though; she needed her exercise to maintain good health and a peaceful frame of mind. Her human caretaker needed the same, so she spoke to the dog as if she understood every word she said and told her they'd make sure get their walk in sometime later.

In an attempt to quiet her nerves, Maggie sipped her tea and prayed to calm her racing heart; the news that Abby did not want to see her was devastating. She'd expected that she'd have supper with her sister and Abby, that they'd talk some more and that Abby would at least listen to her explanation if not welcome her with open arms. Maggie knew full well that Abby loved her; she'd seen it in her eyes and felt it when she embraced her with one of her long, unending hugs. That didn't mean, however, that she still felt the same way. Yesterday, the child learned that Maggie and Kate kept her from knowing about her biological mother, and she was sure that little Abby no longer saw her in the same light. Yet, the way it turned out was so unexpected. Maggie knew that the news would be upsetting, but she hadn't thought about total rejection.

What if it happened this way for a reason, Maggie thought.

Perhaps she wasn't ready, wasn't prepared to tell Abby what she needed to know. Today might be a gift, a day without plans, a day to map out what she would tell the child once she talked to her again. *Oh, God, please give me another chance to do it right.*

The biggest problem with telling Abby everything had to do with Rex, and the fact that he was in jail and would eventually be incarcerated for most of the rest of his life. Maggie had studied enough to know that telling a child that a parent was incarcerated could backfire. She knew that children fantasize and blow things out of proportion to the point of blaming themselves, so they need credible explanations for their parents' problems. Maggie wondered under what circumstances Abby could blame herself. Would she think that her father would be angry with her and blame her because she was the reason her mother ran away? No, she couldn't imagine that the child's thoughts would ever go in that direction, not at her age. What she really wished she could do is tell Abby that she couldn't meet her father because he was out of the country for some reason or another, make up some kind of story…almost anything would be better than the truth…but the poor kid had put up with enough already, hadn't she? And then there was the chance that Abby could hear about her father in the media. She was a bright kid, and it wouldn't be hard for her to connect the dots between the man who beat Maggie and left her for dead, and the man Maggie ran from when she learned she was pregnant almost a decade earlier, especially if they went to trial. Just one more reason to be honest with the child from the onset instead of leaving it to chance, she thought.

Maggie continued to agonize over a way to tell the Abby whole story, but just enough to satisfy her curiosity. Like some parents with incarcerated partners, she couldn't tell her that her father loved her to make her feel better. Rex didn't even know she existed, and she still had no idea how the child would take that bit of information. At least, she'd be able to tell her that the incarceration was not her fault, that it was due to the fact that her parent made a mistake, some huge mistakes, but that would be sugar-coating it, wouldn't it? Did she dare tell her the truth? Did she dare tell her that her father forced himself on her mother? That he said he'd kill her if she ever got pregnant? That she had to run away to save her life as well as the life of her unborn child? No, Abby was way too young to hear the awful truth, but her flesh and blood daughter would have lots of questions that she'd insist Maggie answer. If Maggie simply told her that he'd made a mistake, she'd want to know what kind of mistake. If she said he was cruel and hurt her, the kid would ask her what she meant by hurt. If she said he hit her, she'd want to know how hard, and the last thing Maggie wanted was for her daughter to know what a monster her father really was. Or, even worse, she didn't want Abby thinking she could turn out just like him.

There was a small sized legal tablet on the kitchen counter, a grocery list scribbled on the top page. Maggie needed to organize her thoughts, so she forced herself off the couch to grab the handy tablet as well as the pencil right next to it. As she settled back in, the dog stretched out at her feet, and she started to make another list; this time it had nothing to do with groceries. Instead, she'd make a list of topics she needed to address, the issues that she needed to break down into sentences a child would understand. She decided to number them…the first one being the most important.

1. *I love you more than anyone on this earth.*
2. *I loved you so much that the most important thing to me was keeping you safe.*
3. *I knew that I would never be safe, that he would eventually find me, so I decided that I had to leave you so that he would never find you.*
4. *He hurt me and I was afraid he would hurt you, and then you would grow up to hurt others.*
5. *I wanted you to be raised by caring people who would not hurt you or anyone else.*
6. *I wanted you to grow up to be a caring person, too.*
7. *I knew that my sister would love you as much as I did and would make sure you were safe.*
8. *My sister wanted me to be in your life so when I thought I was safe, I moved back.*
9. *Now that you know all about me, I hope I can be part of your life.*

10.   *You have so many relatives who love you.*
11.   *I'll wait for you to figure out how I fit in.*

When Maggie finished her list and read it, she edited it a couple of times, scratching out whole sentences, and rewriting others until she had two pages of the tablet filled. Mentally exhausted, she curled up on the couch, laid her head on the crook of her arm, and closed her eyes. The tablet slipped onto the floor unnoticed as she slept.

Chapter 23

ABBY

Something was horribly wrong. Something was not right with the world. Abby Genevieve Fogarty awoke in her own room like she'd done every day since she could remember; yet, she'd never felt so sad in her life. She didn't want to get out of bed and didn't care if she ate the special pancakes her mother made every single Sunday morning. She loved going to Sunday school, but she didn't want to think about getting up and getting dressed, brushing her teeth and brushing her hair. It was all too much, and she pulled the covers over her face and cried.

The phone rang and Abby heard her mother answer it. She was laughing. What is there to laugh about? She couldn't imagine laughing ever again. She heard her mother's voice as it got closer and closer until it echoed in the hallway just outside her bedroom door. A rapid knock on her door followed shortly thereafter.

"Abs, can you take a phone call?"

"Who is it," Abby said from under the covers. Before her mother had time to answer, she heard the squeak of the door as it was pushed open and the familiar racket that followed as her blockade…her backpack, shoes and other paraphernalia…scraped through the carpet.

"It's Lily."

"Okay…I'll talk to her."

Abby peeked out from under the covers to grab the telephone from her mother. Once she had the receiver in her hand, she figured her mother would leave. Instead, she plopped on the end of the bed like it was a regular day or something. "Mom...some privacy please!"

Kate jumped up. "Whoa, okay then. Talk to you later." She quickly exited the room, closing the door behind her.

"Why weren't you in Sunday school?" Lily asked first thing.

"Mom let me sleep in, I guess."

"Really? What are you doing today?"

"I don't know."

"Want to go canoeing down the Kinni with us? It's going to be super nice out today."

"I don't know...I guess."

"Can you be ready in about an hour?"

"Sure."

"Okay. We'll pick you up."

"Okay."

Abby might have said she'd go, but her heart wasn't in it. After tossing the phone across the floor, she curled up under her covers. What was wrong with her? She loved being outside, she loved the water, and, most of all, she loved canoeing. She knew that she'd have fun with Lily and Mac...oh, no...Mac would have to go with them! And Maggie would be there, too! They did everything together these days. No way...no way did she want to see her. The tears came; she couldn't stop them because she didn't know why they were there.

Hearing her mother call her name again, Abby held her breath. Now what? Now what was she supposed to do? She felt her mother's weight on her bed, felt hands rubbing her shoulders, heard her mother's voice.

"Are you going to go sweetie? If you are, you've got to get up and get some food in you."

"Do I have to go, Mom?"

"Of course not. Don't you want to go?"

"I don't feel like it, that's all."

"That's okay. There are days I don't feel like going out either. You just want a quiet day at home with Mom and Dad...and Grandma?"

Abby nodded and hoped that her mother saw her move under the covers.

"Okay, hon. I'll give Mac a call. You just get up when you feel like it? We'll be in the kitchen or the backyard."

She gave another nod, felt her mother's hands leave her, and heard her exit the room. Presently, she dozed off. She had a strange dream then, a dream like no other, and when she awoke, her heart was pounding against her ribs, swelling and filling up her insides. She felt the panic she'd experienced after waking from a horrible nightmare, the kind of nightmare that comes in the pitch black darkness of a moonless night. She was grateful that it was daytime, that her room was filled with morning light, but she was scared. Suddenly, she needed her mom and dad more than she ever needed them before and raced from her room to find them. When she reached the staircase, however, she came to a complete stop. She could see her mother at the front door talking to Mac, of all people. What did he want? She said she didn't want to go. Her heart was beating its way out of her swollen chest, upward into her throat. What did he want? Was it bad news?

The door closed and her mother turned. "Mom," she yelled.

"What's wrong honey?"

Chapter 24

KATE

Abby stood at the top of the stairs, sobbing and trembling, her arms wrapped tightly around her waist, and it scared the hell out of Kate. Bounding the steps, two by two, she raced toward her daughter, and Abby launched herself into her mother's arms, forcing Kate to grab the railing, preventing them from tumbling down the staircase.

With her child on her lap, safely sitting on the landing, Kate rocked her inconsolable little girl while she sobbed into her chest. "What's wrong, sweetie? Did you hurt yourself? Are you okay?"

"What was Mac doing here," she cried. "What did he tell you?"

Kate, surprised by Abby's strange reaction to Mac's visit, held her daughter tighter. "It's okay. He was just checking in case you changed your mind."

All of a sudden, the child wriggled free of her mother's arms and stared at the front door directly below them.

"Was Maggie with him?"

"No."

"She's not with? Where is she? Are they going home?"

"Honey, no, they just left for the river," Kate said, shaking her head.

With that, Abby melted into tears, quieter this time, limp in her mother's arms. Kate, trying not to give into her own tears, rubbed her baby's back and rocked her back and forth, consoling her as if she were an infant.

After a while, Abby's crying stopped, but she continued to hold onto her mother for dear life. Kate didn't rush her, knowing that something was seriously wrong, something she knew nothing about.

"Abs...do you want to tell me what's bothering you?"

"I had a nightmare."

"This morning...after we talked?"

Kate felt her precious girl nod against her chest.

"Do you want to tell me about it?"

"I was so scared."

"It's okay...it was just a bad dream, and it's gone now."

"But it was real, Mom, so real."

Kate thought twice about broaching a sensitive subject, but she had an idea that she knew what this was all about. "Was it about Maggie?"

The tears started all over again, the little fists clenching her mother's clothing. "I don't ever want anything bad to happen to her, Mom."

"I know. Me either. What happened in the dream?"

"We were canoeing...Maggie, too. We went under this branch on the edge of the river, and we got knocked into the water. I could see her, Mom. I could see her under the water. She was looking right at me."

Kate rocked and soothed. "What happened then?"

"I yelled and yelled at Mac and Lily...I yelled for them to help, but they didn't...they just told me to get back into the canoe."

"Remember, it was a dream, just a dream."

Abby's shook her head wildly. "No, Mom, she was looking right at me, and I couldn't reach her and nobody would help and I yelled for them to help and they wouldn't."

"Honey...you know if that really happened, Mac would help Maggie, right?"

"But why wouldn't he help? Why wouldn't Lily help?"

"Because it was a dream."

"Mac said it didn't matter, she was dead."

"Oh...sweetie...you know she's not dead."

"Are you sure, Mom? Are you sure?"

"Of course...Mac told me he talked to her this morning. I know she's fine."

"Really, Mom? He saw her, and she was okay?"

"Yes…he said that she just wanted to stay home today."

"Like us."

Kate hugged her daughter. "Yup, like us."

They sat quietly for a few seconds until Abby rubbed her eyes and wiped her nose on her pajama sleeve. After swallowing hard and while gazing into her mother's eyes, she asked a serious question. "How do we know if she's really okay?"

"Let's just give her a call. How about that?"

"No, I have to see her in person, Mom."

"Do you want me to take you to see her?" Kate's heart pounded in her throat.

"Do you think she'd want to see me?"

"Oh, Abs. There's no one else she'd rather see."

"Can we go right now?"

"So you're going in your p.j.'s?"

Abby laughed like her old self, and Kate rocked her one more time. She rocked her out of love, out of gratitude for the chance to raise such a wonderful child, and offered up a prayer of thanks while she was at it.

Chapter 25

MAGGIE

After second guessing about whether or not to go canoeing with Mac and Lily, Maggie shrugged off her regrets and settled in to read the Sunday paper. Horse stood, waiting good-naturedly for her owner to take her for a walk. Eventually, the dog could stand it no longer and began whimpering. Maggie told her to settle down before returning to focus on the paper. In no time at all, the intermittent sniveling became a plaintive cry for attention; the dog had had enough…her patience running thin.

"Okay. Let's go."

Horse wiggled with anticipation as she waited for her human to find her shoes, then put them on and tie them up. She waited for her to find a baseball cap before grabbing the leash and attaching it to her collar. When Maggie saw how excited Horse was to finally get a walk, she patted her on the head, apologizing for being short with her earlier. As if she has any idea how I feel, Maggie thought, smiling and shaking her head.

They left the little house through the front door, traveled down the two wooden steps, and turned left toward the barn and the subsequent path to Long Lake. The dog yanked excitedly on the leash. Maggie told her to heel and, as usual, she obeyed. It was the middle of September, and some of the leaves on many of the trees in Mac's woods were already turning even though the autumnal equinox would not officially arrive for eight or nine days.

As she walked under the canopy of ash and oak, honey locus, red maple and dogwood trees, Maggie kept her eyes focused upward, admiring the beauty that comes to Wisconsin with the change of seasons. She guessed that she should have gone canoeing to see if the leaves on the trees bordering the Kinni were turning because they'd be reflected in the water, offering river adventurers a double dose of autumn's wonder. She reminded herself that she'd have to be happy with walking the trails around the lake where the mirror images of the leaves might be just as good. She wasn't disappointed and her mood improved.

Later, as Maggie and Horse came out of the woods and ambled past the horse pasture and barn, Maggie thought she heard voices. Was someone crying? Who's crying? She stepped up her pace and rounded the corner to the front of her rental only to find Kate and Abby sitting on her stoop, the younger girl sobbing in her mother's arms.

"Oh, God…Kate, what's wrong?" she yelled as she dropped the leash and ran to them.

"Mags, you're home. Abby wanted to see you," Kate said, smiling and reaching for her sister's hand. Abruptly, the child stood, took a couple of steps and wrapped her arms around Maggie's waist, sobbing into the front of her tee-shirt.

Glancing her sister's way, searching her face for some kind of explanation, Maggie asked what happened as she kissed the top of the child's curl covered head.

"She had a bad dream, Sis. She just had to make sure you were okay…alive, I guess."

"Honey, I'm fine," Maggie assured, massaging the back and shoulders of the child as she spoke. "I'm fine. I was just taking the dog for a walk…you know how she loves walks."

Abby nodded and Maggie, at a loss for words, glanced wide-eyed at her sister, hoping for suggestions. *What now?*

Kate started. "Abby…do you want to tell Maggie about the dream?"

The kid shook her head.

"What do you want to do, honey?"

"Go home," she said, releasing her biological mother and running for the car.

Her eyes brimming, Kate turned to her sister. "Sorry…I thought she might want to talk. She had to see you. In the dream you were dead."

Slapping her hands over her mouth and nose, Maggie moaned into them, turned, and hurried into her house. After dropping backwards onto her couch, she held her breath in order to hear the car drive over the gravel in the driveway, but she didn't hear a sound. She sat straight up and before she had a chance to stand, her door opened and the child stood in the center of the door frame. Maggie sat there, staring at her beautiful little daughter, waiting for her to speak. She watched her wipe her nose on the back of her hand and then run both hands through her hair, pushing it out of her face.

"I don't want two moms!"

Maggie leaned forward with her elbows on her knees. "You have one Mom, the one who is raising you. That's your mom…I'm not going to replace her." *My list isn't going to help me with this one!*

"So it will be like it always was? You'll be my mom's sister, come to my things, take me places…we'll just hang out?"

After taking a deep breath and blowing it out, Maggie nodded, but kept quiet.

"I don't want to talk about that other stuff."

"We don't have to," Maggie said, relieved to be able to put off the inevitable.

"I don't care about the secrets anymore. I just want it to be like it was before."

"Then that's the way it will be."

Abby walked toward Maggie. "I love you anyway."

Grabbing the girl in her arms, Maggie said, "I love you, too, always will, and thanks for coming out here to talk with me."

"I thought you were dead."

"You can see I'm not."

"So now you're just my Maggie, right…nothing else."

"Yup."

"Then you don't have to stay away from my house anymore."

"Good because I was getting pretty bored out here all by myself."

Abby smiled for the first time, said good-bye, and turned to leave. Before she was all the way out the door, she said something that made Maggie believe that everything was back to normal, that everything was right with the world.

"Hey, don't forget to come and see me cheer on Thursday."

"I wouldn't miss it for anything."

Standing to walk to the window to watch her daughter and sister drive away, Maggie felt a wave of relief wash over her, forcing her to sit on the nearest chair as her knees weakened, buckling underneath her. *Out of the mouths of babes*...their relationship was more important than the miserable story of Abby's conception and entrance into this world. Abby knew the truth and dealt with it her own way, the only way an eight year old could. She wanted everything to stay the way it was, and the rest of them would have to figure out a way to make that happen.

Maggie got up, walked to her couch, and squatted to pick her list up off the floor. She laughed at herself...she was so sure she needed everything written down, everything she would say to the kid, all planned out ahead of time...but she didn't need it after all. The list was a good one, though, a keeper even, and she'd store it in a safe place until the dreaded subject came up again.

One of her problems had been solved, for now anyway, but another loomed and needed to be dealt with posthaste. Her half-brother had called, wanting to meet her for supper the next day. She'd agreed, keeping the conversation short because she was beginning to question whether it was a good idea to meet him alone. What in the world would they talk about? The weather...politics...religion? Would he be angry that his father might still be in love with her mother, blaming her somehow for the demise of his parents' marriage? When she phoned Claire on the off chance that she'd accompany her, she figured that her mother would be afraid of the very same thing...that the kid would blame her for something...only to learn that her mother's thought process took a drastically different turn. As a counselor with years of experience under her belt, Maggie figured she should have known how her mother would feel about Grant's son, but there was no way she could because she'd never endured rejection the way her mother had.

The mere acknowledgement that Grant had married another woman and that they'd raised a child together when he'd left her to do it all alone had simply reopened a wound, the unhealed wound of abandonment.

    Talking it over with Claire hadn't helped either. Maggie reminded her that Grant had been sent away, but after her mother made some offhanded comments about the lies, she realized that Claire had yet to fully accept his story. She just jabbered on and on about some letters, some letters she never got, and how she knew they had to be a fabrication, a lie, or a figment of Grant's imagination. Eventually, Maggie gave up trying to talk some sense into her and accepted the fact that her mother would not accompany her to meet her brother.

Chapter 26

CLAIRE

Claire's heart ached for her daughters and granddaughter. She'd heard the whole thing…Abby thought Maggie was dead and that she had to go and see her to make sure she was okay. They finally left and Claire sat alone in her light-weight men's style pajamas, curled up on the sofa in the front room, reading the Sunday paper. Her heart wasn't in it, though, but she needed to find a job before she wore out her daughter's welcome. She really didn't want to go back to work and in addition to that, the want ads themselves were hardly worth reading; they barely covered half of a page in the classifieds.

Although Claire knew she could get a job as a nurse because there were plenty of ads for those, but she'd have to get Wisconsin licensure…she didn't know if she could stand to go through all the rigmarole at her age. Most of the other openings were for over-the-road truck drivers. She laughed at the thought of driving a semi…she wouldn't be able to see out of the windshield and there's no way her feet would be able to reach the pedals. She had to admit that she'd be quite a site, though, and would get quite a bit of attention from the burly truck drivers she'd meet at the weigh stations and truck stops. She shivered involuntarily at the thought of meeting new men, dating again, and for the first time since she'd left Mel, she acknowledged what her heart was telling her. She never wanted to be hurt again or hurt another man the way she hurt him; there was only one way to make sure that never happened. She'd have to take herself off the market. How she'd do that exactly wasn't clear, but it was what she needed to do now that she and her daughters had made amends. From now on, they would always come first. The only type of job that really interested Claire anymore had to include service to others. Kate had mentioned that a group in Lake Louise had set up a day shelter for the homeless, and she said that the advisory board was looking for funding to build a shelter. Kate thought that Claire should just walk right in there and tell them what they needed to do. Claire, however, would prefer to avoid stepping on the toes of the hard working volunteers in her new hometown, so she told her daughter that she'd have to figure something else out. After thinking it over, though, she thought she might just volunteer to write some grant proposals for them; she no doubt had the experience they'd need, and they might even welcome her expertise. There was one problem with this plan, however; the advisory board and its members were part of a volunteer organization, and Claire needed money. Of course, she didn't need the Porsche and could get fifty grand for it, but she loved her car. Besides that, it was a gift from Mel so it had sentimental value. She concluded that she'd have to be living in it before she'd sell it. Then there was the money she'd get from the sale of the house in Phoenix, but she still hadn't decided whether or not she would keep the profit. Mel deserved the money…he'd built the place… although he insisted she keep it. She wondered how he was doing. She figured that he must have cut his loses as far as she was concerned because he hadn't called or even emailed since she got there. He'd been her best friend for an entire decade, and she had to admit she missed talking to him, telling him what was going on in her life, and it saddened her to think that he might hate her guts for leaving him.

After refilling her cup of coffee, she padded up the stairs to her room, set the drink on her nightstand, and grabbed her laptop. She needed to do her stretches, but crawled into bed instead, propping several pillows behind her, saving one for her lap. She'd recently read that laptops heat up quickly and that setting one directly on your lightly clothed thighs could turn your skin brown, so she placed the pillow there before setting her laptop down. She figured that the first thing she should do was check the internet for jobs; Craigslist would be a good place to start, she thought. As usual, though, checking her email was the first thing she did before searching for anything else. Surprisingly, Grant's name appeared at the top of her inbox, and her pulse raced with anxiety. She hesitated before opening the reply because he now knew about the serious mental health issues that plagued her. In fact, she really didn't expect to hear from him at all. She figured that he'd consider her nothing but a basket case and who'd want to deal with that? It would be easy for him to stop contacting her; she'd given him the perfect reason to end it. He could still see Maggie and Abby and no one would be the wiser. So what was his motivation for continuing to email? Why didn't he consider it a waste of time?

Curiosity got the best of Claire, and she opened the correspondence. First of all, the email was long…too long…he went on and on as usual. He said he would have been there no matter what. Please! And once again he tried to explain why he was gone…okay, so they took his passport…she'd give him that one…after being threatened by his mother all those years ago, she had no doubt that she was capable of such a thing. But to keep harping on some letters…how could two years worth of letters just disappear? She had no idea why he insisted on keeping up the charade, and it was beginning to annoy her. He wanted her to accept everything that happened so that they could get on with their lives. It sounded as though he wanted her permission to move forward with a clear conscience. She figured that none of what he wanted made any difference in her life. She was getting on with it like she'd always done, without him.

Leaning back against the pillow supporting her back, Claire sighed and closed her eyes. She just couldn't face coming up with a response right now; the whole thing gave her a migraine, so she exited her email program and began her job search. She hadn't hunted for a job since her last home health care patient died. That's when she ended up working at the soup kitchen, and the idea of a homeless shelter took over. She'd built it ten years ago, poured her lifeblood into it, and thought she'd miss it. Instead, she didn't miss it at all because she was right where she needed to be, and the clarity of her decision to move to Lake Louise became immediately palpable when she heard a rap at her door and saw her sweet granddaughter poke her head between the door and the frame.

"Hi sweetie…come on in here and give your grandma a hug," she said.

Abby didn't hesitate for a second and entered the room with an energetic leap onto the king sized bed. Claire closed the computer and slid it off of her lap just as the petite little girl hit the mattress and grabbed her around the neck.

"So what are you so excited about?" she asked, returning the hug.

Backing away, she gave Claire a self-satisfied smile. "Everything is okay, Grandma."

"What's okay?"

"Our family."

Claire raised her eyebrows at the child. "Well, congratulations. So you saw Maggie?"

"Yup," Abby said, grinning from ear to ear.

"And everything is good? You two are talking now?"

"Yup, just like the old days."

Claire was skeptical. "Really?"

"Really. Everything is back to normal except for one thing."

"What's that?"

"You know that guy, the guy on the family tree…the one you said was my grandpa?"

"Sure."

"I still need a grandfather."

"So that's all you need to make life perfect, huh?" Claire said, trying to keep a straight face.

Abby nodded. "Uh huh. Everyone has grandparents."

"Even Lily…she has them?"

"Yup…lots of them. A couple of them live in Florida or something…she calls one of them her step-grandma…I don't get that, but I saw her one time."

"You did, did you?"

"Yup."

Claire hugged her granddaughter to her and kissed the top of her sweet head. "Well, what do you want me to do about it?"

"What's his name again?"

"Grant."

"Where does he live?"

"Madison."

"How far away is that?"

"About a four hour drive by car."

"Yikes…I would hate that!"

Claire laughed. "I know you would!"

"Is that too far…I mean, he probably wouldn't want to come here, would he?"

"He's been here before." She decided not to talk about his ties to Maggie.

Abby got quiet then, and Claire figured she was thinking about the connection anyway. Suddenly, she tossed her curls as if to shake away a thought. "I've got my cheerleading show on Thursday. Could he come to that? Lots of grandparents are coming."

So much for trying to get on with my life without him!

Claire knew that she'd do anything for Abby even though seeing Grant was the last thing she wanted to do. "Do you want me to ask him…is that what you want, sweetie?"

"Uh huh."

"Are Mom and Dad okay with that?"

"Yup. Mom said she knew him when she was little. She likes him."

Claire swallowed her pride and nodded. "Everyone likes him…you will, too. Want me to email him? I can do it today. I'm sure he'll answer right away."

"Okay, Grandma. Thanks."

"Anything else I can do for you?" Claire asked, grinning.

"Nope…that's it."

"Okay. Consider it done." She kissed the child's blonde tresses one more time. "So what's on the agenda for the rest of the day?"

"Mom and I are going to feed the ducks. Do you want to walk the pathway with us? Look at the leaves?"

"I think I'll pass. I've got to get on that email." *Besides, I still don't have the right shoes!*

The dear child stared deep into Claire's eyes, the beautiful green eyes they shared. "I love you, Grandma. I'm glad you live with us."

"Me, too."

Abby took off, slamming the door behind her. Claire laughed, but only for a second. Now that she'd promised her granddaughter that she'd invite Grant to her cheerleading show, she had to follow through, had to get it over with. No better time than the present, she thought.

With the laptop propped on her lap for another try, Claire accessed her email account for a second time that day even though her heart wasn't in it. Oh, she would do it for her granddaughter, but the problem with emailing Grant had nothing to do with her granddaughter, though, and everything to do with the emotions that racked her body every time she had any contact with him whether face to face or through electronic means. Her pulse raced this time, too. She attributed her anxiety to the unknown, the unanswered questions about their collective past. Why hadn't he tried harder to find her…he could have hired people to watch the house…she came home twice a year…he could have easily found her if he'd really wanted to, if he'd really tried. Even though she knew what their parents did, she had a hard time believing that he tried…two years of sending letters, two years out of forty was hardly enough if he really cared. How could he have moved on so quickly?

Claire understood that none of this mattered right now. It didn't even matter whether or not she could stand to be in the same room with him again. What mattered were her granddaughter's wishes. Her requests were the straightforward, no nonsense desires of an innocent eight year old child. Abby simply wanted what she perceived as normal, as typical as every other kid she knew. She wanted to fit in and who could blame her. Claire decided to bite the bullet for the child's sake and reply to his most recent email, keeping it as short as possible and ending it with Abby's invitation. It sounded easy, but she had to calm herself with some deep breathing, some peaceful thoughts first so she leaned back into the pillows, closed her eyes, and counted her breaths in an attempt to block out everything else.

Most of the time, Claire could relax enough to concentrate on the tasks at hand, but there were times when she became too relaxed and would fall fast asleep. Other times, the floodgates would open, and she'd have no idea why. Today, her psyche was overwhelmed, and there was no way she could stop the tears, the tears that became heart wrenching sobs. It was all too much…hearing that Maggie would be meeting his son the next day and contemplating seeing Grant again at the end of the week. Sometimes, she'd remind herself of her strength, of her independence, and snap out of it. This time it was different; this time she cried herself to sleep.

Later, when she heard her name, Claire awoke. At first, she had no idea where she was or the time of day, but recognized the voice of her daughter, Kate.

"Mom, are you okay?" Kate's hand rubbed her back as she leaned over her, whispering.

"Sure, darling…I'm fine. Just needed a nap, I guess." Claire covered her face and rubbed her hands over her brow, all without turning to greet her daughter.

"Want some supper…it's almost ready?"

"It's suppertime? How long have I been sleeping?"

Claire heard Kate giggle. "I have no idea, but we haven't seen hide nor hair of you in quite a while."

Surprised, Claire rolled toward her daughter, "Really? But I just talked to Abby."

"Mom, that was three hours ago. Are you sure you're feeling okay?"

"Yes, Miss 'ever the nurse', I'm fine," Claire joked sarcastically.

"Good! Now wash your face and come on down to supper."

"Okay…sure…just give me a couple of minutes."

"I hate to tell you this, but you're going to need more than a couple…you look like you've been run over by a truck!"

Claire frowned and elbowed her daughter. "Brat!"

Kate rolled off the bed and headed for the door. "I mean it, be there or be square!"

Claire couldn't help laughing at her daughter's orders, but figured she wouldn't be able to follow them because the very thoughts that caused her to lose control only three hours earlier came rushing back. This time she'd find a way to focus on the task at hand instead of roiling in self-pity.

Abby needed her grandfather, and she was the key to getting him for her. If she could let him know that she was comfortable with the whole thing, that having him around didn't bother her, he'd probably agree to come to her show. She guessed she'd lied to men before…she'd recently lied to Mel, hadn't she? Well, she hadn't really lied…she'd just left out the fact that he deserved so much more than a woman who was stupid enough to let her heart rule her brain.

The laptop was on the nightstand. She didn't want to be late for dinner, but it would just take a second to get this over and done with. She flipped open the computer and logged on. After a bit of a search, she found Grant's last email and opened it. She didn't have to read it again because she'd never forget how it felt to question his motives, and she fully understood that he simply wanted her forgiveness so he'd be relieved of any bit of guilt he had left in his heart, any bit of shame that might keep him from moving on.

After hitting 'reply', she decided to keep it short and sweet.

Grant,

Thank you for understanding what I went through. Depression stinks. And I believe you when you say your passport was taken. I've had to deal with your mother, too, and I know what she was capable of.

I agree that we both need to get on with our lives, but haven't we both been doing that for decades? I know I have and will continue to do so, although truthfully, I don't believe I'll ever be able to just accept what happened because there are still so many unanswered questions.

What I'd like to do now is focus on my relationship with my daughters and grandchild. I bet you'd like that, too. So, how would you like to take a drive on Thursday? I know you probably have the week scheduled, but Abby asked me to invite you to her cheerleading show. Even though she doesn't want to face the fact that Maggie is her birthmother, she wants a grandfather. I guess she thinks life will be perfect and her family complete if she has a set of grandparents like everyone else. The junior varsity football game starts at 4, right after

school, and her show is during halftime. I can send you directions if you
decide to come.
Claire

As she hit send, she gave herself a mental pat on the back. She did it without pretending all was hunky-dory or that she'd forgiven him everything. All those years she was sure he must have hated her for their predicament left an indelible wound on her heart. Believing that the one you love hates your guts cuts to the quick. Some people never recover. Obviously, she hadn't.

Chapter 27

MAGGIE

If she were keeping score, Mac would be winning, hands down. He was the committed one, steadfast in his quest to win her heart. In fact, he continued to check in on her each and every evening, and even though she was safe now with Rex locked up, he would find some silly excuse for seeing her just one more time. The memories brought a smile to her face, but also triggered another thought... she'd never asked him out once in the entire time she'd known him. Here he'd taken the time to get to know her and upon learning that she liked to run, introduced her to the university track; yet, he was very accommodating and didn't seem to mind when she insisted on walking her dog around the lake in town instead. He took her out to dinner and dancing, and she never reciprocated. She'd kept secrets from him instead of being honest from the beginning, and he'd forgiven her. He'd searched for her when she disappeared, stood by her while she recovered, and she'd never done a thing to thank him...not one thing. She decided that she was probably lucky he'd hung in there this long because she sure hadn't given him much encouragement.

Unfortunately, she'd been here before, in this very place where it was time to make a decision, to decide whether or not she wanted to move forward with a relationship, and she was feeling the stress. How many men had asked for some kind of commitment from her over the last few years? She could count them on one hand because she'd learned from experience that she couldn't trust most of the men she knew, and the one she thought she could trust turned out to be the most untrustworthy of all. She was no good at reading men, and it was all because of Rex. He treated her like a queen, took her places she'd never been, doted on her, and never pressured her for anything except a commitment. No wonder she fell head over heels in love with him…what girl wouldn't want that…a committed man. She never saw one red flag, never questioned whether he wasn't single, and never saw it coming. Yet, as soon as she agreed to live with him, as soon as her bags were unpacked and her toothbrush had claimed a space in his medicine cabinet, something changed. She didn't recognize it at first; she thought he was possessive because he cared, because he loved her so much, and because he wanted to spend every minute with her. That's what lovers do, don't they?

Then the interrogation began…he wanted to know where she was, who she'd talked to, and what she'd spent her money on. She had to drop her graduate courses because she already had one degree and had to drop her friends because they caused trouble between them. She couldn't pay for her cell phone, so he added her to his plan. Little did she know, but he'd planned it that way so he could keep track of every call she made. He called her names she'd never heard before, degraded her in every way humanly possible including holding her down against her will when all she wanted was a gentle, thoughtful lover. It ended the day he threatened to kill her when she tried to leave him, and he almost got away with it. Now, almost a decade later, he'd tried again. She'd survived both times.

Mac knew all about Rex because, as it turned out, he'd put up with Rex's bullying as a child and later, as a teenager. Once he'd shared that information with his good friend George and his wife, Kate, they knew that Mac would be one of the few people who'd understand what her sister had endured, and Kate began her match-making efforts in earnest. It didn't seem to matter that Mac had been married and divorced… not just once, but twice, Kate found no fault with him and Maggie could do nothing but trust her level-headed sister's instincts.

Kate insisted that they were meant to be together, but Maggie wasn't sure about that. Yet, there was something she did know for sure, something she'd never experienced in the presence of any other man. She felt immediately at home with him, instantly comfortable from the time they met. And that wasn't all. Maggie understood without a doubt that Mac saw her as an equal and for the first time in her life, she could say the same about him. In fact, the focus of their careers was so similar, and their work to rid the world of bullying and domestic violence was so closely related that it scared her. They could be soul mates, she thought, but if the past predicts the future, their trust issues would tear them apart. Both of his wives cheated on him…would he ever be able to trust her, would he throw a fit every time another man talked to her? Was that why she was holding back? She couldn't stand living like that again. Is that why she wasn't putting everything she had into this relationship? She was overcome with sadness at the thought of it, a sadness that reached deep into her heart of hearts and grabbed onto the truth…the last thing she wanted was to lose Mac. There was a certainty to the thought…a sureness that made it real. Maggie decided then and there to take their relationship to the next level, to ask him to come on an emotional journey with her to meet her brother.

Maggie wondered why she didn't think of him right away. It should have been obvious to her because he had the gift of gab, he could talk to anyone. Actually, she had to admit that he was the yin to her yang; he was the talker, she, the listener…a necessary skill in her profession, but it wouldn't be enough for the meeting looming ahead of her. By the time she talked to her mother and sister on the phone later that afternoon and told them of her plan, she'd become completely at peace with her decision. The time was right. Of course, her sister, the hopeless romantic, cheered at the news. Her mother, however, pretended not to care but wished her luck.

It was getting close to suppertime when Maggie glanced out her window to see the jeep, canoe in tow, lumbering up the driveway and past her little farm house. She needed to talk to him before she lost her nerve. Her heart raced and her mouth went dry, but she grabbed the leash anyway, attached it to Horse, and took the dog for another walk…this time hurriedly and in the direction of Mac's house.

Chapter 28

MAC

Mac busied himself with emptying the jeep of all evidence of an afternoon adventure down the Kinni. He had to laugh at the paraphernalia his daughter insisted on bringing with her. First of all, there was the little pink leather purse with the metal studs that she'd purchased with her own money at the thrift shop in town. It was never out of her sight, and she spent a great deal of time cleaning it out and changing its contents. The purse hung over her shoulder at the movies and when she was horseback riding; she took it on fishing trips and canoeing adventures. It went everywhere the eight year old girl went, even hitchhiked on her school backpack. Today, she'd opened it several times to grab her sunscreen and squeeze the contents from the smallest tube he'd ever seen. It also held a tiny jar of lip gloss that her mother had bought her (Mac remembered having to keep his mouth shut so he wouldn't ruin Lily's visit with her mother). He'd seen her apply it more than once and guessed it really didn't bother him; she had to learn about that stuff from someone so it might as well be his ex. As usual, she had to redo her pony tail a few times, change the colorful bands on her wrists to other colorful bands, and show him the little, round plastic animals she'd been collecting, telling him their names and reminding him that Abby had this one or that one, and that she needed a bigger allowance so she could complete her collection. What ever happened to the little girl that loved to canoe, loved to do everything her dad suggested…going to ball games, fishing, boating, horseback riding, and camping? Suddenly, he imagined the purse and all of its contents unexpectedly falling into the Kinnickinnic, he pictured himself jumping overboard in a heroic effort to retrieve the purse, and he envisioned his brokenhearted daughter when he'd come to the surface of the river without it. He couldn't stand the idea of hurting her, but darn it, he wanted his tomboy back and held on to the thought that she'd excel in gymnastics…she did love it, but then he remembered her love of cheerleading and shook his head in the acknowledgement that he had no control over any of it.

Noticing that Lily had fled to the sanctity of the house, Mac accepted the fact that he would be the only one cleaning out the car. After releasing a groan, he got busy dragging the coolers and extra changes of clothes and shoes out of the car, piling them on the ground until he could sort out the dry from the wet, the unopened bottles from the empties, and the salvageable food from the trash. He was so engrossed in his task that he didn't look up until a wet nose poked the back of his arm. He knew the feeling well and turned to pet the humongous dog, and with the sun shining in his eyes, somehow made out the silhouette standing directly behind her. *I'd recognize her shape anywhere!*

"So much for trying to sneak up on me, huh?"

She laughed and changed the subject "You took all of this on your little canoe trip?"

"Yeah, and if you would have come along, this pile would be double in size. Women," he said with a shake of his head. He stood then, reached for her, and pulled her close. Speaking into her hair, he added, "How yah doing anyway?"

"Good, real good. Abby and I have come to an agreement, so all is right with the world."

His eyes popped. "No kidding?"

She smiled up at him. "No kidding."

Mac wanted to kiss her. "This calls for a celebration." He slid one hand into her hair and used the other to pull her close. Somehow the dog ended up between them and the kiss became peck. She had to have seen the look of disappointment in his eyes but giggled anyway.

"Hey, if you want to celebrate, you can come to dinner with me tomorrow night."

Holding her by the shoulders, he pushed her away from him, affecting surprise. "You're asking me to dinner?"

She frowned. "Sure…isn't that allowed?"

"It's just that you…I mean, I just thought you preferred being asked or something."

He got a smile from her, followed by a blush that colored her prominent cheek bones.

"I think I owe you an apology…for never reciprocating."

Rubbing her shoulder, he bent at the knees so they'd be eye to eye. "Hey, I never gave it a second thought. I figured that if you came up with something we could do together, you'd let me know."

A huge smile crossed her face. "You're pretty confident, aren't you?"

"I always knew you liked me," he teased, winking at her. "You're just kind of slow, that's all."

She punched him in the arm. "Hey!"

"Well, you are wearing a cast on your arm!"

"Okay…I'm slow. Still want to go to dinner?"

Mac put his hand to his chin, rubbed it, and then rolled his eyes. "Monday…nothing going on Monday except for cheerleading practice for the girls right after school."

"Kate can take care of that."

"Sounds like you've got it all figured out. What's so important about going out to dinner on Monday?"

Maggie sounded nervous. "I'm a chicken, that's all."

"Why? Is it your dad again? Is he coming around?"

After a shake of her head, Maggie managed a coy smile. "No, this time it's my half-brother. I'm just thinking I might need some comic relief."

"Very funny," Mac said, making a goofy face. "Of course, I'd love to go with you, be there when you meet him. It's pretty exciting, isn't it?"

"I'm not sure what to expect, that's all."

"I can't help you with that, but I sure can change a subject if I have to."

She nodded. "That's exactly what I was thinking."

"So what are you really worried about?"

She chuckled. "I don't know…it's silly, I guess, but I remember Mom saying that Grant's mother thought she was after the family money. I just wonder if the half-brother wants me to sign off on it, too…wants it all for himself. Wouldn't that be something?"

"Wow, I never thought of that. He probably doesn't know that you don't need their money, that you're a world famous lecturer!"

"Yeah, world famous…I guess that'll be my comeback, huh?"

Nodding and wiggling his eyebrows, Mac agreed. "One thing though…um, how do you plan to introduce me?"

Maggie cocked her head to one side, staring into his clear blue eyes while rubbing her free hand over one of his husky arms. She cleared her throat before she spoke and turned the tables on him. "How do you want to be introduced?"

He laughed. "You first." Her mood changed suddenly; he saw it in her eyes and it saddened him. "Okay, call me anything you want…friend, sister's friend, colleague." He heard his own voice; it sounded sarcastic, and he wanted to take it back.

"You're so much more than any of those things," she said, surprising him.

"I hope so," he admitted, happy with her assessment.

Unexpectedly, Maggie jerked the leash on the dog, and Horse moved from between them, leaving her free to wrap her arms around Mac and lean into him. When she spoke, it was barely a whisper. "Mac, if I say it, if I say it out loud, if I commit to you…I'm afraid that things will change…"

Kissing the top of her head and gritting his teeth simultaneously, he thought of Rex and the abuse. He understood that she was afraid that he would turn on her somehow, change somehow, become controlling, possessive…he'd known it all along and he was ready for it, so he took her by the shoulders and pushed her back just far enough so to see her face.

"Look, Maggie…it's no secret that I want to be more than a friend, but I'm willing to wait for however long it takes for you to trust me. All I can do is hope that you'll feel the same way about me someday, so for now I'm just following your lead." *There...I said it.*

He could feel her tighten her arms around his waist, hiding her face in his chest.

"It's not fair...I'm not being fair. You're a wonderful man, you deserve so much more."

Taken aback, he had to let her know the truth as he saw it. He was the lucky one, thrilled to have her in his life. "Are you kidding? You're perfect...perfect...I think you are just perfect."

He heard her laugh into his shirt. "You're crazy."

"No...you're crazy."

"Well, in my case, that's true," she said, her sense of humor returning.

"Now that we've established that, how are you going to introduce me again? Please...don't call me your landlord...that would sound so sleazy."

"Good grief. Of course not."

"And colleague, that's so stuffy."

"Stuffy?"

"It would make me sound like a pathetic old professor!"

"It would not!"

"I know...lover, call me your lover...yeah, I like that one!"

She punched him and laughed. "Hey, that'd make me sound easy!"

"I wish."

"Stop it. Okay...boyfriend...if you behave yourself, I'll call you my boyfriend."

"And you can't take it back later. Once you say it, it's a done deal."

"Oh! For crying out loud. What am I going to do with you?"

Mac couldn't stop a lecherous smile from crossing his face. "Anything you want."

Chapter 29

MAGGIE

After teaching his last class for the day, Mac met Maggie in the parking lot of the Tech, hitched a ride in her Lincoln, and together they headed for the Westward Ho Supper Club on the north end of town. Maggie told him that she'd asked Greg to meet her there because it was less than a mile off the exit from the highway, right on the main drag, so it would be easy to get in and out when he was ready to leave. She told him that she'd be waiting in the bar, in a booth at the far end.

Because they hadn't been dating for very long, Maggie had no idea that the Westward Ho was one of Mac's favorite hangouts. He told her all about the tasty buffet and added that people came from miles around for the 'all you can eat' specials. In fact, Mac frequented the place so often that the hostess, Louise, hugged him when he walked in the door. And it didn't stop there; half of the people in the bar greeted him by name and then there was the bartender, Freddy, who asked him if he wanted the usual.

"How much time do you spend here anyway?" Maggie asked, chuckling as they slid into a booth on the second level of the bar.

"I don't know...I guess I've been coming here since I moved to town. The people at the Tech come here for meetings, luncheons...stuff like that. Besides that, they get all the Sunday football games on the big screens here. Haven't you been here before?"

Maggie shook her head.

"Then how'd you know about the bar?"

"Kate told me about the booths…she said we could sit in the back…that it'd be kind of private."

"I never thought of that…good idea. So how do you want to do this? Have them sit across from us or what?"

"I don't care."

"I think you should sit on the outside…move," he said as he slid out, let her out, then slid back in and toward the wall.

"Why?"

"Because you have to greet them…I'm just along for the ride, remember," he teased.

"You're not going to make me regret this, are you?" While she waited for him to answer, she turned her head away from him and noticed that she could no longer see the big screen television as well as she had before. Instead, he now had the perfect view. "Busted…now I know why you came along."

He laughed. "I have no idea what you're talking about."

While they waited for their drinks, Mac pointed out the Packer memorabilia covering the walls of the popular bar and told her about the players that had visited there, and the autographs he'd collected over the years. She'd heard Mac and George talk about fantasy football and the Pack's chances of winning the Super Bowl, but she'd never heard any of this before and came to the conclusion that their relationship had been based on what was happening in her life. She figured he'd become sick of the drama of her personal soap opera by now and wondered why he stuck around. And even though she was the one who asked him out this time, it was still all about her. She made a mental note to become more involved in his life and learn as much as she could about him. After tonight, she'd concentrate on learning all about the man who seemed to adore her no matter what.

It wasn't long before their drinks arrived and while Freddy waited on them, Greg and his girlfriend showed up behind him. As the server moved away, Maggie saw her brother for the first time. Her heart was in her throat; she didn't know what to do first. Luckily, Mac had his wits about him, gave her a bit of a shove, and she slid out of the booth.

Greg spoke first as he held a hand toward her. "Hi…Maggie…so nice to finally meet you."

She smiled up at the tall drink of water, grabbed his hand in hers, and shook it. "Hi, Greg."

When Maggie directed her attention to his girlfriend, she saw the tears in her eyes, and in an attempt to wipe them away, the girl turned her head. Maggie understood what the girl must be feeling and to show her support, she reached around him, and held out her hand. The girl grabbed it and wiped away tears before looking Maggie in the eye.

"Hi, I'm Jolene."

Maggie smiled confidently, and it dawned on her that she might have to be in charge of the meeting because the twenty somethings she'd just met were emotionally spent.

"I'm so glad you had time to come into town. Here. Have a seat," she said, motioning to the other side of the booth. Pointing toward Mac as she slid in, she added, "Mac MacDermid…"

Mac leaned across the table, reaching for their hands. "Her significant other," he said, winking her way.

Maggie blushed, remembering her promise. He must have sensed how nervous she was and decided to laugh it off. To break the ice, she asked them what they wanted to drink, and Freddy appeared before they could answer.

"So…how did the interview go?" she asked, staring wide-eyed at the young man, imagining what her father must have looked like at that age.

Greg spoke. "Okay, I guess. I have no idea."

"Oh, he's going to get it," Jolene said confidently. "I just know it.

Maggie and Mac both smiled at the confident girl. She was grinning ear to ear as she leaned against Greg, gazing at him admiringly. Greg just shook his head and laughed.

"So you'll be moving to the Twin Cities?" Mac asked.

Greg nodded. "I'd love to live around here…maybe get a place on the St. Croix."

"Whoa, that'll cost you," Mac said.

"I know, but Dad and I might get a place together. He'd like to retire up here."

Maggie felt her face redden. "He's planning to live around here?"

"Well, yeah, I guess…now that you and your mom are living in Wisconsin again. And if I'm working in the cities, well, it'd be perfect."

Taken aback by the direction of the conversation, Maggie was at a loss for words. Grant had told her how excited Greg was to get to know her, to be a part of her life, but she never imagined that either of them wanted to live near her or Claire. She thought of her mother and how his moving there would turn her world upside down. She wished he would have mentioned it to her, talked to her about it before he'd even discussed it with his son. Mac must have misread her discomfort as excitement and innocently added his two cents worth.

"There are some great places for sale on the river, real good deals with the economy the way it is and all. So when will you find out about the job?" Mac asked, leaning closer to Maggie, showing support.

"Well, it's the government, you know…they'll take their good natured time making a decision."

The elder couple nodded.

"They said they'd be in touch by the end of the week."

"I think that's pretty fast for a big time job," Mac said, teasing.

"Not when you're waiting to hear," Greg said.

Jolene reiterated. "He's going to get it."

After a few uneasy moments had passed, Greg cleared his throat and spoke directly to Maggie. "I know this is awkward, Maggie, but I just want you to know how happy I am that Dad is connecting with you. I always knew that something was missing, that he was longing for something. I just couldn't put my finger on it."

Maggie held her breath, listening intently.

"I mean, Dad was great, but sad about something. I knew that even as a little kid. I could never figure it out. He had everything…money, a satisfying career, a nice family…Mom knew about it, too. She tried to explain it to me once, saying that Dad was unhappy about something that happened a long time ago."

"I'm sorry about your parents splitting, Greg. You know it had nothing to do with you."

Shaking his head, Greg continued, staying focused on Maggie.

"All kids wonder if they're to blame, but I knew it was something else. I always knew it."

Maggie decided to get to the bottom of it. "Do you think my mother is to blame somehow?"

Greg got the strangest look on his face and turned to look at his girlfriend. She nodded as if giving him permission to speak. "We know what my grandfather did...I guess your grandmother, too. My father loves her to death, that's all I know."

Maggie's eyes popped. "Loves who to death?"

"Your mother, Claire...he's miserable, actually. He wants a second chance so badly. Do you know how she feels, Maggie?"

Maggie realized then that her half-brother was just a kid looking out for his dad. He had no evil ulterior motives for meeting her...he might want to get to know her, but he was putting his father's happiness above all else. "Greg, I don't know what to say. Her head is whirling right now, you know, with all this new stuff to sort out. I don't think she knows what she wants."

"Really? So she never said she loved him or anything?"

Jolene looked at her boyfriend. "Greg...it's none of your business. Your dad told us to drop it, remember?"

Her heart softening toward the two kids, Maggie decided to let them know what she knew, but before she had a chance, her mother walked in. Maggie spotted her immediately. She stood at the entrance to the bar, searching for them. Before waving her mother in their direction, she warned the kids. "My mother just walked in. Do you want to meet her?"

"Oh, my gosh," Jolene squealed.

Greg turned and his mouth dropped open. "That's your mother?"

Maggie nodded. She knew exactly what he was thinking. "She looks way too young to be my mother, doesn't she?"

He looked stunned.

"She was barely nineteen when she had me."

"Uh huh," he said, nodding. "You told her that we were meeting?"

"Yes. But she wasn't sure if you'd care to meet her." *Nowhere near the truth.*

Staring toward the entry, Greg didn't answer, and Maggie assumed he didn't want to meet her. "I'll steer her out of here," she said.

"No, no…don't. I'd love to meet her." He blew into his hands, slid out of the seat, straightened his clothes, and stood to walk toward Claire. Maggie sat down and watched for her mother's reaction. She saw her mother's jaw drop and a hand slap her chest; she saw the tears stream down her face and felt them on her own. Mac had his arm around her now, his hand rubbing her arm, his lips quickly grazing her temple. Jolene covered her mouth and eyes wide, stared straight ahead. Maggie watched as Claire embraced the kid. She saw him hold her tight, saw her mother wrap her arms around him. *What could they be saying to one another?* After what seemed to be an interminable amount of time, Greg turned and with his arm looped over her mother's shoulder, walked toward them. Maggie stood then, thinking her mother was going to need her, but what she saw through her tears was something from the past, something from 1972, a vision of a younger Claire and her boyfriend, Grant, walking toward her, arm in arm. As soon as her mother reached for her and she felt her touch, the hallucination vanished.

Claire clutched Maggie to her. "I hope I'm not interrupting, darling," she whispered. "I just want you to know I'm all for this…I mean, I don't want this to start with hard feelings."

"I know, Mom…I understand. I'm glad you're here."

Claire squeezed her hard in response. After giving her mother a peck on the forehead, Maggie released her as Greg pulled a chair over so she could join them at the booth. Maggie slid in next to Mac, who patted her leg sympathetically, and Claire sat down, ran her hands under her eyes to erase her tears, and then thread her fingers through her hair, fluffing it into place. Maggie watched her smooth her clothes, straighten her back, and fold her hands in her lap. She heard Claire clear her throat and saw her exhale through pursed lips. Within seconds, she smiled and grabbed Maggie's hand in hers and held on for dear life.

"Mom," Maggie said, shaking her mother's hand slightly. "You haven't met Jolene, Greg's girlfriend."

Claire didn't release Maggie's hand, but glanced at Jolene and greeted her. To Maggie's surprise, Jolene nodded, smiled, and gazed at

Claire with a great deal of admiration in her eyes; in fact, she noticed that both of the young people spoke with her mother as if she were someone they'd always hoped to meet. Maggie hadn't expected it to go this way, but she couldn't have been happier. She sat back and let Claire take over. She watched her interact with Greg and his girlfriend, and as she did, she thought about the reasons they might have to hold her mother in such high regard. There was no doubt in her mind that it had to do with Grant and how he presented their story to the two of them. Maggie figured he must have explained their circumstances and obviously told them how much he cared about her. Maybe he even took some of the blame. He must have shared what he knew of her ability to overcome her unfortunate circumstances and how she used her God given gifts for the greater good. Her mother was quite a woman. Maggie guessed Claire had been admired by many over the years with the exception of members of her immediate family. Little did Claire know, but her daughters could be added to a growing list of admirers. Maggie wondered if she'd told her mother how glad she was that she was here, living in such close proximity to her daughters. She decided she had better tell her soon because she could see that there were a couple of kids who were likely to beat her to it.

Chapter 30

GRANT

Usually, Grant grumbled when he had to bring work home from the office, which was often, but on this particular evening, he was happy that he had something to keep his mind off of his children and their initial meeting.

Hunkering down in his cozy home office, Grant concentrated on the briefs sitting on his desk in front of him. He'd finished his leftovers, knocked off a beer, and now he had no excuse but to get his work done. Leaning over his desk, he read through the computer generated printouts one by one, skimming them for crucial facts and highlighting the most important information for his upcoming case. He figured if he could at least come up with his opening statement, he'd have accomplished something. It wasn't going to happen tonight, though, because his mind kept wandering.

Grant had to do something to keep him on track so he came up with the notion that if he were prepared for anything, he could go back to his briefs. Leaving his desk, he wandered through the house making his first stop the kitchen. After grabbing another bottle of beer, he lifted the handset of his cordless phone and headed back into his office. Next, he searched through his briefcase for his cell and set it on the desk right next to the handset. Staring at them as if waiting for one of them to ring, he had to laugh. If Greg could see him now, he'd harass him mercilessly for not upgrading his cell, a flip phone style of all things; he'd be telling him to get a blackberry or some kind of smart phone or something. The kid should be happy he could text! Grant was simply glad to have a cell so that his son or his staff could get in touch with him no matter where he was. He had his PC for email and the internet; that's all he really needed to do his job. He didn't have time to learn about all the apps…well, maybe if there was an app for the Badgers he'd think about it twice. No, he didn't even need an app for that because all the information he needed about his favorite team was online. Next time the subject came up, he'd remind his son of his age and that he was thinking about retiring and wouldn't need any of it.

Glancing at the corner of his computer screen, gauging how much time had passed, Grant wondered if the meeting was over, if the kids liked each other, and if his son and his girlfriend would be staying in Lake Louise overnight. They promised to call. What was taking them so long?

After giving up on the briefs in front of him, Grant decided his time would be better spent checking his email and replying to the most urgent messages. So with one eye on the phones and the other on his monitor, Grant opened his email program. He didn't know why he hadn't noticed it before, but Claire had written to him the night before. He decided it was a good thing…he got a lot of work done today and wouldn't have if her email hadn't been what he'd hoped for. As it turned out, that's exactly what would have happened.

Talk about cool. She didn't catch his drift at all. Her email read as if it were written by Detective Joe Friday…just the facts, ma'am. No emotion…short and sweet. Actually, there was nothing sweet about it, and the disappointment weighed heavy on his heart. He wondered what questions she had and why she didn't just ask them. He blamed himself. His writing wasn't eloquent enough because she couldn't tell how much he cared. Most of all, she didn't understand that he wanted them to get on with their lives, but together. Perhaps all was not lost…she'd invited him to Abby's show. He didn't care if he had to be there on a Thursday, didn't care what was on his agenda this week, and didn't care about anything but seeing her again.

It was after nine when Grant's cell rang. Grabbing it after the first chime, he spotted his son's name on the screen and flipped the cell open.

"Hey, how'd it go?" he asked.

"Great, Dad…I wish you could have been there."

"At the interview?"

"Oh, no…that went great. I mean, I wish you could have been with me when I met Maggie."

"That's okay, son. It was better…just the two of you."

"That's what I mean, Dad. Maggie's boyfriend was there and then Claire dropped by and joined us, too."

"You met Claire?"

"Yup. Man, Claire and Maggie are hot. How come you never told me that?"

"Because they're family, show some respect! So you talked to Claire?"

"She was going to stay away, but decided that she didn't want hard feelings. Dad, I didn't expect that. And she hugged me so hard you'd think that I was her long lost kid."

"She did?"

"I think it's all going to work out, Dad."

"What?"

"You and her."

"Good grief. What makes you think that?"

"I don't know exactly, but Jolene said she got this sad look in her eyes whenever we talked about you."

"Sad?"

"Like maybe she wished you were there."

"You got all that from a look?" Grant smiled, picturing the kids trying to analyze every little thing. He could hear his son talking to his girlfriend…repeating what he said. Then he heard Jolene yell. "Tell him to tell her how he feels, for crying out loud."

"Just think what she did, Dad. She made sure she met me, made sure Maggie and I got off on the right foot by giving her approval. I think she wants to be part of this, too."

"Maybe."

"Besides that Dad, some guy is going to ask her out. I mean, the guys in the bar were really checking her out."

"I have no doubt."

"She told me she invited you to the cheerleading thing."

"She did."

"You going?"

"I guess." Grant heard his son say 'he's going'.

He heard Jolene yell, "It's time to sweep her off her feet!"

Greg said good-night, and Grant snapped the phone shut. After dropping back into his office chair, he started chuckling; the thought of their matchmaking scheme warmed his heart. Maybe they were right. If he didn't let her know how he felt, someone else would be taking his place. He had no idea why he hadn't thought of it, but now that they'd planted the seed of possibility, he imagined it could happen easily, and then he wouldn't have a chance. He had to do something out of the ordinary to get her attention, but he wouldn't see her for four more days…anything could happen!

After stretching his arms above his head and leaning back in his office chair, Grant racked his brain, trying to come up with something clever, a statement or comment that would warm the cockles of her heart, a remark that she'd never forget. This might take awhile. This might take a gallon of coffee and a case of energy drinks. He really wanted another beer, but any more alcohol at all would surely dull his senses.

Jumping from his chair, Grant headed for the kitchen, took his coffee grounds from the freezer, and filled the carafe with cold water. As he eagerly waited for the coffee to brew, he decided to check the messages from the base unit of his cordless telephone. The LED display had been flashing for a couple of days and he'd ignored it…most people used his cell to get in touch with him now, so the message would have to be some sort of solicitation. He swore to himself that if it was another credit card company promotion or unwanted political questionnaire, he'd be forced to consider getting rid of his land line; no one would be the wiser if he did.

Grant leaned into his kitchen counter, pushed the button, and bent over the telephone to make sure he'd hear the message. *"Mr. Harrison. Please call Wisconsin Savings at 608-something, something, something*

5555 concerning your safe deposit box as soon as possible. Thank you. "

What safe deposit box? He'd never had one. The message had to be for his father, the former president of the bank. They had the wrong Grant Harrison. Now he'd have to deal with his father and that didn't make him happy. He jotted down the number, erased the message, and focused on his coffee pot. The last thing he wanted to do was talk to his father. What was he supposed to do...forgive him? He never even got an apology, not a real one anyway. What was it again...oh yes, 'it seemed like the right thing to do'. Maybe there was a 'sorry' in there somewhere, but he couldn't remember it now.

Later, sitting with his head in his hands, staring at the monitor of his PC, Grant's thoughts about his father's transgressions lead him to wonder if he'd ever apologized to Claire. Had he ever really apologized for not being there for her, apologized for his lack of effort when her mother kept turning him away, apologized for not fighting for custody of his own child, or apologized for not apologizing? He decided to forget about doing something to win her heart; it seemed so trivial now anyway. He owed her so much more than that and remembered that all he'd done so far was make excuses for his own behavior, telling her he wrote her letters for two years, saying her mother knew he was looking for her, figuring she never got back to him because she wasn't interested...excuses...all of them. If he wanted to, he could blame his father and her mother for all their problems. No...he had to take responsibility for his inaction as far as she was concerned. Yes, he was young...yes, he could have rebelled against his parents wishes, fought harder for her...but he didn't know how at the time and now he needed to confront that fact and apologize. He couldn't believe that he'd never fully apologized, that he'd never even thought of it.

Feeling truly remorseful and with the full understanding that what he had done to Claire was wrong, Grant found Claire's last email. He reread it...she'd come off as cool as a cucumber, as impersonal as possible. She hadn't picked up on his statements of affection, hadn't noticed them at all, and he no longer questioned why she hadn't. He'd never been truly honest with her because he'd never been honest with himself, and he decided then and there that it was time to transform their relationship, and it was up to him to do it.

As he sat staring at the cursor, blinking away on the blank space in front of him, he thought that maybe it would be better to handwrite an apology, to send her a letter. His pulse raced at the thought of it, at the thought of all the letters she never got. No, she said she wanted to do this with email, talk things out this way. It was the method she chose, and he knew the importance of following her wishes. Once he decided what he needed to do, his words erupted with emotion.

Dear Claire,

Thank you for the invitation to see Abby's performance. I would love to come. Please let me know where I should go and what time you want me there.

Greg called and told me what a nice visit you all had. I wish I could have been there. Thank you for being there for the kids. I believe that they want to get to know each other better, and your approval means a lot to both of them.

I know there are a lot of questions you feel have not been answered, and I don't know if I'd be able to answer any of them. I would like to tell you, however, that I am sincerely sorry for everything that happened so long ago when I left you to talk to my parents. In fact, I have not regretted anything more in my life. I regret that I didn't fight for us, I regret that I let my parents control every aspect of my life...I should have run away with you...but most of all I regret that I caused you any harm. The last thing I wanted to do was abandon you and our child, but I did and there is no excuse for it. I take full responsibility for the unimaginable hurt I've caused you. You have every right to be angry with me, to hate my guts, and to never trust me again.

Since we can't go back in time, since there is no way to undo the past, I can only pray that there is some way that I can begin to repair the damage I've done. I don't deserve or expect a response. I just want you to know how sorry I am.
Grant

Chapter 31

CLAIRE

In an attempt to be useful, Claire tried to be up and dressed before anyone else. She thought if she could make Kate's family a good breakfast, it would help in some small way to pay her keep; besides that, she felt right at home in the kitchen, and the joy she found in cooking always helped take her mind off her problems. The new routine, however, had gotten in the way of her early morning stretches; she'd have to save them for later because she had to make sure that her immediate family started the day out right.

Before Claire left the lower level of the house, she searched the recycle bin sitting next to the back door for the classifieds in the buyer's guides and shoppers...just some of the items she needed to keep her on the track to finding employment. Sometimes she wished that she were sixty-two so she'd qualify for a monthly social security check, but that was still five years away and the last thing she wanted was for time to fly any faster. She had to work; there was no way around it. Claire congratulated herself, however, for keeping her spending down. She hadn't shopped for shoes, purses, or clothes since she'd arrived in Lake Louise, and she'd stocked up on her cosmetics, prescriptions, and personal hygiene products while she was still in Phoenix. The trip to Madison the week before had been costly, in more ways than one, but other than buying some groceries so she could cook for the family, and the fact that the automatic monthly deductions for her life, health, and car insurances had begun, she hadn't made much of a dent in her new

savings account at the local Wisconsin Savings Bank. She'd opened a
checking account there, too, and was waiting for her debit card and
checks to arrive; other than that and her lack of a regular income and a
place of her own, she'd begun to call Lake Louise her home.

After snuggling into her pillows to peruse the employment ads and
finding nothing, Claire grabbed her laptop. Hoping to keep her mind off
of Grant and his emails, she checked the bookmarked job search sites to
see if there were any recent ads on any of them, but found nothing of
interest. Since there were not jobs to apply for, she reluctantly opened
the email program and sure enough, there was Grant's reply at the top of
the list. Before reading it, however, she made a mental note of the
response she'd give if he was coming to Lake Louise on Thursday. All
she had to do was send him directions or have Kate do it. It didn't matter
either way. With new resolve, she opened his message and started to
read.

Oh my God! As Claire read the apology over and over again, and
with tears blinding her eyes, she took a deep breath, closed her eyes, and
let the apology sink in. First of all, she had to reconcile it in her mind
and recognize the courage it took for him to take all the blame. She
knew that no sane human being would believe what happened just then,
but it felt as though the arteries in her heart expanded and deep within
her chest, the organ beat harder and faster than it had in a very long
time. She felt energized as the oxygenated blood rushed through her
veins and returned to her heart, healing her wounds. Her heart had
softened and the protective shell surrounding it had all but disappeared,
releasing all the built up resentment and anger she'd held there for close
to forty years. She covered her face and gave a sigh of relief as tears
spilled and trailed down her face to settle in the corners of her mouth.

After inhaling a cleansing breath, she read the email again. There
was one problem with it; she had no idea what to do now but understood
with every fiber of her being that she needed guidance, that she had to
make sure she did the right thing for both of their sakes. The first person
she thought of was her daughter, the counselor, and she immediately
grabbed her cell from the nightstand and found Maggie's number in the
contacts. It went straight to voice mail.

Darling, Mom here…I really need to talk to you. Please call me as soon as you can.

Chapter 32

MAGGIE

Maggie had a lot to do so her mother's voicemail came across as an irritant in an already frustrating day. First of all, she was just plain tired. Meeting her half-brother had taken an emotional toll, to say the least, and considering what would happen going forward, especially where her mother was concerned, had kept her awake most of the night. Now, she berated herself for questioning everyone's motives, especially Mac's, Grant's, and now Greg's. She knew she had trust issues with men, and Grant's absence from her life had a lot to do with it, but she'd begun to rectify some of her false assumptions since meeting Mac and now, more than ever, she wanted to trust the other men in her life. Grant seemed decent enough, but she really needed to sit down with him so he could tell her his side of the story. She'd never let him do that; in fact, she'd cut him off when he tried.

Later, when the last student left her office and she'd checked to make sure she didn't have any other appointments, Maggie dialed her mother.

"Hello."

"Mom, it's Maggie."

"Oh, darling, thank you for returning my call. Are you free to talk?"

"Yes…is everything okay?" Maggie said when she heard what she thought was a sob.

"I really need some advice, honey."

"About what?"

"Your father."

"I don't know if I can help you with that, Mom."

"Yes, you can. I need a counselor, Maggie...I need professional guidance."

"I can recommend someone...I'm not sure I..."

"It has to be you."

"Okay...I can try to help. Want to come to my place in an hour or so?"

"Yes...I'd like that."

"Okay, Mom, okay. I'll see you then."

Maggie hung up thinking that her mother didn't sound right, didn't sound good at all. It was panic she heard in her voice; it sounded as if her confidence was gone. She didn't think that was possible. Her mother could be emotional, no doubt, but she was also one of the strongest women she'd ever known.

An hour later, Maggie searched the spanking new cupboards of her recently refurbished rental for a bottle of wine. Her mother loved wine, but Maggie wasn't prepared for company and felt lucky to have found half a bottle of Prosecco in her refrigerator. She remembered that it was left over from a dinner she'd prepared for Mac a week ago or so...she'd pan fried a couple of walleye, and he'd brought the white wine. They both loved sparkling wine, but she wondered if the bubbly had gone out of it. Anyway, it would have to do because she didn't have anything else.

While she let Horse out for awhile, she straightened the place up and tried to think of something to eat because she knew that she didn't dare drink wine on an empty stomach so she decided to make herself a snack. After a bit of a search, she found a loaf of cocktail pumpernickel in her freezer, a box of cream cheese in the fridge, and a cucumber in the vegetable drawer. Good, she could make a little something for herself and her mother as well, but before she could get started on her open faced sandwiches, she heard her mother's car pull in.

Maggie dropped what she was doing and rushed to the door to call her dog...Claire wasn't too fond of Horse...probably because the dog was bigger than she was…who always wanted to kiss her and just about knocked her over every time she'd visited. Horse rushed into the house and returned to her crate, just as she was trained to do, but this time Claire didn't seem to notice, didn't thank her for calling the dog, nothing. She simply followed the dog through the door and with her laptop tucked under her arm, shut the door behind her. She looked frazzled.

"Mom, are you okay? Here, sit on the couch."

Her mother obeyed, straightening out her clothes as she sat. Maggie shoved a glass of wine into her mother's hand and plopped down on the other end of the couch.

"What is it? What's wrong?"

Claire put her glass on the coffee table and fiddled with her laptop, flipping it over and turning it around before lifting the top. Maggie could see that her hands shaking, that she was on the verge of tears. Suddenly, Claire shoved the computer at Maggie. "Here, read this."

Maggie did as she was told, read through Grant's email, and then covered her mouth in surprise. "Oh my gosh, Mom! What are you going to do?"

"That's exactly what I'm here for, darling. I have no idea how to respond."

After closing the computer and shoving it aside, Maggie suggested they make the snack together and talk about how she felt. As Claire separated the little slices of frozen bread, she told Maggie about how she felt when she read the email, about how she was overcome with the feeling that she'd been healed somehow, that her wounds had disappeared. Maggie took her mother in her arms, forcing her to drop the bread onto the counter, and simply held her close.

When they finally separated and got back to work, Maggie opened the cream cheese and handed it to Claire to spread on the bread, then grabbed the paprika from her spice rack before washing and slicing the cucumber. She got a giggle from her mother, the best cook ever, over the simplicity of the food she was asked to prepare.

"Hey, no need to snicker. You're going to love this!"

Claire grinned, nodded, and continued spreading the cream cheese.

"Okay. Let's talk. So you say you feel like you've been healed."

"Uh huh."

"Because of the apology."

"Yes…Maggie…he took all the blame, all of it. The anger's gone. I'm just not angry anymore."

"So what do you want to do now?"

"That's why I came here. I have no idea how to tell him how I feel. I never expected this."

"Okay…well…here's a question for you. Do you believe he's sincere?"

"Yes, I do."

"Okay. Can you in all honesty accept his apology?"

"I think so, Maggie. He sounds so broken up about everything, just miserable."

"Do you think he exaggerated the apology to get you to feel sorry for him? That's happened to me."

"I don't think so…he's never acted like that…before or since he started emailing me."

"So what you're feeling is compassion? You think you know what he must be going through?"

"God…yes. I've hurt people, too, you know."

"Okay…then here's the big question. Do you forgive him for leaving you, Mom?"

"I think I did that a long time ago. I had to let go. I hated being spiteful…I even wanted revenge at some point. My doctors told me that I'd never get better if I didn't let it go. I wanted to move on with my life, Maggie. I remember putting it in Gods hands. Is that forgiveness?"

"I don't think so. I think that you compartmentalized what you were feeling…you put it aside…like in a box…you put it away so you didn't have to deal with it."

Claire nodded. "Yes…that's exactly what I did."

"Okay, sit down, eat something.…I have to think about this." Maggie found a glass and poured herself some wine, then joined her mother on the couch and gobbled a couple of their fresh cucumber treats. Her mother didn't eat anything; instead, she simply sipped on her wine, leaned back into the couch, made herself comfortable, and waited quietly until she obviously couldn't stand it any longer.

"Really…Maggie…are you going to help me with this or not?"

"Let me think…let me think. So you want to know what your next step should be?"

"My God, Maggie…I'll have to see him face to face in a couple of days. I have to do something before then."

"I know, Mom, but you can't rush into something like this."

"Then just please give me some ideas about how to handle this. Don't you think he's sitting there, wondering how I'm going to respond?"

Maggie smiled at her mother. "You really do care about him, don't you?"

"Of course I do."

"Then I think he gave you a gift…an apology is like a gift. Do you accept it or not?"

"I do…I told you that."

"Do you think he opened a door for the two of you?"

"Maybe."

"If you think he did, then you have to let him know that he can walk through it. If you do that then you really can't avoid him anymore."

"Okay, I can do that, but does he want me to say that I forgive him?"

"Can you say that honestly? Do you feel it in your heart?"

"Mostly."

"What do you mean by 'mostly'?"

"I just want him to admit that he never wrote me any letters. He didn't say anything about the letters this time, but there's no evidence of them, Maggie. I just want him to tell me that he's sorry he lied about that and maybe give me a reason why he said it. That's all."

"Why do you think he made that up?"

"I don't know…maybe in hindsight he thinks he should have written to me, so he made it up to get on my good side. I just know Mama and I never saw any letters. I went to the mailbox everyday for close to a year."

"It sounds like there's still some resentment there, Mom. You're not ready to forgive him everything."

Fresh tears spilled onto Claire's cheeks, and she used both hands to wipe them away. "I don't know why I can let go of that one little thing."

"It's because you so want it to be true. Then you'd know for sure he cared…it would be the proof you need."

"Yup."

"What if he sticks to his story? What then?"

"I don't know," Claire mumbled with a shake of her head.

"Well then, how about this. Can you tell him you accept his apology the way he presented it? That part is true, isn't it?"

"Yes, for sure."

"Do you think you could tell him you'll see him on Thursday? That way he'd know that you won't be purposely avoiding him anymore."

"I think I can do that."

"You can do that honestly?"

"Yes. I don't want to make him feel any worse."

"Then worry about forgiveness later…when it feels right…you can't rush it, Mom. It has to come from the heart."

Maggie watched as her mother nodded, sniffed, and stared at her hands. "Is there something else, something you're not telling me?"

Claire nodded quickly, but didn't look up.

"What? What is it?"

"Do you forgive me, Maggie?"

Scooting closer to her mother, Maggie, overwhelmed with compassion herself, wrapped an arm around Claire's shoulder and kissed her on the forehead.

"Mom, there's nothing to forgive."

"Please…I abandoned you!"

"Okay, I was angry, but the day you told us about the depression, the mental hospital and all of that, I understood that you didn't purposely leave us…I knew that there was nothing to forgive. Remember how we cried together? It was as though those tears washed away the years of hurt, the lonely months that went by every year before we'd see you again."

Claire nodded, wiping away new tears. "I never regretted anything more in my life."

"You couldn't help it, Mom. And I'm sorry I didn't tell you how I felt right then. I should have done that."

"It's okay…I think I felt it that day, too. Maybe we didn't need to use words."

"I'm glad you're here with us. Did I ever tell you that?"

Claire shook her head.

"Mom, we really appreciate what you gave up for us. I mean, we can't believe you left your life's work." Maggie eyes welled, and she cleared her throat "Do you ever regret leaving Phoenix?"

"No…I thought I would, but all those years without family…I need my family."

Patting her mother's arm reassuringly, Maggie said, "Me, too." But she had another question. "What about Mel, Mom?"

"I need to apologize to him…I know that now. I doubt he'll ever forgive me though."

"Have you heard from him?"

Claire shook her head. "I'm sure I won't."

"I'm sorry."

"Don't be. It wasn't fair of me to lead him on. He deserved better."

"What do you mean? You two were together for such a long time."

"Yes, but I never loved him the way I love…"

Maggie fairly jumped off the couch. "I knew it. You love him, don't you?"

"Who?"

"Grant. That's what you were going to say…the way you love Grant!"

"Come on, Maggie. It's too late. I can't dwell on that."

"I know a secret…I know a secret…" Maggie sang, dancing in her seat.

Laughing through her tears, Claire shook her head. "Stop it."

"Okay…I'll keep your little secret if you want me to."

"You'd better promise."

"Then it's true?"

"Just promise me…you're not bringing it up again."

With a roll of her eyes, Maggie sang, "Cross my heart and hope to die."

Later, after her mother had left, Maggie sat alone with the bottle of Prosecco. She didn't know why she was drinking the sparkling wine…it had lost most of its effervescence…but she didn't care because she just needed something to sip on while she pondered what her mother had to say. Discussing the topic of forgiveness had stirred up some old memories…the memories of the abuse…the memories of being lied to again and again. After every demeaning thing Rex had done to her in their short time together, he'd come crawling back, looking sheepish and begging for her forgiveness. Sometimes he'd even cry, get down on his knees in front of her and bawl. She'd loved him and wanted nothing more than to believe his every word, so she'd take him back. It would be good for awhile until he'd find another reason to humiliate her, hurt her physically or emotionally or both.

She'd put up with it for months until that fateful day when his wife came into the dealership, the fateful day that she learned he was married, the day that he almost killed her. He'd been lying to her all along…telling her that she was the best thing that happened to him…but he'd been married the whole while. He never apologized for that, but she'd never have forgiven him anyway because being sorry wasn't good enough.

Out of the blue, Maggie thought of her mother. The thing that held her mother back, the reason she was not ready to forgive had to do with the lies. Maggie understood now because lies were the reason she had to leave Rex, and the very reason she could never forgive him. Even though he'd almost kill her twice, it was the lying that hurt her the most. The abuse had broken her spirit, broken her bones, and left her unconscious, but it was the lies she could never forgive and the never ending stream insincere apologies she could never accept. Time after time, he'd broken her heart. Her mother felt the same way about Grant. Of course, it was different. He hadn't abused her, physically anyway, but he'd abandoned her and she was devastated, and the fact that she thought he'd lied cut her to the quick.

It was really too bad, Maggie thought. She had to admit that she'd like to see them together, getting along and taking up where they left off. But she understood now; her mother sincerely believed she'd been lied to. Yet, after the heart wrenching apology she'd received, Maggie wished her mother could overlook it, could take him at his word, but it didn't look like that would happen anytime soon.

Chapter 33

CLAIRE

On the way home from Maggie's, Claire stopped at the farmer's market to pick up some fresh vegetables for supper. By the time she arrived at Kate's, everyone was home, and Kate was already at the stove. Abby sat at the kitchen table doing her homework, but took the time to jump up to give her grandmother a hug.

"Where have you been?" Kate asked, forcing Claire to think about something other than squeezing her granddaughter.

"I stopped to get some veggies...you haven't made a salad yet, have you?"

"No."

"I was going to make supper. I'm sorry I'm late."

"Mom, there's nothing to be sorry about. And you certainly don't have to make supper every night. I told you that. Where were you anyway? Job hunting?"

Claire looked at her granddaughter before speaking...gauging her mood. "No. Just visiting Maggie." Abby didn't look up from her homework or ask any questions. That was a relief.

Kate wasn't about to let it go, though, and continued the inquisition. "Is everything okay? I mean, after last night and everything."

Abby lifted her head. "What happened last night?"

Claire caught a wide-eyed look from her daughter. *Sorry, but now you're in charge.*

"Well, honey. Maggie and I met her brother, Greg, for dinner."

"The Greg on the family tree...the guy you said was my uncle?"

"Yup, that guy."

"Was he cute, Grandma? Remember, you said you thought he'd be cute."

Claire caught a glimpse of Kate's eye roll and decided to ignore it. "You bet he was. Has a really cute girlfriend, too."

"Are they coming to my show? Did you ask my grandpa to the show like you said?"

Kate was probably hearing some of this for the first time, and although the idea of inviting Grant had been hers, Claire thought she'd better bring her up to speed. "Abby wanted Grant to come to her cheerleading show...lots of grandparents will be there. So I invited him for her...I hope that's okay."

Kate flashed an appreciative grin. "Of course. Sounds like a party. Right, Abs?"

"Could we have a party...have everyone over afterwards? The game will be over by six. Could we order some pizza?"

Kate laughed, but must have wanted some clarification. "Now, you two, don't you think you'd better let me know how many people you're planning to invite to this party?"

Claire waited for Abby to respond. The kid liked lists, so she'd probably already made one. She hadn't.

"Just a second, Mom." Abby dug around in her backpack, found a little spiral notebook, and grabbed an orange marker. "Mac, Lily, and Aunt Galen." She scribbled their names on the lined paper.

"Okay, that's three."

"My grandpa and grandma. Did he say he could come, Grandma?"

"Yup, he'll be here."

Kate whipped her head around, staring at her mother. "Really, Mom?"

"Yup...I'll catch you up later, hon."

"Okay, that makes five," said Kate.

"Me, Mom and Dad...six, seven, eight."

"Is that it?"

"What about that Greg and his girlfriend?"

"I asked them…they'll come another time, okay?"

"Okay…I have enough on my plate with meeting my grandpa!"

Claire mussed the hair on her granddaughter's head. "You're a funny little kid, you know that?"

"I'm not a little kid."

Claire didn't want the mood to change. "I know you're not. I just like to mess with you," she teased.

Abby giggled. "Yeah, I know."

"So is the list done?"

"No."

"It's not?" Claire asked, throwing Kate a hopeful look.

Sitting quietly at her spot at the table, Abby didn't look up but said, "I think Maggie's mad at me."

"Why would she be mad?"

"Because I was bossy. No one likes it when you're bossy."

Bending over and kissing the top of her head, Claire spoke soothingly. "I just saw her today. She didn't say anything about you being bossy; she didn't seem mad about anything."

"Are you sure?"

"Yes."

"But I think I said some mean things."

"She doesn't think you're mean."

"But I haven't seen her since Sunday. She doesn't come around anymore."

"It's only been two days, honey."

"I used to see her all the time."

"That's because she lived here. Now you just see me all the time." Claire tickled the girl, hoping to change her mood.

"Stop it…I hate being tickled."

"I'll stop when you tell me what you're going to do about this."

"Grandma!"

Claire continued tickling her granddaughter until she slid off the chair in an attempt to escape. Then, after taking the kid's place on the chair, Claire pulled the girl onto her lap and wrapped her arms tight around her. Looking up from where they sat, she noticed that Kate had left the room. She figured her oldest daughter was also afraid of the worst…that Maggie was staying away on purpose. Claire decided to sit quietly until the child calmed down. When she did, she spoke quietly.

"Grandma, can I show you something I'm making?"

Claire was happy to change the subject. "Absolutely."

Abby hopped from her grandmother's lap, grabbed her backpack, and slid it toward her.

"You need help with it?" Claire asked, thinking it was a school project.

"No, I just want you to see what I made."

Claire watched as Abby dug in one of the pockets of her backpack and pulled out a somewhat crinkled piece of construction paper…actually, it was several orange colored pieces taped together. After pushing her math homework aside, Abby opened up her creation and spread it on the kitchen table, smoothing out the creases as she did.

"What have we got here?" Claire asked.

"My family tree, Grandma."

"Oh, you drew a different one?"

"Yup."

"Can I see it?"

"Yup," Abby repeated as she slid the project toward Claire.

Claire's eyes wandered over the vivid creation. This family tree was much bigger than the original, four times bigger at least, and very creative. In fact, Abby had cut and pasted a great facsimile of an elm tree using brown construction paper and then colored in some believable looking bark. Scattered around on the branches were big green paper leaves; some covered in glitter, of course. Names were carefully printed next to leaves or near the pictures she'd glued on top of them. It looked to Claire as if Abby had it all figured out. She was surprised, though, to see that she had a branch connecting Grant to Claire with Maggie, Kate, and Greg lined up together underneath them. She never imagined that her granddaughter would put it together like that and swallowed the emotions that erupted quickly at the thought of it.

Deciding not to say anything and struggling to take her eyes and mind off of that branch of the tree, Claire spotted George's name under Kate's and Abby's under his. Not exactly the way it's usually done, but it worked. And she hadn't exactly ignored Maggie; she had a tiny brown branch coming off of Maggie's name, curling around until it touched her own. It reminded Claire of an umbilical cord or maybe that was wishful thinking on her part.

"Nice," Claire praised. "Really nice."

"Thanks, Grandma, but I need help finishing it."

"Okay. What can I do?"

"Well, first of all, I don't have pictures of Grant or Greg."

"I can help you with that. We can find pictures on the internet."

"They're on there?"

"Well, I've seen Grant's picture. I bet we can find Greg, too."

"Really?"

"Sure."

Abby's voice quavered a bit. "So Grandma...you're Maggie's mother and Grant's her father, right?"

Claire's breath caught in her throat. "Uh huh."

"So you got divorced like Lily's mom and dad?"

"No...our parents didn't even let us get married."

"But weren't you grown up?"

"Yes, but still pretty young...just college kids."

"But you were at least eighteen, right?"

"Yes."

"Well, then you can do anything...like vote for whatever guy you want for president, go to college or get a job, or get married if you want to ...that's what Mom and Dad told me."

"Sure, but his parents sent him away."

"Really? But he was grown up!"

"Yes...but that didn't seem to matter to them."

"Was he sad that he got sent away?"

"I think so."

"Then what happened?"

"I got sick, my mother had to take care of Maggie, and when he came back to get me, I was gone and no one would tell him where I was."

Abby cocked her head. "But at least he got to see Maggie, right?"

"No one let him see her."

"Gosh, they were mean, Grandma. But he can see her now, right?"

"Yes."

"So she finally gets a dad, and I get a grandpa."

"Absolutely."

"Does he want to see you, too?"

"I guess."

"And you want to see him?"

"Sure."

"So it should be a happy time."

"Yes…especially since we're all going to see you give your cheers."

"And have pizza."

Claire laughed and Abby joined in, but a serious question followed. "So you don't think Maggie's mad at me?"

"Of course not."

"Will you tell her I'm not mad at her either? And remind her to come on Thursday?"

"I'd be glad to."

"I love you, Grandma."

Claire gave the dear child a hug and praised God for her blessings.

***

Later that evening, finally alone in the guestroom, Claire dropped onto the comfortable bed. Covering her eyes with her hands, she moaned out loud. It was time, time she answered Grant's email, and she still had no idea what to say. In fact, she figured it might take her the rest of her life to come up with a decent answer to his heartfelt apology.

After staring at the empty email reply page on her laptop and drawing a blank, Claire decided that writing in her journal might help and hoping against hope that it would, she grabbed her diary from the nightstand. What to write, what to write, what to write! First of all, she had to make note of the date. Now what? She closed her eyes and inhaled through her nose, taking in as much air as she could, holding it and releasing it through her mouth. She picked up her pen.

Dearest Journal,

I have to admit that Grant's apology blew me away. I never expected it and can hardly believe it. All I know is it touched me to my very soul. I'm not fully ready to forgive him, though, but I sure want to. I want this to be over, but I also want full disclosure. Is that too much to ask after all these years? I hardly think so.

Do I think he was trying to make me feel sorry for him? No. Do I think he was sincere? Yes. Would I accept his apology just to make him feel better? Yes, because he shouldn't take all the blame. Maybe that's what I should say...he shouldn't take all the blame.

I think that he's opened the door to forgiveness, and I want nothing more than to give it. I still have a few questions I need answered. If they were, I could let go of the last bits of resentment. Was I just a fool who believed every word he said or did he truly love me? Did he feel he had no control over what our parents did to keep us apart and give up trying to reach me? It sounds that way. Or did he try with all his might only to find roadblocks at his every turn? I'd like to believe he tried.

A rap at Claire's door came just a she'd closed her journal. She could see Kate's dark curls as the door opened, the light from the hallway shining behind her.

"Lucy, you have some splaining to do!" sassed Kate, closing the door behind her.

Claire laughed. "Come here, you!"

Kate leaped upon the bed, stretched out, and while holding her chin in one hand, glared at her mother. "I'm waiting. You want to tell me what's going on between you and Grant?"

After wiggling downward so her head was resting on the pillow, Claire looked her oldest daughter in the eye, grabbed a hand and kissed the knuckles before releasing it.

"Okay. I've been emailing. We just explain ourselves. I told him what happened…that's what he wanted to know…why I left you girls. Then he said he was sent to Brazil, that his parents took his passport so he couldn't get back here. He said not to blame myself for the depression, and that he understood what it does to people."

Kate stared wide-eyed. "So that's true…they really did send him away?"

"Yes, and he talked about the letters he sent explaining it all. I reminded him that I got the mail, and there were no letters. Of course, we know now that our parents worked together to keep us apart, so who knows."

"So after emailing, you got up the courage to ask him to the cheer program?"

Claire nodded. "I said that Abby wanted him to come since learning about him…the family tree and all."

"And he said he was coming?"

"Yes. I just have to send him times, directions."

Kate flopped onto her back. "Are you sure you're okay with it?"

With a shrug of her shoulders, Claire turned and reached for the laptop. Pushing herself up with her hands, she sat, dropped the computer onto her lap, and found her email account. "I've got something to show you. I mean, we emailed back and forth…not getting any closer…emotionally…you know… staying pretty cool…just answering each other questions. Then I got this."

After turning the laptop so her daughter could see the monitor, Claire waited. She saw her daughter's eyes glide across the sentences of the email and watched her cover her mouth in surprise.

"Oh Mom…oh, my gosh! What did you say? How did you answer him?"

"I don't know how, sweetie. I haven't yet. That's why I went to see Maggie. I needed some advice. I don't want to do anything wrong…diminish what it took for him to do this."

Kate was still then, staring a hole into the computer.

"What are you thinking?"

"That this is unbelievable…that you must feel better about him."

Claire nodded. "I do feel better, but what do I say now? He's feeling worse, like he doesn't deserve a thing."

"Well, I'm no counselor, but I'd say accept the apology; accept him, too, for who he is…for the grownup that he's become."

Claire smiled. "I'm going to remember that. What a good way to put it! So since I have to answer this, where and when on Thursday?"

"Well, we want her to be able to concentrate on her cheers, so I think he should come here to meet her first, and then we can all go to the game together. Let's get the initial meeting out of the way. How does that sound?"

"Okay, like three?"

"Yup…two or three…it's a half day of school, so the kids will be home all afternoon. I took it off, and I'm not on call either."

"Good for you. You need a break. And I'll take care of getting back to Grant."

Kate leaned over her mother and gave her a quick hug. "Thanks for doing this. I think it's another important step for Abs, don't you? I mean, one more piece to the puzzle."

Claire nodded.

"Besides that, Mom, I'm looking forward to seeing him, too. I remember him. I know I was only two or three the last time I saw him, but some of my first memories are of him."

"Really honey?"

"Yes. I distinctly remember him throwing me in the air and catching me. And horseback rides. I remember riding around on his back. Was that him?"

Choking up, Claire nodded. "Yes."

"I remember Uncle Harry…Grant's dad, too. Mom, he was great, he really was."

"I'm beginning to think he and Mama truly believed we shouldn't be together."

"Could be. Whatever it was, I know Grandma loved you. She tried to hide her feelings, but I'd hear her in her room, bawling her eyes out after every one of your visits."

Claire could barely speak. "I wish she would have told me."

"She wasn't good at that, Mom. She never showed her feelings. She was just trying to do what she thought was best…best for you and us…best for everyone."

"And I suppose you're going to tell me that Uncle Harry helped."

"He was a lot of fun, really. He took us everywhere, like on vacations that Grandma would never have been able to afford."

"Okay, but just answer me one thing," Claire said, blowing her nose before continuing. "You really thought he was an uncle, a relative of Grandma's?"

Kate nodded enthusiastically. "I always thought he was her brother…you know…the old bachelor brother."

Claire sighed. "He put on a really good act, didn't he?"

"I guess so…he never gave us a reason to doubt him."

***

Once she was alone, Claire pondered her reply to Grant's apology. There was one thing she knew for sure, and it baffled her. She'd been wounded when he never contacted her and wished him ill, but then she'd shut down emotionally, blocking out all memory of him. But now, since his anguished apology, she no longer wanted him to suffer, not for one more minute, not for one more hour. It was all she could think about, all she really cared about now. His wellbeing had suddenly become paramount; he'd humbled himself, he'd admitted wrongdoing, and her wounds were healed.

Claire really wanted to hear his voice, but she'd have to wait. There was no way she'd be able to talk to him now; she wouldn't be able to form the words. Email proved to be her best option for a while longer, so she settled into the only chair in the room, and with the computer on her lap, she began to key the most important words of her life.

Dear Grant,

I don't really know what to say except to thank you from the bottom of my heart for your apology. It meant more than you'll ever know. You've opened a door for us…a door that's been shut for an interminable amount of time…and I will never forget it.

You had to have known that you were everything to me. When you never came back, I assumed that it was because you didn't feel the same way toward me. I assumed that our relationship was a lie. Today, I learned differently.

Grant, I want you to know how proud I am of the courageous man you've become. You contacted me without knowing whether or not I'd reject you. Did I ever tell you how thrilled I was to hear from you? I'm sure I didn't. Then, facing possible rejection again and with noticeable humility, you contacted our daughter. Did you know then that you'd answered my every prayer? And now you've proven your courage once more with your heartfelt apology. Truthfully, I couldn't ask for anything more except to talk to you in person very soon.

I hope you believe me when I say that we are all looking forward to seeing you on Thursday. Please join us at Kate's home, 440 Pathway Place, before three. Abby understands your connection to our family and is thrilled to have grandparents like everyone else.
Yours,
Claire

Chapter 34

GRANT

It was Wednesday evening before Grant could give any attention at all to his personal email. In actuality, he'd been distracted the entire day…not by his heavy workload…but by the news of a safe deposit box he couldn't remember renting.

When Grant finally returned the call from the Madison branch of the Wisconsin Savings Bank…one of the many in his parents' fleet…he was told that the safe deposit box was registered in his name as well as his mother's. His father's name was not listed on the lease. After being informed that the yearly fee was due on the box, he was told that since his mother had passed, he should come to the bank with his key and remove the contents or pay the rental fee for another year. Key? What key? If he chose to do neither, the box will be reported as abandoned and the contents turned over to the state's unclaimed property office.

Grant thought he must be losing his mind. He had no idea that he shared a safe deposit box with his mother…ever. When he explained that he was never assigned a key, the teller told him that he couldn't access the box without it. He had to have the key to match the bank's own guard key, plus a signature and password. What the hell? He could care less what his mother kept in some old safe deposit box. Besides, he'd gone to the reading of her will like a good boy, learned what she had left him, and told her attorney to donate it to his favorite charity. He ended the short meeting by asking her lawyer to send him the receipt for the donation and marched out leaving his father and son sitting there, stunned. And now this. It was the last thing he wanted to think about, but he supposed he should call her lawyer to find out if he knew anything about the key or what was in the box so he could get on with the more important things in his life like sit around and daydream about the various responses Claire could come up with regarding his most recent email.

Tired and starving, Grant had no energy to cook a decent meal, but found some leftover roast beef and made a sandwich instead. Thinking that he probably shouldn't drink beer every night of the week, he poured himself a large glass of milk and headed down the dark hallway. It was mid September and dark by 7:30 now, so after taking a quick peek at the three-quarter moon, he flipped the switch to the lamps in his home office, giving the pine covered walls a comforting, warm glow...just what he needed.

Grant figured he'd better down the sandwich before checking his email because Claire's response just might spoil his appetite or make him vomit or even worse, give him a heart attack. He chuckled...he was in too good a shape for a heart attack... or maybe not. He swallowed his last bite and crossed his fingers before opening his email program. His temperature rose when he saw her name on his list of mail, so he quickly downed the ice cold milk. All he got out of it was a brain-freeze. It didn't cool him off like he'd hoped. All he could do now was ignore the headache, open the message, and hope for the best.

As it turned out, Grant couldn't have hoped for anything better. Sitting alone in his office, overcome with relief, he collapsed against his desktop, his forehead landing on his folded arms. Decades earlier, the pain of losing her had brought him to his knees. He'd had hope while he was writing the letters, hope that she'd read them and wait for him because if it was the last thing he did, he'd find a way back to her. It didn't happen that way because her whereabouts were kept from him, and since he wasn't given access to the family money, he had no means at his disposal and, therefore, no way to find her.

His studies became his obsession and later, his work as a defense attorney took over. He regretted, however, that his marriage and family took a back seat. He knew his ex-wife had forgiven him; she was the most compassionate person he'd ever known...and his son certainly held no grudges as far as he could tell. And now, after hearing from Claire, all was well with the world. He'd see her soon and this time, she'd be able to look him in the eye.

Chapter 35

CLAIRE

On Thursday, Claire awoke with the dawn, and it wasn't long until she began worrying about seeing Grant again. She faithfully stretched her way through her five rites before showering and dressing and making breakfast for the family. Try as she may, she couldn't stop thinking about Grant even though it was all about Maggie and Abby and their budding relationships with him. The interaction between the three of them was of the utmost importance now, especially since the youngster needed to figure out how she fit in with her biological family and how it would work from now on.

Perhaps she should just stay out of the way, Claire thought. She should just stay in the kitchen…her comfort zone…while the rest of them hovered around him. No one would be the wiser if she did. Yet, she couldn't help wondering what type of relationship he'd want now. Would they simply carry on as usual, emailing once in awhile and maybe run into each other when he was visiting Maggie or Abby? She guessed that she could do that without any problem. After spending years assuming he hated her for her part in the pregnancy, his heartfelt apology had cleared the air, so to speak, and they could move on with their lives like he'd said.

Unbeknownst to Claire, Kate had made appointments for the two of them to have their hair and nails done first thing that morning. Her daughter insisted she'd made the appointment way ahead of time, that it had nothing to do with the fact that Grant was coming to town that day.

Claire rolled her eyes, letting her daughter know that there'd better not be a hidden agenda, no ulterior motive. Kate simply asked her to take a look in the mirror. It was time. Truth be told, she hadn't been to a hairdresser in a month; her roots were showing and her nails were a mess.

Kate drove. In fact, she insisted on following her regular routine which included stopping for drive-through coffee on the way. They'd be sitting there for awhile, she said, with hair that needed coloring, cutting and styling not to mention getting their nails in shape; they'd be lucky if they'd be done by lunchtime.

When they were in the car and on the way, Claire asked Kate why they had to drive so far out of town, what was so special about the place. Kate laughed. She told Claire how thrilled she was when she found Attitude Galore because Carlene, the owner/operator, ran an exceptional place of business. Not only was it a full service salon, but Carlene had her own naturally curly hair to deal with. She was a miracle worker, Kate said, and since the two of them were similarly blessed, they needed an expert in the field; Carlene would know exactly how to color and style their unruly manes.

Shortly after they'd arrived at the salon, Claire noticed another reason for supporting the beauty shop. There on the walls were posters about an organization called "Cut It Out". She noticed business-type cards promoting the group at the checkout counter and in the restroom. Kate explained that the organization has partners all over the country…hundreds of salons belonged to the group, pledging to join the fight against domestic violence. Claire asked if Maggie had been to the beauty shop yet. Kate confirmed that she had and told her that Maggie would be doing a presentation there later to raise funds for the local women's shelter. Claire was reminded once again that her daughters' knew what they were doing, and what they were doing was for the greater good.

Two hours later, Claire and Kate, fresh from the beauty shop, headed to the elementary school to pick up their favorite third graders. Kate said that since Mac was committed until three and she had the cheer outfits at her place anyway, the girls might as well spend the afternoon in the backyard preparing for their show. When they got home, Claire made the girls some lunch, but they hardly touched a thing. Cheerleading had become their life, and the backyard, their stadium.

Leopards! Let's win!
First and Ten!
Do it again!
Leopards! Let's win!

Their cheers echoed throughout the neighborhood, down the pathway, and across Lake Louise. The women spent most of the afternoon in the kitchen, intermittently watching the girls cheer their hearts out or reminding them to save some energy for their show. Abby still insisted on ordering Pizza Palace pizza after the game. The women agreed that it was the girls' prerogative to plan what they wanted to eat for their party, and while everyone loved the popular hometown pizza, Claire wanted to celebrate by making lasagna. The adults would prefer it, she said as she tried to convince her daughter of the fact. And some garlic bread wouldn't hurt either. Claire, of course, got carried away with the menu, adding anti-pasta salad and green beans. She'd taken over the kitchen like she figured she would anyway, sending Kate off to the grocery store for supplies and then to the liquor store to find some good Merlot. Kate told Claire that she thought they needed a cake, too, and decided she'd pick up a chocolate Dairy Queen cake…Abby's favorite…on the way home.

Chapter 36

MAGGIE

As soon as Maggie knew the date of the cheerleading fest, she made sure that she could leave work early that day, blocking out the space on her calendar so she wouldn't accidentally make appointments only to cancel them later. The students she counseled needed her services and canceling appointments on her end would not be fair to any of them. In fact, a couple of them had very serious problems; calling off their sessions could set either of them back. She was there to help, not hinder their progress.

It was close to two when Maggie pulled up to the curb in front of her sister's house. She didn't get out of the car immediately; instead, she leaned back in her seat and said a prayer. She needed God's help with Abby, needed some direction, and hoped to find the right words when she saw her daughter.

After letting herself in, Maggie found her mother and sister in the kitchen, chatting away...seemingly without a care in the world. As she wound her way through the kitchen, she spotted the girls in the backyard. Before she could say anything, her mother's arms were around her, her lips bussing her cheek.

"She'll be so happy you came," Claire said, shaking her gently.

"I hope so."

Kate came around the kitchen island then and added her two cent's worth. "She gets it now, Mags. She's accepted as much as she's able...for her age."

Maggie nodded, repressing her true feelings. "Yup, okay."

"We've decided to have a celebration, darling. After all, it's much like a family reunion, isn't it?" Claire ventured.

"So Grant's coming?"

"I believe so. I told him two or three."

"Good. Now put me to work. I need something to do," Maggie ordered, breathing deeply and exhaling, releasing some anxiety.

Claire laughed. "It's going to be fine…believe me, honey…just fine." She handed her a knife and a long loaf of French bread. "You know how to make garlic bread?"

"Of course," Maggie answered, smiling.

"Garlic bread? I thought we were having pizza?" It was George, talking as he walked into the room. "Hey, what's going on? I see real food!"

Kate left her station to give her husband a hug. "It's your lucky day. Mom's cooking. You've still got to order pizza for the girls though."

Feigning relief, the slightly overweight teddy bear wiped his brow. "Thank you, Claire. You saved my life. The thought of having pizza again just about did me in."

Claire laughed. "Hey, you've been eating pretty good since I got here."

George patted his belly. "That's true, and I've got the figure to prove it."

Kate rolled her eyes. "We all do."

Maggie had just sliced the bread and started to butter it when the girls came flying in the back door.

"We're thirsty," Abby yelled before plopping down on a chair, exhausted, her head dropping onto her folded arms. Lily followed, falling into a chair next to her friend, head back, eyes closed, panting loudly.

"Okay," Kate said, "you can have some milk, but eat those apple slices and cheese, too. Then head upstairs and change your clothes."

Lifting her head and turning to look at her mother, Abby started to whine about 'who knows what' when she spotted Maggie standing at the island. Maggie's stomach did a flip. Her prayers had not been answered; she had no idea what to say to the child. As it turned out, she didn't have to say anything. Abby stood, staring at Maggie, mouth agape, before running around the island to make contact with her biological mother. Wrapping her arms around Maggie's waist, she hugged her as hard as she could.

"I'm sorry I wasn't nice to you," Abby whispered into Maggie's shirt.

"I understand. This is hard, honey," Maggie said, kissing the blond curls.

The sweet girl looked her in the eye and smiled. "But this is a good day, isn't it?"

"Yup, for sure."

Suddenly, the child turned to her grandmother. "What time's he coming, Grandma?"

"Anytime now, so eat up and get dressed or we'll be late."

Abby must have noticed what the women were doing because, suddenly, a scowl came over her brow. "Why are you cooking all this stuff? I thought we were getting pizza?"

Kate laughed. "We are. Dad is going to call when they open at five and order it. We just wanted a little extra because you're going to be starved after all that cheering."

"Good idea, Mom." Abby seemed satisfied with her mother's explanation and bounded out of the room to race her friend up the stairs.

"Good save," Claire said, chuckling under her breath.

"I've been doing this for awhile."

Maggie walked toward her sister, grabbed her shoulders, and began a soothing massage. "And what a good job you've done."

Kate turned her head, giving her sister a buss on the cheek. "Thanks for giving me the chance...and, oh, oh, keep doing that!"

***

Mac had spoken to Maggie earlier in the week, told her that he had a staff meeting he couldn't miss, and said he'd meet them at the football stadium instead. He said he'd be sure to save some good seats since he'd probably beat them there, considering she had a house full of women to get to the game on time. Maggie told him that George would be bringing the girls as soon as Grant showed up.

When Grant hadn't arrived by 3:30, Maggie grabbed her smart phone, touched the contact icon, and then tapped Grant's number. There was no answer. She called his home, followed by his office; the result was the same…no one was answering any of his phones. She left messages at all three places just in case, but the girls had to get going so George had no choice but to leave with the two of them in tow. The three women followed, albeit reluctantly, shortly thereafter.

The parking lot of the university stadium where the high school teams played was packed, so Kate drove around until she found parking on a side street about a block away. She mentioned then that she'd never seen so many cars in the lot for a junior varsity game. The women laughed; Abby had proudly informed them earlier that all the girls on her little cheerleading team were inviting their grandparents, and it looked as though she was right. As they crossed the busy highway at the intersection, Maggie tried to contact her father; still no answer…the call went straight to voicemail.

As she walked, Maggie could feel her head begin to prickle and her face flush. Her heart lodged in her throat; her pulse quickened. *Dear God, Please don't let anything happen to him now…not now!*

As the three women hurriedly crossed the street, Claire grabbed Maggie's arm and pressed against her. "Where is he?"

Maggie, in a desperate attempt to ignore her anxiety, answered calmly. "He might already be here. Maybe he was running late, so he went directly to the stadium."

"Yeah, okay. Or maybe he simply turned off his cell so his staff couldn't get in touch with him. I'm sure they're plenty busy…probably didn't want him taking any time off."

Nodding, Maggie patted her mother's arm. "Yup…it's probably something like that."

Maggie had no idea why junior varsity football was such a big deal until she saw the 'Welcome Parents' banner above the entrance to the stadium. The parking lot was packed, people stood in line for tickets, and she could see a concession stand on the other side of the gate. She guessed she was happy that Mac, the smart aleck, was saving them seats. Otherwise, they'd have been plum out of luck.

After climbing the metal steps to the first level of bleachers, the women searched the place for Mac and George...and hopefully, Grant, too. Of course, they spotted Mac almost immediately, standing and waving his arms above his head to get their attention. Maggie couldn't help noticing how adorable he looked in his jeans and Lake Louise Leopards sweatshirt. She gave him a warm smile as she returned the wave, indicating she saw him and hoping he'd sit down before he made a fool of himself. As the women neared Mac, they saw George and Aunt Galen sitting there, spread out across the bleachers, holding their precious spots for them. Galen sat in the first row, her purse and her sweater saving their seats. Claire sat next to her, followed by Kate who sidled up next to her husband. Mac patted the spot next to him directly behind her sister and mother. Maggie couldn't resist the invitation, and Mac gave her a quick kiss after pulling her in next to him on the bleachers.

"Where's Grant," he asked after second or two.

"Never showed up," she whispered. "I haven't been able to reach him either.

Mac grimaced. "I hope everything's okay."

"Yup, me, too. Abby was really looking forward to this."

"He could still show up. Maybe he's one of those guys who won't answer the phone in the car. You know...a cautious driver...following all the rules."

Suddenly Kate turned toward them, poking their knees to get their attention. "They're coming out. Oh...look how cute they are."

A couple dozen little third graders raced across the football field to the home team side of the stadium. Maggie noticed that Abs wasn't the same little girl that left the house earlier. In fact, the entire group of girls had their hair in lopsided ponytails, held together with golden pompom-like ties. She leaned toward her sister. "Do you see makeup?"

Kate turned, nodded, and rolled her eyes. Then they both got the giggles.

After forming a very long line directly in front of the bleachers, the girls began to cheer. Abby and Lily stood right next to each other, close enough so their parents could see them easily and, of course, waved their pompoms enthusiastically.

Clap, clap, cheer, cheer
We are the leopards from LLHS
Here to prove the blue and gold
A step above the rest!

When the cheer was over, the younger girls jumped and shook their pompoms. The teens did cartwheels close behind the cheering youngsters. The parents, grandparents, as well as friends and family of the players, cooperated with the youngsters, clapping right along with them. More cheers followed as the junior varsity players ran onto the field.

Leopard fans
Stand up and cheer
This is our year!

The stands erupted with stomping and yelling. Everyone joined in…the enthusiasm was infectious, to say the least.

During the plays, the girls sat on the sideline, their pompoms lying neatly in front of them. Every so often, one of the girls would turn to look for her parents. Mac gave Lily a thumbs-up when she looked his way. She'd simply grin and then turn to face the field. Abby, however, did not turn around as often; instead, she could be seen pulling grass out of the turf. The destruction of the field didn't last long, however, because the JV cheerleaders would have them up and cheering for every touchdown and extra point, then again between the downs, timeouts, and kick off's. Sometimes they'd leave the pompoms on the sideline and simply clap along with their cheers.

One, two, three, four
Go Leopards, go!

Chapter 37

CLAIRE

Concentrating on her granddaughter and her cheers did little to stop irrational thoughts from invading Claire's brain. God was going to get her for every hateful thought she'd ever had about Grant. It was true that there were times in her life she'd wished he were dead. Back then, it was simply a logical reason for his absence, and it was better than thinking how much he must have hated her for ruining their lives. God had to know that everything she'd imagined those many years ago were nothing more than emotional responses to abandonment. There would be no reason to punish her now. But then, where was he? And what possible reason could he have for not answering even one of his phones?

By half-time, Claire was beside herself, her train of thought taking off in the direction of déjà vu. But why? Why would he abandon them again? She berated herself for accepting his apology; it was simply a farce, an evil charade. She tried to shake off, forced her mind to concentrate on the present and faced forward as the girls did a cheer dance in the middle of the field to a popular hip-hop melody.

I wanna see you move, move, move.
I wanna see you shake, shake, shake.
I wanna see you drop, drop, drop.

The stands were rocking with the girls' song; fans, parents, and grandparents singing right along with the budding cheerleaders. Claire stood to do the same, but when the blood rushed to her brain, and her hands and feet began to tingle, she dropped onto the bleachers to breathe. *How could I be such a fool?*

Kate didn't seem to notice that her mother was no longer singing, or standing for that matter, but Maggie bent toward her from behind and touched her shoulder.

"Mom, you okay?"

Claire shook her head without looking at her daughter and concentrated on her breath.

"Do you need to leave?"

Claire, sensing a breakdown, nodded, and then heard Maggie tell Mac that she had to take her mother home. Momentarily, Kate figured out what was going on and quickly handed Maggie her car keys.

When they were alone in the car a few minutes later, Claire could no longer hold back the tears. "I'm so sorry Maggie. I wouldn't have told him about you if I thought he'd do this. I thought he'd act like a grownup, you know, want to be a father, want to take responsibility."

"I know what you're thinking, Mom. You're remembering the hurt...it's all coming back, isn't it? You think he did this on purpose or something, don't you?"

Claire nodded, grabbed tissues, and blew her nose.

"Mom, don't do this... he'd never hurt you again. Ever!"

"You don't know any such thing," Claire chided, livid.

Maggie grabbed her mother's knee and gave it a shake. "Mom, he really cares about you. He's told me that...Greg told me the same thing. Something else has happened. Something else is going on."

"I wished him dead, you know? God knows I didn't mean it...I really didn't."

Claire covered her daughter's hand with her own. Maggie shook her leg again and told her to stop it...everything would be okay. Claire thought otherwise, but kept it to herself. *God forgive me.*

Chapter 38

MAGGIE

After lecturing her mother on Grant's virtues until she couldn't stand the sound of her own voice, Maggie suggested that Claire wash her face and straighten up…the family would be coming through the door any minute. She returned to the main level, and while she was alone in the kitchen, Maggie tried his numbers one more time. It went straight to voicemail. It didn't make any sense at the time, but she figured that they'd eventually learn what happened. Good news or bad, what mattered now was Abby and Lily and their little party. Thinking about how cute the girls looked, makeup and all, brought a smile to Maggie's face and put her in a better mood. The girls did a great job and deserved a celebration…and they'd get one no matter what.

Since the food was prepared ahead of time, Maggie simply warmed the lasagna in the oven along with the garlic bread. She pulled the salad out of the refrigerator, topped it with dressing, and tossed it before shoving the tongs into the bowl. Kate had set the table before they left, so all Maggie had to do now is fill the glasses with water, lemon slices, and ice. And, when the doorbell rang, she opened it to find a Pizza Palace delivery boy standing on the porch…not Grant, as she'd imagined.

The food was ready and the house would be full of people in a matter of minutes, so Maggie headed up the stairs of her sister's house to the room she once called her own and knocked. "Mom? Ready?"

"Uh huh."

"Okay…they'll be here soon so hop to it."

The door opened then and Maggie saw her mother looking as good as new, but she couldn't help giving her a little more encouragement. "Everything will work out. Come on…let's party!"

Claire grabbed her daughter and gave her a warm hug. "What would I do without you?"

"Just fine, I'm sure!" Maggie retorted with a giggle.

"So you haven't heard anything yet?"

"No, Mom. You'll be the first to know."

"Okay, okay…let's do this then."

***

As far as the girls were concerned, the party was an unequivocal success. Abby was quieter than usual, but Maggie explained that things like this happen, that something very important must have happened to force Grant to miss her cheer show. She explained how he could have been called into court, that a new case could have come up, and that he was the most important attorney in Dane County. She told her that if someone committed a crime against anyone in that county, he'd work very hard to put that person in jail. Abby agreed that she didn't want a bad guy running loose either. Maggie's explanation must have satisfied her because her mood changed for the better. Her mother's frame of mind was another story. Maggie could see that she was trying her best, smiling at the girls' antics and laughing at Mac's goofy jokes. But every once in a while, she'd see her staring out the window or down at her hands. Maggie figured that was all she could expect considering the circumstances.

It was way past nine when the girls became surly and before Maggie could say good night, her cell chimed. She ran to retrieve it from the kitchen counter as the others in the room shushed one another in order to eavesdrop on her conversation.

Maggie smiled and covered her phone. "It's Grant," she said, turning to face the family before giving him her full attention.

"Are you okay?" she asked, keeping an eye on her mother the

entire time.

"Yes…honey…I'm so sorry."

"Just so you're okay. You know how imaginations run wild," she said.

"Yes…well…I couldn't use my cell at the hospital."

"Hospital? What happened?" Maggie asked as she watched her mother's hands fly to cover her mouth.

"It's my dad…he's had an episode…a massive stroke. He's not going to make it, honey. They have him on life support."

"Oh…Grant, I'm so sorry," Maggie said before dropping onto the nearest kitchen chair.

"So Greg and I have been at the hospital since before noon…we felt we had to sit right with him in case something happened…you know what I mean?"

"Yes…I understand. It's no problem. We figured something went wrong."

"Can you tell Abby how sorry I am that I wasn't there?"

"Yes…of course."

"And Claire…I so wanted to talk to her."

"I'll tell her." Maggie promised, giving her mother a shy smile.

"Okay, honey. I've got to go. We have to figure out what to do. I'll call you tomorrow. Okay?"

"Yes…I'm so sorry, Grant. Thanks for letting us know. Bye."

***

Later, when the house was quiet again, the women collapsed on the large sofa in the living room. Feeling a chill in the air, Kate decided to ignite the pilot light on the gas hearth in preparation for the coming winter. Claire hadn't acclimated to the cool Wisconsin evenings anyway and wanted nothing other than to cuddle with her daughters in front of the toasty fireplace. They sat, sipping their favorite beverages, mesmerized by the flames flickering behind the glass.

Finally, Maggie decided to break the silence. "Mom" she said quietly. "What are you thinking?"

Claire shook her head and stared a hole into her wine glass. "Nothing."

"Come on. We have to talk about it."

"Sometimes you're such a pain...you know that?"

Maggie, surprised by the comment, backed away from her mother.

Claire quickly grabbed her daughter's hand and kissed her knuckles. "Sorry, honey. It's just hard, that's all. I've done nothing but think about it. I mean, on one hand, that man and my mother did whatever they could to keep us apart. On the other, they took really good care of you girls when I couldn't."

"Good old Uncle Harry. He was a pretty good grandfather after all, huh?" Maggie said, her voice softening.

Kate nodded. "I'm not even a blood relative, and I thought the world of him. Too bad we didn't keep in touch after Grandma died."

"We were grown up and gone by then, Kate. Besides, now we know she was the one he really cared about," Maggie reminded her.

"You couldn't prove it by me. Remember how excited we got when we knew he was coming to town?"

"That's because Grandma would be in a really good mood while he was visiting."

"But we figured that we were in for some fun, too," Kate added.

A frown came over Claire's face. "I still can't believe that I never heard about him when I visited. I mean, I stayed with you for a few days each time...you'd think it would've come up."

"We probably talked about him...just called him our uncle or something. You probably didn't think anything of it because Grandma had a couple of brothers."

"Why didn't I ever run into him or Grant either for that matter?"

"Mom," said Maggie, "the timing of Uncle Harry's visits was most likely planned that way, don't you think? If they were keeping you and Grant apart, they'd have to do some serious scheduling."

"Yeah, we were pretty horrible...Grant and I," Claire said mockingly.

Maggie ignored her mother's sarcasm, her voice taking on a serious tenor. "Do you hate Grandma for it?"

"No. And I don't really know why I don't. I just can't, I guess."

"Why do you say that?"

"Because she knew that I was in no condition to raise you two, and she was right about sending me away for help. I'm indebted to her for that, you know."

"And what about Uncle Harry?"

"Well, he did clear some things up for Grant and me, didn't he? In some small way I guess I'm grateful for that. I just hope the two of them got a chance to talk…you know, clear the air."

"Because you and Grandma didn't," Maggie stated matter-of-factly.

Claire nodded. "Maybe she would have confessed or something. Come to think of it, did I ever thank you girls for taking care of everything…the funeral arrangements and all? "

Kate answered that one. "I'm sure you did. Besides we were close by…you'd moved to Phoenix by then."

"Oh, that's right," Claire said before turning to face Maggie again. "Grant said they had him on life support, huh?"

Kate piped in. "That's not good. Probably no brain activity. He may already be gone."

Maggie heard her mother take a ragged breath.

"Poor Grant," Claire said, tears brimming her eyes. "I hope he's okay. We should send flowers."

The girls, sitting on either side of their mother, patted her, and one of them wrapped an arm around her. The other merely pressed her head against her mother's shoulder and nodded.

Chapter 39

CLAIRE

Claire barely slept, churning fitfully throughout the night, so when her cell chirped at ten in the morning, she groaned in agony. Even though she was half asleep and because she was used to being on call for Martha's Place, she rolled over in bed and quickly grabbed her cell from the nightstand.

"Hello?" she croaked.

"Claire...it's Grant."

Startled, she rattled, "Oh, Grant."

"Dad's gone, Claire. He never regained consciousness."

"I'm so sorry."

"The service is Tuesday at 10. We're having it at the largest church we can find. Lots of people knew Dad."

"That's good, so you'll have lots of seating."

"I think we're going to need to seat a thousand or so."

Claire blinked in surprise. "You expect a thousand people?"

"He was well known. We're planning to feed that many afterwards, too."

"Well, if they don't show up, you can give the non-perishables to the homeless shelter or food pantry."

Claire heard Grant chuckle. "Leave it to you to think of that."

"Just saying."

She heard him clear his throat. "I'd like you to come."

"Me? Come to the funeral?"

"Yes…you and Maggie and Kate…and the rest of the family if they'd like."

"Are you sure? I mean, your son…your ex…I'm not sure we belong there, Grant."

"Yes, you do… all three of you."

Claire was at a loss for words.

"Did you hear me Claire? I need you and the girls with me. I want my family with me."

"Your family is there."

"Yes, I have family here, but you were the first, my first family…you and the girls."

A vise gripped her heart. "Grant…I don't want to interfere..."

"Interfere? You belong here. The girls loved my dad. Maggie told me that."

"Okay…I'll tell the girls what you said."

"Claire. Please. I need all of you here. Please."

"I wouldn't feel right, Grant. He didn't want me around, remember?"

"But he tried to make it right by taking care of the girls for us."

"But your ex …I just don't want to make anyone uncomfortable."

"Listen. Holly has known about you since before we were married. She'd love to meet you. And Greg would like Maggie to be there."

Claire could hear his voice crack, and it broke her heart. "Okay…we'll talk about it."

"And remember…I was going to adopt Katie…she was going to be mine, too. I lost all of you! Promise me, Claire. I can't do this without you."

"Yes, you can. You've done everything without me."

"That's before I found you, Claire. I don't want to do this or anything else without you ever again."

Claire snapped her phone shut, curled up, and cried for the lost years.

***

Since she'd overslept and then cried herself to sleep after Grant's call, it had to be about noon. Feeling disoriented after sleeping so late and thinking everyone must have left for the day, Claire wandered out of her room without throwing on a robe over her men's style pajamas or getting dressed first. When she arrived at the bottom of the stairs and turned into her daughter's kitchen, she saw that she was anything but alone. There sat Maggie with her back to her, facing her sister as they sat at the kitchen table.

"Good afternoon, sleepyhead," Kate greeted, leaning to one side.

Maggie swung her head around. "Hey."

A frown crossed Claire's face. "What's everyone doing home?"

"No school…in-service for the teachers, I guess."

"And I just stopped by for lunch," Maggie added.

Claire padded past her daughters to the coffee pot. "Why didn't someone get me up?"

"You needed some rest…yesterday was an emotional roller coaster," Maggie said.

Claire nodded. "I guess. Where's Abs?"

"Birthday party…all afternoon. Tomorrow it'll be the Homecoming parade. She and Lily beg to go every year. Mac and George always take them. It's tradition."

"Kids still like parades?"

Kate chuckled. "They don't really care about the parade…just the candy that's tossed from the floats."

"And the guys want to take them?"

"No need to feel sorry for them…there's a football game afterwards."

"Another football game?"

"And then the Packers play the Vikings on Sunday. The guys are in seventh heaven!"

"Yeah, testosterone heaven!" Claire smiled, shook her head in dismay, and sat down next to Maggie because she had the daily newspaper in front of her. "Done reading this?" she asked.

"Sure," Maggie answered as she slid it toward her mother.

"You girls want to go to the Mall of America or something? I haven't been there in years."

Kate shook her head. "No thanks. We just need to sit and talk."

"Talk about what?"

"You know…Tuesday. What are you going to do about Tuesday."

"What about it?"

"Grant called both of us, Mom. We know the funeral's on Tuesday," Kate said.

Claire concentrated on her coffee.

"We're going," Maggie stated. "Kate and I are going."

"I figured as much," Claire confessed.

Maggie grabbed her mother's arm, accidently spilling some of her hot coffee.

"Stop it," Claire said, frowning.

"Sorry, Mom. Are you coming with us or not?"

"I haven't decided."

Maggie bent over and peeked up at her mother. "We want you to come. He does, too."

"I know. He told me."

"We're going down on Monday evening so we don't have to get up so early to make the drive."

"Really?"

"Yup...staying at the Concordia...your favorite hotel!"

Claire shook her head. "I don't know."

"You've got something else planned?" Kate teased. "Job hunting perhaps?"

Claire, ignoring her daughter's attempt at humor, swallowed hard. "I don't belong there. I feel like…I don't know…like the black sheep or something."

"Hey, there are plenty of them on both sides of this family."

Claire raised an eyebrow in agreement. "I don't have anything to wear."

"Oh, please!"

"My car only holds two adults."

Maggie chuckled. "We're taking mine."

"Come on, nobody wants me there."

"I can name a couple who do…no one else will even know who you are."

Claire rolled her eyes. "Can we sit way in the back?"

"Sure."

"We aren't going to hang around afterwards, are we?"

"Just let us know when you're ready to leave and we'll leave."

"Promise."

"Of course, Mom. We get it. We know this is hard for you. We just want to make an appearance for Grant and Greg…that's all…show them we care. That's it."

Chapter 40

GRANT

Thursday had been the longest day of Grant's life, and Friday wouldn't be much better; he had a lot to do before the funeral. His assistant, Barbara volunteered to spend the morning contacting the press and state employees. Grant met briefly with his father's lawyer who told him that his father wanted to be cremated…simply another surprise… and then offered to contact the members the state bankers' association. Greg said he'd take care of the relatives, calling the handful he knew of and asking them to spread the word about the arrangements for his grandfather. He'd also made arrangements for serving food after the service. Grant surmised that Greg was a lot more mature than he was at that age, and his heart swelled with pride.

Later on in the day, Grant met with the family's pastor who told him that his father had planned the service in advance. In fact, he learned that the music, prayers, and bible verses had been hand-picked by his father shortly after Grant's mother passed away. Grant had no idea about any of it, but the fact that his father did something without his knowledge was nothing new anymore and only served to remind him of his mother and the surreptitious safe deposit box. Grant made a mental note to give his mother's lawyer a call on Monday. The man had to know about the safe deposit box and whether or not there were any other skeletons in his mother's closet. He wanted to tie up all the loose ends as far as she was concerned because he'd soon have to deal with his dad's stuff and one parent's baggage at a time was plenty as far as he was concerned.

Saturday flew by as Grant and Greg continued contacting everyone they knew. Thank God for Sunday…the day of rest. Grant could finally put his feet up, that was true, but truly restorative rest eluded him. Exhausted mentally but unable to sleep, Grant spent Sunday morning preparing brunch for his son. As was their tradition, he'd be over to watch the Packers at noon. Spending the afternoon with his son would prove to be the first time in a long time that Grant thought about something other than his unhealthy relationship with his deceased father and his desire to reconnect with Claire before it was too late.

Monday arrived with the dawn, and Grant had only one thing on his mind. He made the call at 8 AM, and sure enough, his mother's lawyer had something for him and told him he was glad he'd called. They agreed to meet that afternoon and when they did, the attorney simply stated how sorry he was to hear about his father, but according to his mother's will, what he needed to give him could not be handed over until his father had passed on, too. They shook hands and Grant secretly prayed that he'd never have to see the guy again. He'd been his mother's lawyer and anything that had to do with his mother left a bad taste in his mouth.

Grant walked out of the office with a 9 x 12 catalog style envelope in his hands and unfastened the metal clasp as he scurried into the dimly lit stairwell where he'd hope to have some privacy. After firmly closing the door behind him, he stood on the third floor landing and opened the envelope to find a key, a small card with a series of numbers written on it, and a plain square envelope. The envelope was open; in fact, it looked as though it had never been sealed shut. Grant felt his blood drain from his body as he slumped against the cement wall and slid downward until he hit the steps. *What was so important that his mother had to keep it from him until they'd both passed on!*

After shoving the key and the smaller card in his suit coat pocket, he pulled a small, unimpressive piece of card stock from the envelope, his hands shaking with the fear of the unknown. He attempted to read the note, but there was barely enough light in the stairwell for Grant to make out the handwriting. Was it written in pencil? He could see that it had faded…it was barely legible…so he stood and held it as close as he could to the bulb in the stairwell.

To my precious son,
    When you read this note, your father and I will be long gone.
    Enclosed is a key to a safe deposit box and a code. Take these to the Wisconsin Savings Bank on State Street, and they will allow you access to the box. Everything will be explained when you open it. You may choose to ignore my request. Please don't. You will understand everything when you see the contents.
Love, your mother

Spurred on by the note, Grant continued down the stairway until he was out of the law building. After recovering from the blinding sunlight, he hurried the three blocks to the Wisconsin Savings Bank, jaywalking and swerving through traffic as he ran. He entered through the wide, heavy duty glass doors and slowed his pace as he crossed the marble floor of the magnificent foyer of his father's bank, the first in the franchise. When he approached the first teller's window, one of the others recognized him and offered her condolences. Several of the tellers chimed in then and after politely acknowledging them, Grant finally asked one of them how to access his safe deposit box. The familiar employee, a bright, cheery woman dressed in the bank's uniform…navy skirt and gold jacket…lead him to an office in the back of the bank. There he was greeted by Carroll John, a vice president and good friend of his father's, who asked him to take a seat.

"So sorry to hear about your father, Junior. You have my sympathies."

"Thank you, Carroll. Now about my safe deposit box. Can you tell me when it was that I signed for it?" Grant asked, hoping to get the show on the road.

"Of course." The elderly man opened a drawer in the desk with a key from his pocket, pulled out a manila folder, and opened it on the ornate cherry wood desktop. After pulling out a form, he slid it towards him. "Have a look. You and your mother signed this in May of 1970."

"Wow, I don't remember that at all."

"Well, what were you doing at the time?"

"May of '70? I was just graduating from high school."

"Hmm, perhaps your mother thought you needed the box for your birth certificate, passport, or savings bonds. Things like that."

"It doesn't ring a bell. Well, anyway, I'm here now so I guess I should check it out."

"Okay then. Just sign your name and fill in the password."

Grant did as he was told, signing his name and carefully copying the code from the small card he'd found in the envelope earlier.

"Good...now the key."

Grant rummaged around in his suit coat pocket and finally handed him the key.

"Okay, great. Follow me please."

They both stood and Carroll passed in front of Grant and walked to another door in the back of the bank. He unlocked the door, pushed it open, and the two of them stepped down the stairs to some kind of vault. Using the secret combination of numbers, Carroll spun the tumbler, unlocked that door, and motioned for Grant to enter. He did as he was told although he was surprised that the vault was there. He'd never been in that part of the bank the entire time his father was president.

"Box 4102," Carroll stated firmly.

They both searched for it, but Grant was the first to spot the metal door, toward the back of the room, at waist level. The elderly man used two keys to open it; Grant's and one belonging to the bank. The door swung open, and Carroll slid out the long, metal box and carried it to a nearby table.

Holding his palm outward, John motioned to Grant. "I'll leave you alone now. Just call for me when you're finished."

Grant nodded before turning to pull a metal chair out from under the table. He sat, placing his shaking hands on either side of the box. Ignoring the knot forming in his stomach, he took a deep breath and lifted the attached cover from the box, letting it hang off of one end.

His next breath caught in his throat. There, tied together with ordinary twine, was a collection of envelopes, the one on top addressed to Grant. After cautiously sliding it from the bundle, he spotted Claire's name and her Rock Creek address on the next envelope. His chest burned with indignation when he recognized the Brazilian postage stamp on the red, white, and blue airmail envelope and noticed that it wasn't postmarked. *What the hell!*

Despite the fact that he was in shock and sick to his stomach, Grant felt as though a miracle had taken place; indeed, there was a God. He really didn't care what the top letter said. All he cared about were the letters he'd written to his beloved. He piled them onto his lap, counting out loud as he shuffled through them. There were seventeen in all. He couldn't remember just then how many he'd written, but he'd never forget what it felt like when she never wrote back. Eventually and with a heavy heart, he had no choice but to give up trying to reach her.

Flooded with an astonishing sense of relief, he now understood why she never wrote to him and knew she hadn't lied about never getting the letters either. Her mother hadn't kept them from her, and his father may have known nothing about them. The explanation had to be hidden within the first envelope; he ripped it open, angrily tossing the envelope to the floor.

My dear son,

Please forgive me. I did not want you to ruin your life, and I did whatever I could to make sure that wouldn't happen. You had so much potential, and you were throwing it away.

When I learned that your girlfriend already had one child, I could only imagine why she went after you. You, my poor boy fell for her…you didn't have a chance. I'd seen her from a distance, spoken to her on the telephone. I'd seen that lovely face, that figure…I'd heard the sweet voice. There was no doubt in my mind that she knew exactly what she was doing. My job, dear boy, was to protect the family fortune…protect it for you, protect your future.

Once you were safely in the hands of my father in Brazil, and I had your passport in mine, I assumed that my job was done. My father informed me otherwise. His dear friend and confidant, the postmaster, brought your first letter to my father. He wanted his permission to send it on. Oh, you had the correct postage, you had addressed it properly, but the postmaster knew the details surrounding your visit. He wanted to honor the family by following our wishes.

My father called me to tell me about the letter. I told him to keep it, to keep them all. He did just that, and when he returned to the U.S., he handed them to me unopened. I kept them at home, but then when my health deteriorated, I decided to drop them into this box.

I've been thrilled with your fine career, your wife, and your son. You made wonderful choices after all. I don't know if the letters even mean anything to you now, but I promised my father that I'd give them to you someday. He'd always had mixed feelings about keeping them from you in the first place. So this time, I'm following his wishes. Love, your mother

Suddenly transported back in time, Grant again experienced the crushing blow, the anguish he felt when Claire never wrote back. *Yes, Mother, her name is Claire.* This time, however, the sucker punch had been delivered by his mother, his dead mother. He thought he knew what she was capable of, but this was a new low. Always cold, controlling, and calculating, she continued to interfere in his life from the grave. He wondered if this despicable offense was enough to send her straight to hell.

The letters! I have the letters, and Claire will no longer doubt my love for her. Unbeknownst to his mother, Grant had a new lease on life. What do they say about the thin line between love and hate? He couldn't remember, but as much as he hated his mother, he loved her for saving the letters, for not destroying them like she probably wanted to do. And then there was his grandfather…he really owed him. He always knew how much his grandfather loved him. He'd seen it in his eyes and heard it in his voice when he praised him, especially when he'd spend his free time working with the poor. Grant wished he could talk to his dead grandfather right then and there, but he knew that was impossible. Perhaps the man could see him from heaven above, he thought. Grant raised his eyes to the ceiling and thanked his grandfather properly.

Chapter 41

CLAIRE

Claire really dragged her feet getting ready for the trip to Madison for the funeral. She'd recently said goodbye to the place, hoping never to set foot in the town again. But here she was…expected to attend the funeral of a man who did everything in his power to keep her and Grant apart. She knew deep down in her heart of hearts that he took good care of her girls, but he'd also conspired against her, and that hateful revelation cancelled out any good he'd done. Her daughters needn't worry, though; she'd get ready to go and she'd do so in a timely manner because she'd promised herself that she'd never do anything to disappoint them again.

After loading their overnight bags into the trunk of Maggie's Lincoln and before piling into the car, Kate began begging to sit in the front. She still got carsick, she said; she still hadn't outgrown it after all these years. Claire learned something new about her girls whenever they were together lately; the story about car sickness was news to her, too.

Settled in the back seat, Claire began her inquisition. "So when was the last time you were sick?"

"I don't know. Twenty some years ago, I guess."

"What makes you think you'd still get sick?"

"Because I will never forget the last time."

"What happened?" Claire asked, thinking this was serious.

Kate turned in her seat and faced her mother. "This is gross, Mom. Remember how I said I was a cheerleader? Well, this was eighth grade.

I'd had orange soda at the game and didn't think anything about it at the time. I hadn't gotten sick in a while I guess. Anyway, on the way home in the backseat of my gym teacher's car, I had to vomit. I had no idea what to do, so I just opened the shoebox holding my brand new white sneakers and threw up on them. I was sure nobody saw me so I just put the cover back on the box and stared straight ahead."

"Weren't there any other people in the back seat?" Claire asked, amazed.

"Yup. Girls on both sides of me."

"And they didn't notice?"

"I guess they pretended not to."

"What about when you got home? Mama must have had a conniption."

"I just handed them to her, told her what happened, and off she went to clean them up."

"I can't believe that...I would have gotten yelled at," said Claire.

"Yes, but remember, I never did anything wrong."

"You would have to remind me."

The women laughed at their mother and since they had a lot of time to kill, must have decided that Claire owed them a tale or two.

"Okay, Mom. You must have some stories about your childhood," Maggie suggested as she glanced at her mother through the rear view mirror.

"All I can remember is anxiety...about everything...planting, harvesting, too little rain, too much rain. Hail damage...crops ruined...bankers circling the place, bill collectors too.

"Shoot! Well, then you must have some good stories about Grant. Tell us about how you met," Maggie continued.

"Really? It's not very interesting."

"Come on, just one story then we'll leave you alone...promise."

"You're going to make me wish I'd stayed home," Claire complained as she turned her head and stared out the window.

"One story. Please," whined Maggie.

"Okay. I met him my first day of college. He and I were in the same class." Claire said before pausing and returning her gaze to the scenery flying by the window.

"That's not a story…that's a couple of sentences. Okay, here's a hint. What did you think of him when you first laid eyes on him?"

Claire chuckled. "I'm not telling my daughters that kind of stuff?"

"Well, if you tell us stuff…we'll tell you some juicy stuff, too. Okay?" Kate cajoled.

"Man, this is going to be a long trip."

"Come on, Mom, spill," Maggie teased.

"Okay…he had a hangover, followed me into class, and I had to move because he reeked!"

Maggie gasped. "No kidding? What happened next?"

"The next time that class met…he was waiting for me. He sat next to me and apologized. He cleaned up good, that's for sure."

"Now, that's more like it."

"Yes, but he blew it when he told me he was taking the class for the second time."

"Oops!" said Kate, covering her mouth for affect.

"Really girls, I didn't need him. I mean, I wanted good grades. I thought he was flunking out or something, partying all the time, so at the end of class period, I said something snotty and left."

"Holy cow…and he came back for more?" Maggie asked, having a hard time keeping her eye on the road.

"I think you'd call him a stalker today. I suppose I could have told him I had a child…that might have gotten rid of him. Anyway, there he was, chasing after me again the next class period." Claire laughed at the memory.

"What's so funny?"

"So I see him coming toward me. He's dressed to the hilt…he'd even shaved. And he's carrying an expensive leather briefcase."

"College kids carried briefcases in the '70's?"

"Very few…most of us carried shoulder bags made out of canvas…that's why it's so funny. Then he really turned on the charm. You aren't going to believe this one. He opened his spiral notebook and made sure I could see that he'd rewritten all of his notes. And he had his textbook with him, too."

"Way to wow the girls," Maggie said with a giggle.

"He sure tried. Anyway, I had some learning problems, so I had my tape recorder with me, and I had some different ways of taking notes. Well, he'd never seen that before, so he asked me if I'd teach him how to study…since he'd flunked out once already."

"Smooth talker."

"It didn't work on me, though. He'd have to prove himself. I told him he'd have to have his next assignment done by Monday and show it to me. He'd have to prove he was serious. Then I said I'd let him know if he deserved my help."

"Man…you weren't any fun! I'm surprised that he ever talked to you again," Kate said, turning in her seat to stare at her mother.

"Just my luck, he did just as he was told."

"That's not very romantic," Kate added.

"Well, all I know is I wanted to make out with him the minute I saw him."

"Mom!!!" Claire's daughters yelled in unison.

"Well, you should have seen him…that unruly black hair, that jaw line…"

"Grandma would have killed you if she knew that."

"Exactly! That's why I put him through the paces. I had to make sure he was a decent guy and that he just wasn't out for 'you know what'."

"How long before you told him about me, Mom?" Kate asked sheepishly.

"I never told him. But one of his fraternity brothers was from Rock Creek. He'd seen us together and warned Grant that I was after his money or something because I already had a kid."

"And Grant didn't dump you right then?"

"Nope. He never even told me he knew until a couple months later."

"Wow, Mom," Kate said.

"I know. And I'd lied to him, too, telling him I had to go home every weekend to work. He kept saying that he wanted to visit me on a weekend. I was a wreck, wondering what he'd do when he found out the truth. I guess he could tell that I was nervous because one day, out of the blue, he told me that he already knew. Then when he met you, Katie, he fell madly in love with you. For a while there, I thought he liked visiting me just so he could play with you."

Kate giggled. "Well, I was adorable."

"That you were."

Kate cleared her throat. "Mom…Grant told me that he wanted to adopt me."

"He did?"

"Is that true?"

"Yes…he was so optimistic then…we were going to get married and raise both of you no matter what his parent's thought about it. He said he'd figure it out."

"You didn't have a chance against them, did you?"

"Nope."

Just then, Claire's cell buzzed from inside her purse. She rustled through it and when she pulled it out, spotted Grant's number on her screen. Her heart swelled to fill her throat, and she swallowed hard, hoping to find her voice.

"Speak of the devil," she said before flipping the cell open. "Hello."

"Claire?"

"Yes."

"It's Grant."

"Hi"

"Umm, what did you decide?"

"About the funeral?"

"Yes."

"We're on our way."

"Now?"

"Yes…we're staying at the Concordia tonight so we'll be there on time tomorrow."

"You, Maggie, and Kate?"

"Yes."

"Oh, I thought…I mean, I want to apologize…I had no right to insist you come…no right at all...."

"It's okay, Grant, really. It's a stressful time."

"The visitation's at 9…can you come then?"

"Okay, sure…that'll be fine."

"Greg and I will be looking for you then. You know the way?"

"Yes. Maggie's got the address in her GPS."

"Thank you so much, Claire. Thank you for doing this."

"Grant…I'm okay with it…really I am."

Grant said goodbye and Claire returned the cell to her purse.

Maggie stared at her mother through the rear view mirror. "So, you're not going to accuse us of dragging you along against your will?"

Claire shook her head. "No…he needs us."

***

Settled into Maggie's Lincoln first thing Tuesday morning, the women set out to find Beltline Church in Middleton. According to the GPS, they had to head southwest out of Madison to Hwy. 12. It should take about 20 minutes, Maggie said, and they'd be there in plenty of time.

About a mile off of the highway, the mega-church rose out of the countryside, its majestic steeple reflected perfectly on the still waters of the pond below it. As Maggie pulled into the vast parking lot, she accused Claire of getting the time wrong. It wasn't anywhere close to nine o'clock, and the parking lot was already packed. Claire insisted that she was right about the time while Maggie drove up and down the rows, looking for a place to park. Eventually finding an empty space at the far end of the lot, she quickly pulled in to claim it. To Claire's chagrin, Maggie's grumbling didn't stop there. Having to walk in her heels past hundreds of cars on their way to the front doors of the church, she continued her whining until Claire reminded her that she should just be grateful for the mild autumn morning…they could be walking in pouring rain instead.

The immense non-denominational church appeared to be a fairly new structure, the architecture a mixture of modern and traditional. Once inside the brightly lighted lobby, which Claire guessed to be much larger than most sanctuaries, the women were immediately struck by the size of the huge steel beams that ran from the floor to the skylights interspersed in the ceiling…not to mention the mob that stopped them in their tracks.

"Can you believe this crowd?" Claire asked, incredulous.

Slowly shaking her head, Maggie said nothing.

"How are they ever going to find us?" Claire wondered out loud.

"No need to worry," Kate piped in from behind. "Grant is heading this way as we speak."

Claire surveyed the crowd until she spotted him. After that, she was hard pressed to stop the excessive beating of her heart, and even though she knew that Maggie was his number one concern, she wanted more than anything to take him in her arms and comfort him. When he reached them, he gave her that smile she knew so well and grasped her hand in his. Maggie and Kate each gave him a quick hug, one right after the other.

"Kate, finally," he said, giving her an extra squeeze.

"Come on," he said, his glance bouncing off of each of them in turn. "I have someone I want you to meet."

Without releasing her hand, Grant pulled Claire through the crowd. Maggie and Kate followed, stopping abruptly now and then as Grant accepted condolences from people he seemed to know. A short time later, they entered a small chapel at the back of the church. Claire guessed that the people milling around the room were Grant's relatives, chatting away and catching up on each other lives. When he finally stopped and let go of her hand, he was standing in front of three women seated closely together in a row. Claire recognized his assistant, Barbara, who stood, gave her a warm smile, and held a hand out to greet her. Claire graciously took it, giving it a gentle squeeze. When Grant introduced Claire to Annette, his father's housekeeper, the woman choked up, but managed to take Claire's hand and welcome her.

Finally, a tall brunette with a willowy figure, the physical opposite of Claire in every way, rose to greet her. "I can't believe it, Grant. Claire…you're here!"

Suddenly remembering the news articles and photographs she seen, Claire couldn't stop the rising heat of a blush. Grant patted her back and smiled warmly. "Claire...this is Holly."

Holding out her trembling hand, Claire reached for Grant's ex-wife. Then, when she got up the nerve to look her in the eye, she saw nothing but warmth and acceptance radiating from the woman. In fact, her eyes welled with tears as they spoke.

"So nice to meet you," Claire said sincerely.

"And you. We're all so glad you could make it."

"Thank you."

Claire felt Grant's hand on her shoulder again, patting her, as he turned to look for Kate and Maggie who'd entered the room directly behind him. When he introduced Claire's daughters to Holly, the brimming tears slid down her face, and she grabbed Maggie and pulled her into an embrace while reaching for Katie to do the same.

"Grant has told me so much about you. Welcome to the family," she said. She turned then and motioned to someone to come over to where they were standing. "Darling, come and meet Claire and her daughters."

A stocky but outrageously handsome man, standing a few feet away, talking with a group of men, turned and walked toward the family. Holly smiled proudly and introduced her husband, Lucas Taylor. Claire glanced up at Grant, thinking he couldn't be happy about this, but the look on his face wasn't what she'd expected; in fact, she'd never expected any of this.

"Hello," Claire said.

"I can't believe this. I finally get to meet the famous Claire Holmes."

She blinked in surprise.

He laughed. "I was in banking with Mr. Harrison, Claire. I was with him when we heard you speak at the banker's convention in Phoenix. In fact, you were so convincing, I gave up a hunk of my money for Martha's Place myself."

"I'm happy to be able to thank you personally." Claire said, smiling, as she presented her hand and he took it.

"I hear you left the place, moved back here."

"Yes, but I left it in good hands."

"You know, Madison needs someone like you. We could definitely use more services in this town."

"I guess you don't know why I moved back then." Claire turned toward the man's wife who still had her arms around Maggie and Kate. "These are my daughters, Maggie Borgerson and Kate Fogarty."

Kate held out her hand; Maggie followed.

"Great to meet you," he said.

"They're finally living in the same city, so I thought I'd join them. Besides, I can find homeless people anywhere these days, so I'll have plenty of work to do even in Western Wisconsin."

"Well, when you're ready, I can put you in contact with a bunch of people who have to find a place for their money. In fact, there are quite a few of them around here today. I'll have to introduce you."

Holly scolded her husband. "Lucas. We're not here to talk business."

"Oh, sorry. I guess I've been told," he said, winking at Claire.

Grant interrupted by tapping Claire on the shoulder. "Let's see if we can find Greg."

Claire followed Grant out of the chapel and to the other side of the building where wide glass doors opened into an auditorium style sanctuary that was slowly filling with mourners. Claire noticed the half circle of chairs lined up, beginning at the front of the large stage and ending at the top of the oversized room. Heavy purple drapes hung behind a shiny, black grand piano on the large, mostly empty stage. The place was implausibly stark, but breathtakingly beautiful in its simplicity.

"How many people does this place hold again?" Claire asked as Grant changed places, moved behind her, and pressed her forward, his hand resting at the small of her back.

He shrugged. "More than a thousand, maybe two."

"Wow."

"Yeah, wow. It's the largest church in the Madison area. I heard they're planning to grow to 4,000 members."

"No kidding."

Maggie and Kate came up behind him, asking the same questions. Grant happily repeated himself. Then, when Greg spotted Grant and the women, he waved, motioning for them to join him. As they approached him at the stage, an ornate, wooden cart housing an urn behind its glass walls came into view. Claire stopped suddenly as if she'd forgotten why they were there, and Grant bumped into her, almost knocking her over. He grabbed one of her arms, helping her right herself.

"Sorry, are you okay?" he asked before releasing her.

She nodded, frowning. "He wanted to be cremated?"

"Yes...I didn't know about it either."

"Claire," Greg called from behind her. She turned, and he pulled her into an embrace.

"Is Maggie here?"

"She should be right behind me."

Greg lifted his head. "Hey, Maggie...glad you're here."

Maggie hugged the kid when she reached him and then introduced him to her sister. They shook hands, Greg caressing hers in both of his.

"Jolene's around here somewhere, too," he said. "Well, as long as we're all here I'll fill you in on how this is going to go."

Greg seemed to be in charge, and Grant simply listened, letting him take the lead.

"Okay. So the family will stay in the chapel until everyone is seated. The minister will let us know when it's time to walk in."

"Where would you like us to sit?" Claire asked, cooperating with the confident young man.

"What do you mean?"

"What row do you want us in...how many are going to be taken by family?"

Greg raised his eyebrows in surprise. "Claire...you, Maggie, and Kate will be with us...with the family."

Slowly shaking her head, she declined. "We don't belong there, Greg. We'll just find a place back there," Claire insisted, motioning away from them.

"Claire," Grant interrupted. "I'd like you to sit with me. We want the girls sitting with us, too."

Claire frowned, holding tears at bay. "Grant, that wouldn't be right. He didn't want me to be part of the..."

Grant stopped her mid sentence. "I want you with me."

"No, Grant, I can't..."

"Listen, I just want to present a united front. In case he can see us from above, I want him to know he couldn't keep us apart forever."

Claire, shocked by the anger heard in his voice, could see that he was serious. His jaws were clenched; his grip tightened around her arm. "But Holly should..."

"Holly will be a few seats away. She agrees that you should be with me."

Claire could feel the tears coming. "Grant, it's Maggie who should...she's the one..."

"Just sit next to me. That's all I ask. Just for today. I mean, Annette and Barbara will be sitting with us. They're close friends of the family, too."

"So I'm just another friend."

"If that's the way you want it," Grant said, emotionless.

Chapter 42

GRANT

Grant could finally breathe. Claire had agreed to sit with him although she'd made it abundantly clear that she wasn't especially happy about it. He couldn't tell whether she still cared about him or not. In fact, she seemed to be deliberately ignoring his attempts at reconciliation. How in the world did she miss the meaning of his intentions when he wrote "I don't want to live the next forty years without you"? He'd chalked it up to the impersonal nature of email at the time, but now he was having second thoughts. He even wondered if giving her the letters would make any difference at all.

As they sat in the chapel waiting for the minister to give them the go-ahead, Grant watched as Claire interacted with his friends and the few relatives who showed up. Totally at ease, she seemed to be in her element…not on edge like she was around him. Of course, she was used to having women around, helping women, working with other like minded women. She chatted with Holly and the others as if they were old buddies. Coincidently, she seemed oblivious to the men in the room…the ones who stared unabashedly.

Talk about staring…Grant couldn't help notice that she looked better than ever. He imagined that she finally felt comfortable in her own skin. In addition to that assumption, he could see that she'd learned how to dress; her hair and nails were impeccably done. The black dress she wore draped over her figure like it was made for her. Perhaps it was. She was much thinner than she was at eighteen, but her hourglass shape could still compete with the best of them. Maggie had inherited her mother's small stature and body type, but Grant could see that she was more athletic than Claire, her muscular calves obvious under her skirt covered knees. Then there was Katie…he remembered her being the cutest little kid he'd ever seen…and she'd grown into a beauty in her own right. Much taller than her mother and sister, with dark brunette hair and an olive complexion, and unlike her mother and sister, she was blessed with hips like a boy. Pantsuits were invented for her, he imagined, because today she looked like a supermodel.

Grant couldn't have been prouder of the women in his life. Not because he thought they were beautiful, but because they had taken good care of themselves, because they were self-sufficient and successful…no thanks to him. Then there was the way his ex-wife Holly had taken Claire and her daughters into the fold, engaging them in conversation, taking in their every word. Ten years ago, he couldn't have imagined any of this. He and Holly were having problems and once they faced them, once they brought them out in the open, there was no going back. Yet, she'd become a true partner when it came to what was best for their son, and to overcome the problems that come with joint custody, they'd learned the meaning of compromise and in the process, forged a bond stronger than they'd had when they were married.

Grant's reflections stopped abruptly when the minister entered the room. It's time, he thought, as walked toward Claire and grasped her hand in his.

"Let's go," he whispered softly.

She nodded and walked beside him to the door of the chapel. When he turned to see who'd be following, Greg was there with Jolene, but had allowed Kate and Maggie to walk ahead of him. He gave Claire's hand a squeeze and when she didn't pull away, glanced at her, caught her eye, and mouthed a silent 'thank you'. To his surprise, she leaned into his arm.

As they walked into the packed sanctuary, the sounds of a wonderful, old fashioned church organ echoed throughout. Shortly after taking their seats in the front row, Grant reluctantly released her hand as the clergy began his words of welcome and lead a responsive reading of Psalm 23. The congregation was then asked to stand to sing the opening hymn, "How Great Thou Art", and the vast room echoed with voices raised in song.

When the crowd was seated, the pastor read the comfort of God's word from Ephesians and the book of John before delivering his message. Grant listened attentively as the man talked about his father and told stories about a man of great faith, a man he barely recognized as his dear departed father. He told of a man who planned his own funeral down to the last detail; he spoke of a man who had such strong faith that he couldn't wait for the day he'd meet his maker in heaven. The pastor said he'd been impressed by a man who believed in no uncertain terms that he'd be meeting his wife at the pearly gates and seeing his parents and grandparents once again. *Or was it Martha he was hoping to meet!*

Grant heard the minister ask those congregated there to rise and join him in singing "The Old Rugged Cross", a favorite hymn of Grant Leland Harrison II. Slowly shaking his head in disbelief, Grant still managed to stand with Claire and muddle through all three verses.

Days earlier, Greg had asked his father if he wanted to speak at the funeral. Grant told him that he'd rather not and assumed his son felt the same way. Now, he sat there stunned as the minister introduced his son as the only grandchild of Grant II. He watched as Greg, dressed in the suit he'd bought him for graduation, confidently ascended the stairs to the stage and approached the podium. Grant felt Claire shift uncomfortably in her seat; he heard her clear her throat and turned to see Maggie grab her hand. After that, all Grant could do was stare straight ahead. The lump in his throat wouldn't dissolve, wouldn't go away no matter how many times he swallowed.

There wasn't a sound in the room as Greg picked up the microphone and started to talk.

"Good morning. Thank you all for coming today. I'm the youngest grandchild of Grant Harrison, the second. I thought I was his only grandchild until recently when he began to tell me stories about two girls, girls he'd known as children...one of them his granddaughter and the other her half sister. He said he spent a lot of time with them when they were growing up, but hadn't seen them in many years. He said that he hoped that I'd be able to meet them someday. I'm happy to say that I have met them, that they also have fond memories of my grandfather, and that they have joined us here today.

You know, I didn't always appreciate my grandfather. He was as tough on me as he had been on my father. He told me that he wasn't going to baby me like other grandparents did. He said that if he did, I'd never grow up, I'd never be able to stand on my own two feet. On the other hand, he was always there for me. He was there when my parents divorced; he was there to make sure that I didn't take any blame.

My parents were great, but they had busy careers so I spent a lot of time with my grandfather in his golden years. He taught me how to save money, but he also taught me the importance of giving back. My grandfather was the one who introduced me to the area Boys and Girls Club. I went with him to meet the kids, helped him organize fundraisers and field trips. He took a lot of those kids under his wing, befriending them, helping them with their problems whenever he could, and I did the same. I'll sure miss those kids when I move to Minnesota.

Mostly, I'll miss the hours we spent over the cribbage board or playing euchre or chess. But I have a feeling he'll be watching me from up above as I start my new career, my new life. And I hope that I'll have the same strong faith in God that my grandfather did. He told me that he wasn't perfect, that he'd hurt a lot of people in his life, and he only hoped they he'd be forgiven some day even though he didn't think he deserved it. I know he made some strides toward that end before he died."

Grant noticed that his son looked right at him when he spoke those words. The mass in his throat wasn't about to leave him now. And when he dared take a peek at Claire, he saw that she was having a hard time holding it together herself. Maggie had closed in, her head resting on her mother's shoulder. He wanted to wrap his arms around her and hold her forever, but he was sure that she wouldn't appreciate it so he concentrated on getting the lump to leave his throat by swallowing his tears as his son continued with his farewell.

"If there is anyone here who happens to have a story or fond memories of my grandfather, we'd welcome hearing from you."

Grant held his breath, sure that no one would step up to the plate, but there was a rustle behind him, and he turned to see an unfamiliar man coming down the aisle to take the steps to the stage. He wasn't alone. Several people stood in various places throughout the sanctuary and began to move forward.

The first man nervously approached the podium. His hands trembled as he held the microphone, but he soon regained his composure.

"Mr. Harrison saved my life. He was the only banker I'd ever met who gave a damn. I was laid off, and it wasn't long before my savings were gone. I went to Mr. Harrison because I didn't want to lose my house, too. At first they wouldn't let me see him…he was the president of the bank after all. The mortgage officer talked to me, but gave me no options, so I wrote Mr. Harrison a letter explaining my circumstances. He called me and invited me to come in and see him. I did and he worked with me to come up with a plan to save my house from foreclosure. My family and I will forever be grateful to him."

As soon as the man stepped down, there was another to take his place. There was the employee who'd been diagnosed with cancer and couldn't pay her bills. Mr. Harrison threw a fundraiser for her, paid the bills that she couldn't, and made sure her job was waiting for her when she was able to return to work. Another woman talked about how she couldn't pay childcare for her children on a teller's salary. She told how Mr. Harrison called a meeting to find out how many of his employees were struggling the same way. Within a month, there was a daycare center across the street from that bank and many others throughout Wisconsin. The childcare fee was cut in half for employees who used the services if they would volunteer at the bank sponsored food shelf once a month.

The last speaker was a teenager, baggy pants and all. He looked sheepish, but once he started talking, he had nothing but glowing reports about how Grant's father picked him out of the crowd at the Boys and Girls Club because he was always making trouble. The kid said he was angry about being poor, about moving every time the rent couldn't be paid, about having to stay with relatives when things got bad. Mr. Harrison took him out for ice cream, talked to him about what he wanted in life, and then gave him a job at his home keeping his yard in good shape. He said that if it weren't for him, he'd probably be in jail.

After several people talked, the minister reappeared and gave a blessing. He asked everyone to stand and join him in the Lord's Prayer. He followed that with the Benediction and the organ began to play the postlude.

Grant sat flabbergasted. He felt as though the blood had been drained from his body. He was limp as a wet rag and felt like one, too. Why hadn't he noticed all that his father had done in the community? Where was he when all this was going on? Because he was a kid, hadn't he paid any attention to his parents' extracurricular activities? Or, had his father turned a corner after he left home? Had he changed for the better after having a grandchild? Or was it because of Claire's mother? Had she influenced him in some way? This last thought forced him to glance at Claire. She looked as stunned as he felt. He heard his name and looked up to see his son motioning to him to stand. He grabbed Claire's hand and pulled her up with him…whether she wanted to or not. They followed the pall bearers and the cart with the ashes out of the room, walking like zombies held in a trance. Once the family was in the lobby, the funeral director handed the urn to Grant. He could do nothing but accept it, and lucky for him, his son was beside him and led him back into the chapel where the urn could rest until the day was over.

Chapter 43

CLAIRE

As far as Claire was concerned, she'd served her time. But no, her daughters were not ready to leave, telling her they needed to stay longer to talk to Greg, to get to know him, to show their support. Claire had had enough and when they were finally alone in the restroom, she let them know just that.

"Really, girls," she whined. "Let's get out of here."

"Why don't we have some lunch, relax a bit. We'll know when its time to leave," Maggie suggested.

Claire was livid. "I've had enough. You said we could go when I was ready."

"But why? Aren't you curious about all those people who remembered Grant's dad? I want to hear more about that, don't you? I mean, he took care of us, but all those other people?"

"And he treated Grant and me like dirt!" Claire cried.

"Oh, I'm sorry, Mom. I wasn't thinking. Okay, okay…we'll go. Let's just say our goodbyes first," Maggie cooed, wrapping an arm around her mother.

The three of them left the room, walked down a hallway, and entered the fellowship room. It looked to Claire as though everyone at the service had stayed for lunch. She had no idea how they'd find Grant in the crowd. In fact, she found it disconcerting. They'd never get out of there now; they couldn't even call his name…he'd never hear it over all the commotion in the room.

Little did she know, but Grant had been looking for them, too, and came into the room right behind them.

"Claire, please stay for lunch. I'd like to talk about what we heard in there. You have to be as shocked as I am."

Claire couldn't look at him. "Really, I just want to go."

"Please don't," he pleaded.

Claire lifted her head, and her eyes met his. When she saw the look of dread on his face, tears burned in her eyes. "I've heard enough, Grant. I don't need to be reminded that he thought so little of us and so much of all of them. I can't believe it."

"Me either. In fact, I sat there thinking I had to be at the wrong funeral," Grant said with a shake of his head. "The father I knew was all about making money. I never saw his philanthropic side. But I think I know what happened. I think I know why my son experienced a different human being than I did."

Claire wanted to run, she was sick of hearing about him…she just wanted it to be over. "I don't care."

"Mom, come on…just listen to what he has to say. Please," Kate pleaded.

Grant reached for her then, touching her shoulder gently. "Claire…at first he wanted a relationship with Maggie, but then it became about Martha. Don't you see? He couldn't stay away…he knew he'd made a mistake and didn't know how to rectify it, so he did the only thing he knew how to do…he made sure Martha had whatever she needed to raise his granddaughter, and it started by buying the farm. But I think there was more to it."

Claire, silent, clenched her jaw.

Continuing to rub her shoulder, Grant leaned toward her. "Just tell me one thing, Claire. Did your mother do things for others? I mean, was it at all a priority in her life?"

Maggie prodded her on. "Mom?"

Claire rolled her eyes. "Of course. She was a good Christian woman. I don't know how many times I had to help her make meals for the shut-ins or sick. And if she learned that someone needed money to keep the electricity going or whatever, she'd fill an envelope with cash and put it in their mailbox. I think she gave away money when she shouldn't have."

"You're right, Mom," Maggie said, interrupting. "When we moved to town, she'd drive people to their doctor's appointments. I know because sometimes we'd be dragged along, and sometimes with other little kids in the car. Remember Kate?"

Kate chuckled. "Oh, yes, because I'd get carsick!"

Claire smiled at her daughters.

"That's what I figured," Grant said.

Claire cocked her head then, finally giving him her attention. "What do you mean?"

"I don't know how to say this, Claire, but I think my father changed after meeting your mother. I know he was there for the girls, but I think Martha influenced him somehow. He never went to church when I was a kid. I went with my mother...she had to run things there, too...but never Dad. Now we learn that he believed in God and that he wasn't afraid to die."

"Well, that's great. If they were such great Christians, why did they do what they did to us?"

"I think it all goes back to the fact that they thought we were going down the wrong path, that we needed straightening out or something. My dad always used tough love with me...and you were sick, Claire."

Claire was incredulous. "So now we're letting them off the hook?"

Shaking his head vehemently, Grant explained. "No, of course not! It's just that they had any idea how much we meant to each other. I mean, I think your mother knew, but she was afraid for you. I don't think she trusted me for a second. And, my mother and father never saw us together. If they had, they would have seen it."

"Seen what?"

"They would have seen how much we cared about each other...how we were meant to be together."

Claire blushed, stared at him, and this time, did not look away. She was speechless as she watched Grant redden and felt him nervously remove his hand from her shoulder to shove it into his pocket. Glancing at her daughters, she saw that they were on the verge of tears. Time stood still.

Grant was the first to speak. "Um, are you staying to eat?"

Claire was already shaking her head. "We've got to get going."

Maggie gave her the evil eye, but didn't interrupt.

"I'm sorry you can't stay," he said. "Can you just wait a minute, though? I have something for you in my car, Claire."

Surprised, Claire agreed. "Maybe you could walk out with us. We'll just say goodbye to Greg. Okay? Come on girls," she said, taking control, as she walked into the crowd.

***

A while later, Claire was settled in the back of Maggie's car, waving to Grant as he stood watching them leave. He had a strange look on his face, almost mischievous, she thought, like the cat that swallowed the canary. It made her smile, and he must have seen it, because a huge grin spread over his face. What was he up to?

They'd barely made it to the highway, when the inquisition began.

"What's in the package, Mom?" Maggie asked, peering at her through the rearview mirror.

"I don't know. If it's something his father left for me, I don't want it."

"Come on, open it. Maybe it's money, and you'll never have to work again!"

Claire laughed, but gave her own assessment. "Yeah, like a wad of cash...a payoff for past damages."

"Maybe it's something of Grandma's," Kate offered. "Something she'd given Uncle Harry. It's probably just pictures of us."

"Well, whatever it is, Grant sure was insistent that you get it today. He could have mailed it, you know. He's got it packaged as if he were going to anyway," Maggie added.

"True...that's true, I guess." Claire pulled the large, padded mailer from the seat and onto her lap. It was sealed as if it were to be mailed like Maggie said. "It's sealed tight. I have nothing to open it with."

"Hold it," Maggie yelled. "I have a first aid box in the glove compartment. Kate, open it…there's a scissors in there."

Katie did as she was told. Sure enough, an unused, white plastic box was lodged there just as her sister had said. She grabbed it, snapped it open, and began searching for the scissors. As soon as she located them, she turned, handed them to her mother, and cheered her on. "Hurry up!" she screamed like a little kid on Christmas.

"Good grief…hold on, will you?" Claire said as she painstakingly cut the end off of the envelope.

"What is it?" Maggie asked from the driver's seat.

Claire pulled out a wad of letters held together with a beautifully tied, pink ribbon. The top envelope had Grant's name printed in capital letters. Underneath it was a handwritten note signed by Grant himself. She read it silently.

Dearest Claire,

I found these in an old safety deposit box of mine. You need to read this letter from my mother in order to understand any of this.
Love, Grant

Claire looked up at Kate, choking out the words. "The letters…these are the letters Grant said he mailed to me."

Claire watched Kate gasp and cover her mouth, and heard Maggie say, "No way!"

When Claire regained her composure, she slipped the letter out of the first envelope and read it to herself. Looking up, tears in her eyes, she spouted, "His mother made sure they never got sent. The postmaster kept them and gave them to Grant's grandfather. He saved them, but insisted his mother give them back to him."

Blood rushed to Claire's head, her heart was beating in her ears and her throat was swollen with tears. *The letters were real…he never lied to me!* Throwing her head back, Claire grasped the letters to her chest and began to sob. She could sense the car slowing down, hear it hit the gravel on the side of the road, and feel it come to a complete stop.

Maggie turned in her seat. "You going to be okay?"

"I'm fine," Claire said through her tears.

Both of her daughters had turned in their seats just to make sure.

"What do you need, Mom? Just tell me. Do we need to go somewhere? Do you need to be alone? What?" Maggie begged.

Claire could barely speak, but managed to answer the question. "I need to see Grant right now."

"Do you want me to turn back?"

"Oh, no, he's going to be at the funeral for hours," she stammered.

"Call him," Kate ordered.

"Now...while he's there?"

"I bet he doesn't care...he wants you to call."

Claire didn't know what to think, so she dug around for her cell, found his number and hit it. It rang one, two, three times. Claire thought she should hang up, thought this might be inappropriate or that he turned off his phone, but he answered anyway.

"Hello," he whispered.

"Grant?"

"Claire?"

"Can I see you?"

"Now?"

"Whenever you say."

"Where are you?"

"I don't know...outside of Madison somewhere."

"Do you want to meet me someplace?"

"Sure."

"Want to come to my house? I can be there in an hour or so."

"Okay."

"Do you have my address?"

Claire covered the cell. "Mags...do you know Grant's address?"

"Yup. I put it in my GPS just in case we had to go there today."

"We can find it," she told him.

"Just head back the way you came. See you then."

Claire snapped her phone shut. "Maggie, take me to the first car rental business you can find on that thing."

Chapter 44

GRANT

Grant couldn't have asked for better news, and now, he couldn't wait to get home. He found himself cutting people off in the middle of conversations by thanking them for coming. He moved from person to person as they sat around the tables, eating the catered meal. He shook their hands, smiled, and nodded in appreciation of their sincere condolences. Several people asked him to join them. He declined, telling them that he couldn't eat if he tried. There were lots of questions about Claire and her daughters. He shrugged his shoulders saying it was a long story, and he tried to remain civil when they mentioned that his father was a great man and assumed he'd miss him.

The crowd was thinning, so Grant tried to leave, saying goodbye to Annette, Barbara, and Holly. When he found Greg in the chapel, his son shoved the urn at him, telling him to take it home for now. It was the last thing Grant wanted to do, but Greg explained that since he was the executor of his grandfather's will, he'd find out what he wanted them to do with his ashes when he met with his lawyer later that day. Grant wouldn't have to house it for long. Besides that, the urn gave Jolene the willies. Grant could do nothing but oblige his son, grab the thing, and head for his car, but not before he told him to call if the will held any surprises

After setting the urn on the floor in the back seat, Grant left the mega-church parking lot and headed out of Middleton toward his home on Lake Mendota. As he drove he thought about his father's disapproval of everything including his decision to buy the house on the lake. He was an adult, capable of making his own decisions, but thank goodness, none of the things that his father warned him about ever happened. There hadn't been a flood, noisy boating enthusiasts hadn't ruined his summer nights, and the value of his house hadn't decreased even in a down economy. His father told him that the prairie style house would go out of fashion, and the lake would become polluted, so he'd most likely lose his shirt on the thing. His dad wanted him to buy a modest home until he inherited the mansion in Maple Bluff, and he didn't understand why his son wouldn't want to live in the most upscale neighborhood in Madison. Even his father's death couldn't take away the joy of living on the lake, having his own boathouse, and being close the University and the Capital. That was one time he'd made the right decision and stuck to his guns. Other times, not so much. Before he knew it, he was pulling into his garage, closing the double-wide door behind him, and entering his kitchen. The joy of home ownership suddenly took a back seat to the heady realization that the love of his life would be joining him soon.

After rushing upstairs to his bedroom to change into jeans and a button down shirt, he started to panic…he didn't have anything to feed Claire and the girls when they got there. Once he returned to his kitchen and began searching his cupboards, he realized he had plenty and relaxed somewhat. The refrigerator had beer and white wine, but he wasn't sure what beverages they preferred. There were a couple bricks of cheese in one of the drawers and lots of salad fixings in the other. Were any of them lactose intolerant? He hoped not. The freezer held some steaks, pork chops, chicken, and frozen vegetables. He decided that he could whip up something if he had to…if they wanted to stay, that is.

Since he couldn't see who was coming up the driveway from the inside of the house, Grant had a camera installed when he first moved in some twenty years earlier. He made sure the computer screen in the kitchen was set to view the driveway so he could watch for Maggie's car. While he waited, he eyeballed the first floor rooms to make sure his junk was picked up. He gathered up some newspapers and threw them in a basket before grabbing a glass off an end table and a coffee cup from his desk, hiding them in the dishwasher when he circled back into his kitchen.

The kitchen was in good shape. He wiped off the counters for good measure and then checked the powder room nearby to make sure the women wouldn't think he was a slob. To his surprise, his weekly housekeeper had everything in tip top shape…the first sheet of toilet paper folded into a V and lovely hand towels lay on the granite counter, a scented candle nearby. The room smelled amazing. Funny, he'd never noticed that before.

Leaning over his counter in the kitchen, Grant nervously downed a tall glass of water as he watched the computer screen. He stretched his arms over his head, brought them down, shook them out, and gave his neck a roll. His heartbeat slowed some; he was finally breathing normally. In that moment of calm, he began to wonder why they were coming back. He figured they simply wanted to thank him for the letters in person. Or since they weren't postmarked, did they think they were fakes…letters he'd written since he found Claire…letters to get on her good side? It seemed like a ridiculous assumption, but they were in such good condition that someone might actually think that very thing.

The phone rang unexpectedly, interrupting his train of thought. Greg was calling from the lawyer's office. He just wanted him to know who was mentioned in the will and told him that the law firm needed some addresses before sending the will to probate. Grant was not surprised by list of names considering the recent turn of events and agreed to email the addresses as soon as he could.

Just then, a car pulled into his driveway, but it wasn't Maggie's Lincoln. His heart sank; he didn't recognize the dark blue sedan as belonging to anyone he knew, so he watched to see who'd emerge from the car before leaving his kitchen to greet his surprise guest. He'd have to figure out a way to get rid of whoever it was posthaste.

To his surprise, it was Claire who poked her head out of the car and glanced at the house. He could see a frown cross her face. Oops, she's thinking she pulled into the wrong driveway. Well, isn't that why he bought the place? No one could guess by the entrance that there was anything special about his house and that was just the way he wanted it.

Why was she driving that car? Was she alone? Had she come to see him because she wanted to be alone with him? High hopes pushing him forward, Grant hurriedly started for the stairs to find out.

Rushing down the sidewalk to the driveway, Grant shouted Claire's name because she wouldn't be able to see him from where she was standing. When he came around the corner of the garage, he spotted her behind the car door. It looked as though she still hadn't made up her mind about staying, that she hadn't heard him yell her name. When she finally saw him coming around the corner, she looked relieved, stepped away from the car, and closed the door. That's when he saw that she had the letters wrapped in her arms at her waist.

"Claire...you found the place."

She nodded.

"Where'd you get this car? Where are the girls?"

"I rented it and sent them home."

Grant stood stunned. "They're not with you?"

She shook her head.

"Oh."

"I wanted to talk to you about the letters...alone, I mean."

"Okay...sure," Grant said, holding his emotions in check while motioning for her to come toward him. When she reached his side, he gently touched the small of her back, guiding her down the sidewalk to the doorway and stairs that lead to the kitchen. "Come on in," he said, giving her a wide smile as she passed in front of him.

Claire walked up the steps into the kitchen. "You got your dream house."

Surprised that she'd remember such a trivial thing, he blushed. "Well, it isn't exactly a Frank Lloyd Wright, but it's close enough."

When she wandered into the dining room, he followed.

"What a great view of the lake, Grant. You know, when I lived in Arizona, that's what I've missed the most...the lakes...all the water we have around here. Did you build it?"

Shaking his head, Grant answered. "No, but it was relatively new when I bought it. I was just thinking about that. My dad hated it."

"I'm sorry," Claire said quietly.

"It's okay. I stuck to my guns that time. I wished I would have had the guts when I was younger though."

Shaking the bundle of letters in her hands, Claire turned his way. Cocking her head to the side, she validated him with a simple statement. "I don't think you had a snow ball's chance in hell."

The way she said it brought a smile to his face, but he wanted to clarify. "We didn't have a snowball's chance!"

He watched her blush and lick her lips...he'd made her nervous. Shoot. That was the last thing he wanted to do. He wanted to make her comfortable; he wanted her to stay forever. "Claire? Do you want to sit down? Can I get you a glass of wine or something?"

She nodded and continued to stroll in the direction of the living room with its expansive fireplace and wall of windows. "This place is just gorgeous, Grant."

"I'm glad you like it. Can I get you something?"

"You mentioned wine before?"

"Yes. I've got some pinot in the fridge. I think I have some merlot somewhere if you'd prefer that."

"The pinot sounds great."

Grant left her to grab the wine. He could finally breathe. Was he holding his breath the whole time? He could have been...his chest ached. Or was it simply his heart aching for her? As he reached for a wine glass, the thought crossed his mind that perhaps his dreams were coming true. Here she was, sitting in his favorite place on earth, and they were totally alone for the first time in almost forty years. He exhaled through pursed lips, poured two glasses of wine, and returned to the living room.

As he walked toward her, he noticed that she'd made herself at home. She'd thrown off those expensive stilettos and curled up on the couch facing the lake, her feet tucked under her...just like she used to sit when they were studying in the library or in his room so long ago. The site sent a wave of raw emotion to every nerve in his body.

"Here you go," he said as he came up behind her, hoping to be able to hold it together.

She glanced his way as he circled around, handed her the glass, and then plopped down on the other end of the couch. "Cheers," he said.

She repeated the toast and took a sip. "Hits the spot," she said.

He nodded and noticed that she'd dropped his letters onto the craftsman-style coffee table.

"I'd never leave this couch if I lived here," she said.

"I don't believe you...all that energy you have?"

"Okay. I'd never leave it on the weekends!"

He laughed. "That's exactly the way I feel." He hesitated before broaching the next subject, unconsciously clearing his throat before he spoke. "Maggie said you had a house for sale in Phoenix. Have you sold it yet?"

She shook her head. "Nope. The market's not cooperating."

"What kind of a house is it?"

"Typical of Arizona developments...a one-story stucco, red-tile roof, in a gated community...sprawling and expensive."

Grant licked his lips nervously. "Maggie said you lived alone."

"Uh, huh."

"Oh, I thought you were engaged or something," Grant said, his voice tentative.

She looked at her hands. "I was, but we never lived together."

Grant smiled to himself, relieved by her answer. "Oh...you were an old fashioned sort of couple."

She smiled but didn't look his way. "I don't know about that, but he still had kids at home. I didn't want to raise anyone else's kids."

"I think that'd be hard."

Chapter 45

CLAIRE

I didn't want to raise anyone else's kids because I never had a chance to raise my own! Bile rose from her stomach; she thought she would vomit. She had no choice but to tell him everything. Her heart was beating its way out of her chest. Hands trembling, she set the wine glass aside, turned his way, and spewed her story.

"Grant, I didn't get the chance to raise the girls either. Maggie was just a few weeks old when I was hospitalized. I thought I'd be back in a blink of an eye. Mama said I could have custody if I could support them, but I never made enough money until they were grown. Then it was too late."

He nodded. "I figured she was holding something over your head."

"You did?" Claire asked, surprised that he wasn't shocked by the news.

"Yes, and you explained a lot in your emails."

"I never did make a lot of money, you know…when the girls were young or even later after I established the shelter. I mean, I was really good at raising money, but I never kept any of it. Everything went into the shelter accept for a monthly stipend. That was good enough for me."

She watched him nod; he didn't take his eyes off hers until after she threw out her question. "Did you ever hate me for leaving her, for not raising her myself?"

Grant gave a quick shake of his head. "No! For heaven's sake, no! I never felt that way for a second. I knew there had to be a good reason for you to leave her…you were such a good mother to Katie. Really, I couldn't figure it out, so I tried to find you on my own."

"You did? How?" She wasn't convinced.

"When your mother wouldn't tell me anything, I asked my dad to help me."

Claire cocked her head to the side. Had she heard him correctly? "He helped you?"

"I think he may have started at one point. The search for you most likely led him to your mother. I'm sure she told him how she felt about me…maybe he tried, but couldn't convince her of my virtues. I don't know. Anyway, he probably gave up and decided to do what he had to do to see Maggie."

"You really think that's how it happened?" Claire asked, scowling.

Grant gave her a determined nod. "I have a vague memory of my dad coming to me, all apologetic, saying something like he tried, but there was no trace of you."

"You believed him?" she asked, squinting, skeptical of anything Grant's father might have had to say.

"At the time, yes. I didn't think I had any reason not to. I thought my mother was the bad guy, remember?"

Tears welled involuntarily in the corners of her eyes. "And now I find out that you really wrote me letters." Inhaling a shaky breath, she covered her face with her hands and rubbed her fingers over her eyebrows.

"You didn't believe that I wrote you letters?"

He sounded angry; she shook her head and sniffed. "No. You kept mentioning them, but there was never any evidence they existed. I thought you made it up to get on my good side, maybe so I'd be more supportive of your relationship with Maggie or something."

"Wow," he huffed. She heard disappointment in his voice. "I had no idea …"

Noting his distress, she didn't want to make matters worse, but there would never be a better time to tell him everything. "I'm sorry, but lots of things went through my mind while I was waiting for you. That you hated me, that you lied to me the whole time we were together, that you just used me or that you were dead or you would have come back. You name it; I thought it."

"And I figured you never forgave me for not being there from the beginning and that's why you never wrote back." He reached over and took her hand in his. "So now you have the letters, and you know that I would never have abandoned you."

Claire nodded and without looking at him, wiped her nose with the back of her free hand, and whispered a thank you when tissues appeared out of nowhere. As soon as she finished blowing her nose, she heard him clear his throat.

"Did you read any of them?" he asked timidly.

She dabbed the tissues under her eyes, slowly shaking her head.

"You didn't…I thought you'd rip them open immediately," he said, his voice rising.

She could hear the panic, feel his pain. The last thing she wanted to do was hurt him. Managing a smile, she finally lifted her head and gazed into his eyes. "I don't need to read them. I know they exist. I know that you wrote them…that you tried to reach me."

As Grant nodded, tears began streaming down his face. She watched him lick his lips as he wiped his fingertips across his cheekbones. "I never forgot you…never forgot what we had."

Claire, momentarily speechless, shifted her weight and closed the gap between them. "Me either." She barely got it out before he wrapped his arms around her in an all encompassing embrace. Closing her eyes in response to the hug, she felt his lips caress her forehead before he pressed his cheek next to hers. She opened her eyes when he started to back away and watched him swallow nervously before speaking.

"When you do read the letters, you might want to skip the last few."

"Why?" she asked as she wrapped her arms around his bicep and pressed her head against his shoulder.

"I remember the outrage I felt when you didn't answer them. I probably wrote some things I shouldn't have. Sorry."

Lifting her head, she captured his gaze and held it. "No need to apologize. You didn't understand why I never answered them. Anyway,

I always felt something was wrong or you would have come for me."

"Something was wrong all right."

Claire nodded, her cheek rubbing against his shoulder.

Grant kissed the top of her head, whispered in her hear. "Could I have a do-over?"

Claire giggled. "Where in the world would you start?" She cocked her head to get a better look at him and spotted the grin she'd missed so much.

"Well, I need a date to this thing."

"What thing?"

"I have to clean out my dad's place...put the house up for sale. I figured you'd know exactly what to do since you just put your house on the market."

Claire rolled her eyes for affect. "That's how you're going to start your do-over? Put me to work?"

"I think it'd be a perfect way to start!" Grant claimed, releasing a chuckle.

"Why would you think I'd ever want to step inside that house again?"

"I just thought we could do some snooping together. Maybe we'd find something of your mother's or maybe you'd take a fancy to some piece of furniture and want it for yourself."

Backing away, blinking, and shaking her head in dismay, Claire began to question his sanity. "What are you talking about? He wouldn't want me there, looking through his stuff."

"I think you're wrong about that."

Claire could do nothing but glare. "You're out of your mind!"

Wide-eyed and smiling, Grant continued. "No, I'm not! You're in the will, too. So are the girls."

Confounded by the prospect, she sputtered, "Don't be ridiculous." She slid to the edge of the couch, but Grant grabbed her shoulders to hold her in place while he advanced his theory.

"Dad thought money could buy anything. I bet he figured if he left it to us, it would pave his way to redemption."

After taking a deep breath and blowing it out, Claire calmed enough to think rationally and express what was in her heart. "I can't speak for Maggie and Kate, but I don't want it, Grant."

"But Claire…I know you're job hunting…you wouldn't ever have to work again."

With a vehement shake of her head, Claire set him straight. "I don't care."

"Are you sure?"

She nodded without hesitation.

"Well, then we can make sure your share is sent to Martha's Place or some other charity…whatever you want. That's what I'm going to do with mine."

Taken aback, Claire searched his face for clarification. "Don't you want it?"

"Absolutely not. I gave my mother's money away, too."

"But why?"

"There are plenty of people who need it more than I do."

Her heart swelled with pride. *There he is…the man I fell in love with.*

"Besides, I don't want to give them the satisfaction. They can't buy my love, Claire."

Cocking her head to the side, she gave him a wry smile. "News flash. They're gone. They wouldn't know the difference."

"It's just in case they're watching," he said with a lift of his eyebrows.

Her smile became a giggle. "Whatever you say." *I've missed you so much.*

"Anyway, I'd rather give it away for free," he said with a wink.

"The money?" She couldn't take her eyes off him. *Breathe, breathe.*

He gave a shake of his head. "No…my love."

Claire felt the heat of a blush rise to cover her cheeks. "Who's the lucky girl?" she whispered.

"You know."

She nodded into his shirt, hiding her tear stained face. His arms wrapped around her, holding her tight as he begged for a second chance.

"I couldn't stand it if it didn't work out," she sniffed.

"It'll work," he whispered.

"It'll have to be long distance...I'm not leaving the girls again."

"Don't worry. I'll move."

"You can't move!"

"I sure can. Besides, I've always wanted a place on the St. Croix."

Stunned by the news, Claire backed away to get a good look at his eyes. "Since when?"

"Since I knew you were back."

THE END

Some of the readers of Maggie's story in *No Longer Afraid* asked me if I had more stories to tell about her family. I did, indeed. Since Maggie's mother, Claire, took everyone by surprise in book one, her story became the obvious choice for the second book in the *Home to Lake Louise* saga. Of course, Claire's steadfast daughter, Kate, has her own story to tell in book three, but for now, just enjoy her Baked Apple Pancake…see the recipe below!

Thanks so much for letting me know how you feel about my little tomes! I'm forever grateful. Bobbie Jean

From the kitchen of Kate Fogarty

Baked Apple Pancake

Ingredients:
¼ cup butter
3 Tbs. sugar
¾ tsp. cinnamon
2 apples, peeled and sliced

4 eggs
2/3 cup milk
1/3 cup flour
1 Tbs. sugar
½ tsp. salt

Melt butter in a 10" fry pan. Combine the 3 Tbs. of sugar with the cinnamon and sprinkle it over the butter. Arrange apple slices over the sugar mixture in the pan. Cook over medium heat for 3 to 4 minutes. Cool slightly and pour into a 8x8 glass baking dish or 9 inch pie pan.

In a separate bowl, beat eggs, milk, flour, sugar, and salt together until smooth. Pour mixture gently over the cooked apples.

Bake in a preheated 400 degree oven until the sides are puffy and golden brown…about 15 minutes. Serve immediately.

Helpful References

Lucy's Family Tree by Karen Halvorsen Schreck
Illustrated by Stephen Gassler III

Down Came the Rain (My journey through Postpartum Depression)
By Brook Shields

Family and Corrections Network; The Incarcerated Fathers Library
www.fcnetwork.org